THE TUG
OF WAR

The Tug of War
Copyright © Julia Sutherland 2016
Published by daisyPress Fiction

ISBN 978-1-910358-12-2

British Library Cataloguing in Publication Data.
A catalogue record for this book is available from the British
Library.

With thanks to Meg Humphries at Green Star Proofreading

Typeset in Charter 11/15

daisyPress fiction is an imprint of Daisypress Ltd
Bristol
England

daisypress.pub

THE TUG
OF WAR

Julia Sutherland

daisyPress
FICTION

To Gareth, Macsen, Frank and Gill
and to my parents Beryl and Harold
who served during the Second World War.

Chapter 1

'Stop daydreaming, Andrew Thomas.'

I looked up from the letter I was writing and saw a hand waving towards a notice board along the hallway.

The voice belonged to my friend, Ian, and he continued, no longer shouting now he'd got my attention.

'Leave – a whole seventy-two hours from Monday eighteen hundred hours.'

Another voice from down the hallway confirmed we indeed had leave.

I quickly joined the excited group jostling around the notice board. The hum of voices making plans filled my ears. All modes of transport were being considered by the men, but I wondered if buses would still be running at night. The voices were a cacophony of sound surrounding me, and I shook my head to clear my thoughts.

A loud voice penetrated my brain. 'Yes, gentlemen, the War Office has given you a little holiday, don't just get drunk now, will you?'

The regimental sergeant major had appeared. We hadn't noticed his arrival until his voice bounced off the walls.

'Yes, sir. No, sir.' An obedient chorus rang out from the men, but we knew a few pints of the landlord's best would be consumed nonetheless.

I stood gazing at the notice board, lost in thought, until another voice rose above the noise around me.

'Andrew,' said Ian. 'You going home?' Ian Smith was my best friend, and a tank crew comrade. We met on join up and had stayed together ever since, despite the Army's best efforts to separate us.

'Andrew!'

I jerked my head round to face Ian.

'Are you going home?' he asked again.

'Sorry, Ian,' I said. 'Of course, home to Mum and … Pamela. What are you doing?'

Ian was now standing right next to me. There was a short pause before he replied.

'Going to London to try and see my sister.'

I looked at the light-haired man beside me; I didn't know he had a sister, but I let it go for now. I ventured a proposal. 'OK, we can travel up together and I'll get a train home from there.' We hadn't travelled to London together before, there had always been an excuse not to, so I'd never actually met Ian's family.

'That's no problem, Andrew. I'll check the train times and let you know. It'll be a busy train with us lot on it.'

'I'll stand all the way if I have to,' I said, grinning

wide. I was happier than I had been for weeks. I was going home.

Ian laughed. 'With this crowd on leave you'll have no choice but to stand if you want to go and see your lady love.' Ian winked and thumped my arm. 'Pamela isn't it?'

'Pamela, yes.' My face felt hot in a second. 'But family come first.'

Ian smiled at my reply.

With our faces filled with excitement, we all dispersed slowly back to barracks. There was a buzz among the men, even the ones who had no real family to go home to. I knew they would visit friends or even just find their local pub and spend their free time drinking. The thought passed through my mind that some may not leave barracks at all – the ones who had no one left after the bombings.

'Hey, bud, why all the happy faces?' An American accent met my ears. 'Don't you guys know there's a war on?'

'Hi, Brad,' said Ian, 'we have leave.'

Brad was a skinny American who had recently taught us to play stud poker. He was leaning against the doorway, a broad grin across his face, arms folded, relaxing before he went on duty.

'Great news.' Brad pushed himself away from the wall. 'Visit the kitchen before you go, see what the cook has spare.'

I looked sceptically at him. 'Can we?'

'Sure,' he said, nodding. 'All you Brits do it … well, the ones we tell anyway. Butter, sugar, milk, anything you guys want.'

'Fantastic, thanks, we will,' said Ian before I could ask any more questions.

Ian and I exchanged looks. We could take some treats home, rationing was hurting everyone, and I knew my family wouldn't trade on the black market. But a question mark lingered in my brain at Brad's offer, though Ian seemed fine with it.

The next two days went past at a snail's pace. I began to think the officers had some power to make time pass more slowly. But when Monday crept round, Ian and I approached the double doors leading to the kitchen with some trepidation. I opened one door halfway before we sneaked a look to see who was working.

'Yeah? What d'ya want?' A large man wearing grubby white clothing shouted down the kitchen at us.

I felt uneasy and rubbed the back of my brown hair; I was doing this more frequently nowadays. I was sure a small bald spot was forming at the back of my head or, at the very least, the hair was thinning where I rubbed it. I hadn't had things on the black market before – surely this counted as black market, it certainly wasn't on ration book. There was a catch in my voice as I spoke.

'Um, we were told we could pick up a few things to take home on leave, you know, for our family.'

Ian pushed the doors fully open as I spoke, though he hadn't said anything – hedging his bets, no doubt, like usual. I'm sure it was never deliberate, but he always managed to keep out of trouble, and I ended up carrying the can when things went wrong.

'Oh, sure thing, what do you fancy?' The man's mood seemed to change in an instant. Judging by the food stains on his clothes, I guessed he was a cook. 'Sugar, butter, peaches, condensed milk, bacon. You name it, we got it.'

He walked towards us wiping his hands on a pristine white cloth. 'Got lots of jelly. Sorry, jam you call it.'

'Anything you can spare would be great.' Ian and I nodded at each other. It was going to be all right; we weren't being set up by the Yanks, something that would have certainly resulted in us losing our leave. I let out a small sigh of relief.

'Come right in, got a bag for some sugar?' With a plump hand the cook motioned us further into the kitchen.

'Here, will this do?' I waved a bag in the air, a shoe bag I thought would be enough to carry all the provisions we'd be given.

'Sure will, give it here.' The cook began pouring what must have been pounds of sugar into the open bag. I realised I would be getting more food than I'd thought.

'Hey, steady on,' I said, reaching for my bag. 'I have to tie it closed.' I put my hand on the bag to steady it. The bag would be overflowing if he continued pouring at that rate.

'Oh, right.' Cook stopped pouring the sugar and I tied the bag up.

'Now. How about some peaches? Butter, tinned meat, jelly?' Cook grinned like a benevolent uncle, hands on his hips. 'Anything else you guys want?'

'Dried egg if you have it?' said Ian, with rising intonation.

'Sure, hang on a minute.' Cook disappeared into a storeroom and came back with tins of dried egg and milk. He dropped them on to the kitchen work surface and slid it all down towards us. He was like one of those bartenders in the American Westerns I'd seen in the camp cinema. I managed to catch them without any falling to the floor. It was harder to do than it appeared on the films.

'That's more than generous,' I said sheepishly. 'Thanks.' I thought of the reaction when I handed the food over to friends and relations, and felt even more grateful.

'No problem.' Cook smiled. 'We know the rations you lot get.' Then he turned away, picked up a ladle and banged it on the counter top, shouting down the kitchen, 'Where's my coffee?'

He suddenly looked back at us as though a thought at occurred to him. 'Hey, want some coffee too?'

I had to laugh, but I shook my head. We had no need for coffee. Cook wandered off, grumbling, probably in search of his hot drink.

We both stood there staring at the piles of food. I had not, in my wildest dreams, thought we would get so much. We quickly gathered it all up and returned to our bunks before anyone spotted our bounty. We packed it in our kit bags, making them rather heavy to lift, but I hardly cared.

The train slowly chuffed its way through the English countryside toward the capital. Despite the failing light, I started to see the devastation caused by the German bombing raids. I saw the stark remains of buildings, rows of jagged houses like rotted teeth, once someone's home. Searchlights cast around the sky, seeking out the enemy, but so far we were lucky: no raids interrupted our journey.

Alighting at the main station we were soon swallowed by the swarming crowd. Spotting a tea wagon, we made our way over for a warm drink and a sandwich.

'Mmm,' I said through a mouthful of bread. 'It's amazing what you get used to eating and end up actually enjoying.'

'Yup, hunger does that to you,' said Ian, half-heartedly. He was eyeing up the girl making the teas.

I swallowed the last of my sandwich, tapping Ian on the arm to get his attention. 'I'll see you here Wednesday lunchtime for our return, yes?'

'Yes, all right, see you then.' Ian continued to smile at the young girl, who beamed back at him. He broke off the eye contact long enough to say goodbye to me as we clasped arms, before I picked up my illicit goods and headed off in search of my train home. At the end of the platform I stopped to look back at Ian. He was waving goodbye to the girl, who was now holding a paper napkin. I suspected there was the name of a public house or other meeting place scribbled on the paper. As I gazed at my friend waving to the girl, I thought about Ian's sister, and whether there were other family members he hadn't mentioned. I thought, with a chuckle, if she was his only sibling, he was carrying a lot of food for her to eat. I then hoisted the kit bag on to my shoulder and began walking to find the train to take me to Birmingham and family.

The final train journey seemed to pass in a haze of cigarette smoke and sleep. My eyes felt sore with tiredness so when I was lucky enough to squeeze into a compartment with one empty seat, I fell into a deep sleep, the kit bag safely stored under my legs.

The juddering of the train coming to a halt woke me with a jolt. For a moment I was unsure where I was, but I came to quickly and checked, through the window, it was the right platform. I was home. I stood awkwardly and stretched, gathered my bag and coat and left the train. The platform was full of uniformed men, many swarming around the tea canteens, gulping from tin mugs. I took a welcome hot cup of tea and a bun, and watched the world go past for ten minutes. I wasn't taking in the confusion but letting it wash over me until I'd finished my tea and polished off the last crumb of my sandwich.

The buses, as I'd guessed back in barracks, weren't running, so I took the first step of the long walk home to Mother, coming home safe.

The long street, dimly lit by the moon, was silent in the early morning. Only my boots disturbed the silence, their metallic clicking sound on the cobbles echoed from the sleeping houses as I marched up the street to my home.

I pushed open the gate to our garden, hoping it didn't squeak, and stepped up the short path to the front door. The tiny garden was barely long enough to push a lawnmower, but it boasted a few spring flowers, which blurred in my vision as they swayed in the light breeze. A late daffodil, still standing proudly in the soil by the path, made me smile. It almost made me cry.

I reached up and put the large key in the door, turning it slowly until I heard the click, then pushed the door open into the hallway. To the right was the best room, hardly used, the piano standing in pride of place along one wall. I'd spent many hours on that thing trying to learn scales. Only Mother now played. I could bash out a tune in the mess, as I had done on many a drunken night, but I couldn't play as Mother did – no amount of practice would make me as good. Mum had a gift that, sadly, she hadn't passed on to her eldest son. To the left was another room where we ate at a large table that dominated the room. It was a gift from a deceased member of Mother's church where she played the organ for Sunday services. A beautiful table, but too big for our little home. You could spread the Express newspaper out fully and still have room for cups of tea and plates of food. And that was unextended. I couldn't recall seeing it fully open in the ten years it had been there.

I wasted little time dropping the heavy bag by the door. I shook my arm loose and I looked up the stairs, but no sound or light came down.

I was pleased I hadn't woken them, so I crept along the narrow hallway to the kitchen. I opened the door and found a cup for water, drinking from it greedily. Taking off my coat and leaving it over the bottom banister, I went into the best room and sat on one of the not-so-comfortable chairs. But despite this, I promptly fell into a deep sleep until I was woken by a scream. As my eyes came into focus, I saw Mother rushing toward me, desperate to welcome her son home from the war.

'Andrew!' she cried. 'Andrew, you're home.'

I struggled up from my chair and was immediately clasped in my Mother's embrace.

'Mum, I'm fine, really I am. Got a little leave, back Wednesday night.'

Mother squeezed me tighter and kissed my cheek.

'Leave off, Mum,' I said, but then locked my arms around her back and kissed her, ignoring my own protestations for her to leave me alone.

'How can I leave off?' she said, shaking her head. 'Are you OK, no wounds? Are you eating good, are they treating you alright?' She paused to draw in a breath and look over my body as though she might find some war injury.

'What are you up to?' she said, hugging me again. 'Oh, I know you can't tell me that. How long can you stay? You said Wednesday. Oh darling, it's so good to have you home. Want to eat something?' Another breath. I let her ramble on, asking questions while we held each other tightly.

'How long have you been here, why did you not wake us? Are you tired? Do you want to sleep?' Mother finally ran out of breath and she just held me. As the questions were asked, tears had found their way down her face. I hadn't seen Mother cry with happiness before. My arms dropped away from her.

'I'm OK, Mum. Back Wednesday, so I'll be leaving morning time. I'm fine, really.' I took Mother's hands and shook them gently. 'Mum, it's fine.'

A noise from behind made me turn my head towards

the doorway. My father stood there, quietly watching.

'Sorry, Dad, did I wake you?'

The older man took a few steps into the room and gently squeezed my shoulder.

'No, son, I was awake when you came in.' My father rubbed an eye. 'I thought you would need a sleep, so I didn't wake your mother. Tea?'

'A cup of tea?' shrieked Mother. 'Of course he wants a cup of tea. And breakfast.' She pushed herself away and bustled from the room on a quest to feed her returning son. I heard Mum filling the kettle then clanging it down on to the stove. Plates rattled.

'How you keeping, son?' Father looked me in the eyes.

I knew what he meant. He'd been in the war, the Great War he called it, when I first went to school. Father didn't talk much about his time in France.

'I'm OK, Dad. Good mates, hard work. On tanks like I said last time. You must have seen them in the news-reels about Africa.' I took a step towards him to give him a hug but he took my hand and shook it hard.

'I'm OK,' I repeated. 'They've just put me back in big tanks, no longer recon – after all that training. Told us yesterday.'

Father shook his head. 'Same old Army, not knowing what it's doing. Oh well, son, keep out of trouble.' He turned away to find his favourite chair just as the sound of rushing feet came down the stairs.

A whirlwind of a fourteen-year-old boy fell through the door and jumped into my arms. James, my brother, had arrived.

'Andrew, you're back!' My brother almost knocked me over with his yelling. 'Have you killed any Germans yet?'

James's question shocked me and I glanced at Dad.

'Have you driven those new tanks?' he continued. 'I've seen them in the paper.'

'James, I'm OK,' I said, gently lowering him to the floor. 'Yes, those tanks are big, as you are. You've grown again.' I could smell soap on my brother and suddenly I realised Mother and Father smelt of it too. Home. I pulled James towards me again and nuzzled his hair as I felt my eyes begin to smart.

I looked up and saw Mother standing in the doorway, smiling.

Mother gave a little sigh and spoke quietly. 'Yes, he does grow, I can't keep up with him – clothes and shoes, have to use your old clothes now.

I let go of James and looked at the shoes that had just thudded on the worn carpet. They'd been my best shoes a few years ago.

'He's taller than you, Mum … and heavy.' I made a show of rubbing my biceps, only half pretending. 'Tea brewed?'

'I've just put it on the table next door. Come on and tell us what you can.'

'Just a tick,' I said. 'I have to go outside.' I left the room and went through the back door to the outside toilet; my parents had put a bathroom in a lean-to before the war. I washed my hands and splashed some water on my face. When I returned my family were eagerly waiting for me around the large table. Breakfast was started and we ate in-between speaking of friends and relations then, full, I lent a little back on my chair and smiled at Mother.

'Thanks, Mum, that cup of tea was great, just hit the spot.' I patted my tight belly. 'We're with the Yanks at the moment and we get more coffee than tea. It makes a nice change, though. Lots to eat – strange food, but fills us up.'

Mother beamed, as I knew she would, and cut another slice from a loaf, pushing butter and marmalade in front of me. 'Go on,' she said. 'You must be hungry.'

'Thanks.' I grabbed up the butter and spread a thin layer on the bread, watched closely by my family. I was still hungry despite the food I'd had on the train. I was grateful for the silence since it helped me clear my head and relax, though just being home had that effect.

'Oh, I have some things for you,' I said, remembering the food the American had given me. 'In the kit bag.' I nodded my head towards the hall.

'I'll fetch it, son,' said Dad. 'You stay and eat your breakfast.' He dragged the bag into the room and methodically undid the knots that tied the top securely. 'You didn't want anyone to get into this, did you?'

'No, Dad,' I said, covering my full mouth as I spoke. 'I slept on the train with it under my feet. I wanted to keep it safe.'

'Look, Mother,' he said. He always called her that in front of the family. 'A tin of jam, dried egg, milk. What's this?' Father held up the tightly bound bag to show me.

'Sugar, Dad.'

My dad's face turned serious. 'How did you pay for

all this?' His sharp eyes bore into me like they did when I was a kid, when I was trying to hide some misdemeanour from him. 'And where did you get it? Not black market I hope, son.'

'No, Dad,' I hastily replied, unable to escape his scrutiny. 'I told you, I'm with the Yanks. They give it to the boys who are going on leave – those that ask, that is.'

Father's eyes smiled at me again.

'Well I'm most grateful.' Mother laughed, breaking the tension. 'I must write a short note in thanks for when you go back. This lot will come in handy.' Mother nodded to herself as she looked over the welcomed food. 'Now eat up.'

'Well, son.' Father coughed. 'I have to go to the shop now, pop in if passing and see your father, won't you?' He scraped the chair back from the table and looked fondly down at us, his small family.

I took a break from chewing the last of my bread and butter. 'Yes of course. Anything to do in the garden?'

'No, I dug it over last week. If I'd known you were coming I would have left it. Did my back no good, I can tell you. I'm just getting over the soreness.' Father rubbed the small of his back as he stood by his chair. 'Chickens are laying well, but the rats are about again. See you later, son.'

As Father left the room, James leaned over towards me and whispered conspiratorially, 'Have you seen any Germans yet? What are they like? Are they that good an army?'

I frowned. 'They are good, but we are better.'

I saw that James's eyes shone with excitement at the thought of one day fighting them himself. I would do anything to stop that happening.

'No,' I said, shaking my head. 'I've seen them on the newsreels like you.'

I looked at Mother and raised an eyebrow. She took the hint. Mother ruffled James's hair and gave him a gentle push to get off his chair.

'Shush! Off you go to school. You'll see your brother at teatime if not earlier. Now scoot.'

James reluctantly obeyed, getting off his chair and traipsing from the room, stopping at the door and turning slightly to look at me. 'I will see you at tea time, won't I?'

'Yes you will,' I replied quickly. 'I've some things to do, then home for tea.'

'Great.' The door slammed shut behind my brother.

I winced at the bang. 'Did I make so much noise moving about when I was his age, Mum?'

'Yes, Andrew, you did.' Mother collected my plate and teacup. 'You off out now?'

'Yes, a quick wash then out to see … a few friends.' It felt like I'd trailed off at the end; perhaps I was a little embarrassed about my desire to see Pamela.

'Most are away now, son,' she said. 'A few come back on leave, not many, but …'

I watched her closely as she gazed at the table.

'I've got to tell you, Andrew, Matthew is never coming home.' She looked at me, her bottom lip caught, just for a second. 'He has gone to the angels.'

'Not Matthew!' I stared at my mum. 'No … what

15

happened?'

'A bombing raid at his RAF base,' she said, her eyes filling up. 'I didn't want to write to you, Andrew. It happened a while ago.'

'Not Matthew,' I whispered again. I felt my throat constrict. 'He always wanted to fly.' I picked up the bone-handled knife and looked at it intently, trying to avoid meeting my mother's gaze. My eyes smarted. Matthew, the little boy I'd started school with, grown up with; the same class all through school, climbing trees together, getting into trouble. Fond memories flashed through my mind. I sniffed as I finally looked at Mother. 'Yes, he did want to fly, didn't he?'

Mother gave a slight nod while clearing away the remains of the breakfast. 'A few more will join him before this war is over.'

She shook her head, ever so slightly, and looked up at me. 'Matthew is flying with the angels now.' Her eyes sparkled with unshed tears.

'Not to dwell,' she said, sniffing and seeming to brighten. 'Off you go.'

I sat for a few moments, numb with the sentiment. The sound of feet running down the hallway shook me from my thoughts. The front door opened and slammed shut, loud footsteps echoing through the open window as James ran down the street towards his school. I realised James was very like I was at that age, late for everything – and noisy.

I rose and dropped a kiss on the top of Mother's head and went out to the bathroom where I had a strip wash using a kettle of hot water Mother had placed by the basin for me. Feeling refreshed, I put on a clean shirt, leaving my dirty laundry out for Mother to wash even though it wasn't wash day.

I walked down the hall towards the front door, Mother stood in the doorway of the sitting room, watching me.

'I'm off out now, Mum. See you.'

'You take care, Andrew.' She pecked my cheek as I passed her, pausing slightly so she could place the kiss. As I left I could feel her eyes following me.

I found myself almost running to the pavement from the house, my boots making as much noise as James had on his dash to be at school on time.

I collected my thoughts and looked up and down the road. No bomb damage near here, I silently thanked the Lord. I then faced left, put my shoulders back and began marching up the road towards the object of my desire. Acknowledging greetings from neighbours who had known me since I was a baby, I made my way towards the little general shop where Pamela worked. As I walked along I occasionally patted the top pocket of the coat I wore.

As I pushed the green glass-panelled shop door, the doorbell hanging behind sounded the familiar ding-ding, and everyone in the shop turned their heads to see who had come in. Smiles greeted me, some knew me, others didn't, but they all seemed pleased to see a soldier who looked unharmed.

Pamela wasn't there, but Mr Vincenti was, serving

and laughing with his customers. He had little to sell that wasn't rationed, but he did his best. There were a few tins of fruit, some fresh vegetables, grown in local back gardens, which he sold on for a small commission. It worked and no one had complained so it must be legal, he told his customers. Despite his name, Mr Vincenti was born in London, he spoke no Italian, but was proud of his secret ice cream recipe. How I loved that ice cream! I dreamed of it some nights, hoping the war would end soon so that his ice cream making could start again. I could almost taste it as I stood in the shop, its familiar smells all around me.

'Hello, Mr V, Pamela in today?'

'Andrew my boy!' Mr V threw his arms wide to greet me, but didn't move from behind his counter. 'She has a day off today, sorry.'

He made a sad face but brightened almost instantly. 'Can you help me a few minutes, my son? I need some boxes moved so I can get these ladies what they want.' He nodded in acknowledgement to the ladies who were waiting patiently in line to be served.

'I have some extra dried milk out back but I had a delivery of potatoes yesterday and they've gone and dumped them in front of it.' Mr V opened up the counter top and invited me through.

I gave a little inward sigh. 'Sure, Mr V.' I moved quickly through the raised counter past Mr Vincenti and into the back room of the shop.

Half an hour later I finished moving 'some boxes' from one place to another, but I didn't mind. Mr Vincenti was an old man now and really needed more physical help in the shop than he could expect Pamela to provide. She was dainty, not built for hard work at all. I smiled at the thought of her.

Moving off once more down the street, I acknowledged more hellos and greetings of joy from neighbours, glad to see me hale and hearty. It was a short walk to Pamela's house and I soon reached her street, stopping in horror at what I saw. The factory at the top of the road had been bombed and some of the bombs had fallen wide of their target. There were gaps where houses had once stood, gaps perilously close to Pamela's house. I shuddered at how close they'd dropped to Pamela's house.

Pamela's door opened right on to the pavement, not like ours with the little front garden.

I knocked firmly on the wooden door and I heard footsteps approach, first hurrying then slowing as they got louder. Eventually the door opened a few inches to reveal Pamela's mother.

'Well, well, if it isn't our Andrew. How are you?' She ran a hand through her hair, pausing only for a second before she continued. 'How is your mother and father? I haven't been out recently, had a cold, and I didn't want it to move to pneumonia. I thought I had better stay in. Better now, a bit of a cough though.' The woman hardly paused to allow me to answer as she stood there in the half-opened doorway. Like my own mother, she could talk for England. 'How are you, my lad?' she repeated.

I wondered if she was going to ask all her questions again, one at a time.

'You'd better come in. No smoking, mind, not with my chest.' She opened the door fully and let me move past her into the front room. There was no hallway in her house.

'Well, thank you, Mrs Harding.'

As I passed her she yelled at the bottom of the stairs, 'Pamela? Pamela, you have a visitor.'

'I'll be right down.'

I tensed at the voice. Pamela. I realised with a jolt how nervous I was about seeing Pamela again. My stomach did a flip as I heard her voice.

'Coming.' Bed springs creaked, and a bang, which I took to be a book dropping to the bare boards, suggested Pamela was wasting no time in coming down. I swallowed nervously; and then a clatter of little heels on the landing. She was coming down the stairs towards me. I looked up and there she was. Pamela.

Chapter 2

'Hello, Pamela,' I said. 'You look great.' I just had time to finish the greeting before she clattered to the bottom and threw herself into my arms.

Mrs Harding tut-tutted, but I didn't care. Pamela was in my arms and I nuzzled her neck.

I reluctantly put her down and smoothed her blonde hair back off her face so I could see her more clearly. I wanted to kiss her nose but daren't with her mother looking on.

'Hello, Pamela,' I said again, smiling at her broadly. But then I felt a little uncertain. 'I have a few hours leave and wondered if you would like a walk ... maybe take in a movie.'

'Mum,' she said, without taking her eyes off me. 'I'll be out for the rest of the day.' Pamela gazed solidly into my dark brown eyes. I felt my stomach flutter for a second.

'Oh, really? And who's going to help me with the

housework?' Mrs Harding moaned at her daughter. 'This cough isn't getting any better, you know.'

Pamela threw a quick kiss at her mother and took her coat from a hook on the wall next to the front door. 'Shall we?' she said, opening the front door.

I pinched the front of my beret and quickly followed the fair-haired girl out on to the street.

'It is wonderful to see you,' said Pamela, stepping back to close the door that, in my haste, I'd left open. 'Stan Park is still beautiful, even without the daffodils. Do you remember we went there in February?' Pamela gave a little giggle. 'Shall we go there?'

Pamela stopped to put her coat on.

'Fine by me,' I said, helping her feed her left arm into the hole; she didn't button it and it swayed around her legs as we began to walk down the street – to the accompaniment of twitching net and blackout curtains. After a few steps, Pamela put her arm through mine, and the further we got from her mother's house, the closer we walked together. The Park was empty, save for a few people looking at the ducks; only one lady, a rather sad-looking lady, was feeding them with the remains of what looked like a very stale loaf.

'Gosh, I haven't seen a stale loaf for a long time.' Pamela giggled. 'No food stays around long enough to go stale in our house.'

I smiled and nodded in agreement. 'I think that's the same in every home these days, even my brother is eating more than Dad now.' I squeezed her hand. 'I thought you would be working in the shop. I went there first – Mr V got me moving boxes and things.'

Pamela answered quietly. 'Yes, that's the hardest part of my job. He's getting infirm, and I am not big enough to move all the bigger boxes for him. But we manage most of the time.' She patted my arm. 'You've saved me some hard work tomorrow. Thank you.'

I squeezed Pamela's hand again. 'Happy to help,' I said. 'I expect you ask all the strong young men who come in to move deliveries around.'

Pamela looked a little sheepishly up at me then giggled. 'Sometimes, but only the good looking ones.'

'Do I count?' I didn't consider myself as handsome, I was OK, but no Clark Gable.

'We actually get lots of offers of help,' she said, clearly ignoring my question. 'I suppose they're hoping we can increase the ration, but, of course, we can't.'

Pamela shook her head and let out a little laugh. 'The arguments and the soft-soaping of Mr V is something to be seen. You know Mrs A – Mrs Armitage – from the next street? She offered to darn his socks yesterday.'

'Mrs A?' I said with a frown. 'Why? She gets Mrs Windsor to do that for her, Mum told me a few years ago.'

'Yes, I know,' said Pamela. 'I see her going in Mrs Windsor's house sometimes. Mrs Windsor does all the alterations in the area now.' Pamela paused a second. 'To be honest, Andrew, I was thinking of getting my darning needles out for profit.'

'Watch out for the fly boys!' I said, only half joking. 'Or they might want you to do more than darn their socks.'

I didn't want her dallying with the RAF – the brylcream boys, we called them – or worse still, the Americans. They seemed a bit too fast and loose with our girls.

Pamela smiled up into my face. 'Oh, Andrew, you do say some funny things sometimes.' Heaviness came over her face and she made a little sigh. 'You heard about Matthew?'

'Yes, Mum just told me. I wonder if he ever got to fly much.' My voice got a little softer as I spoke, the American threat fading from my thoughts.

Pamela gave a quick smile. 'Yes he did, he trained to be a navigator. He told me last leave, he was so happy to be flying.'

I stopped and looked at the girl linking arms with me. 'Well, at least he achieved his dream and, as Mum put it, he's flying with the angels now.' I felt I had to be positive about something to overcome the awful news of Matthew's death.

'What a lovely way to think,' Pamela said quietly. 'I will tell his Mum next time I see her, if she's all right, that is.' Pamela looked away for a few seconds, then back at me. I saw tears forming in her eyes and I wanted to kiss them away.

'Shall we sit on the bench?' I nodded towards a small wooden seat.

Pamela gave a little sniff and wiped her eyes. 'Our bench,' she said. 'I come here … I suppose I shouldn't really say that, should I? Our bench.' Pamela spoke quickly, as though embarrassed at what she was saying. 'But it was a lovely day. Do you remember? The daffodils were just out, and so warm.'

The bench we had sat on in February was unoccupied and we sat down arm in arm, chatting a little, or sometimes happy just to sit in a companionable silence, occasionally acknowledging the greetings of passing friends and acquaintances. I realised I was content just being with Pamela.

The sun had reached its watery zenith as we later strolled around the edge of the lake and watched the ducks cavorting in the middle of the cold water. Several ducklings swam around nervously as dogs, unleashed by their owners, stood barking at the water's edge.

We talked of nothing in particular: the latest film she had seen with her girlfriends, how handsome Rhett Butler was, whether we really liked Vera Lynne, the new fast music from the USA brought over by the American GIs. Trivia, really.

'Vera is too maudlin,' I ventured. Pamela agreed quietly. The topic of weather came up, of course, and how it didn't yet seem like the end of spring and beginning of summer. Time passed comfortably and I was happy.

Hunger pangs led us over to the park's small café and we ordered a tea each and one bun to share. We sat outside, watching people walk by as we drank our tea, Pamela ate the bun, I'd eaten too many over the last twenty-four hours and I knew I would have a large meal later with the family. I remembered the tins of meat brought home as well as the much-lauded sugar and butter.

'Oh, I nearly forgot, Pamela,' I said, digging into my coat pocket. 'Here, I have this for you.' I produced a blue packet of sugar and held it towards her. I'd seen a small packet on the kitchen top and I'd carefully decanted some sugar before leaving the house.

'Oh, Andrew, the nicest present I've had this week.' She laughed. 'I can drink tea without but I do prefer sugar in it.' She took the packet and put it in her black leather handbag, the clasp not quite closing properly afterwards. 'Mum will be so pleased. It's not black market, is it?'

'No,' I answered, shaking my head, and then … 'Who else has been giving you presents this week?' A thought had shot through my mind: other soldiers, Americans maybe? I tried not to think of men knocking on her front door.

She immediately coloured bright red. 'It's just an expression. Really, Andrew, no one else.' Her hair fell forward over her face obscuring the blush of her cheeks.

'I do hope none of the Americans are causing you or your friends any problems. They aren't, are they?' I tried to look serious. I'd heard the talk of the Americans after they'd returned from a trip away from the camp. I had not liked what I'd heard. I was glad I didn't have a sister, not after hearing some of the stories. But I was sure Pamela was not like those girls.

Pamela shook her head so vehemently that her hair, cut in the peek-a-boo style of a film star, bounced around her head. 'No, Andrew, no problems. I keep away from the Americans. I should be getting back, Mum is really not well.'

I raised an eyebrow.

'Really not well,' she said, emphasising the words.

'It's not the cough – something to do with her heart. But she won't admit it.'

'Is it bad?'

Pamela looked sombre. 'She passes out. I found her at the bottom of the stairs the other day. I go home at lunch time, and other times if I can, to check on her.'

I took her hand and rubbed it gently. 'I am sorry.'

'It's OK. I am prepared for the worst.' She sighed and stood up from the tea table where our empty cups stood. 'I must go now.'

I remained seated, I felt unsure of what I should do if I stood up; I wanted to kiss her but dare not with so many people passing by. 'Can I see you later, the pictures, and another walk?' I hoped I had an imploring look on my face as I spoke. I was unsure of myself, but I did so want to continue seeing her on this leave, it may be the last time I saw her.

'I'm finished with walking, but the pictures would be good. Come after you've had your tea, there is a late showing, we can catch that if you like.'

She wanted to see more of me! I got up from my seat, took my beret off and ran it around my fingers. 'Great I'll see you then, can I walk you home?'

'No don't be silly, Andrew,' she said, brushing off my offer with a curt shake of the head. 'I'm perfectly all right. You go and see some of your friends, a few are on leave too.'

Pamela put out a hand and touched me lightly on the arm, then left me standing by the table weaving my beret slowly between my fingers.

Tea was a rather noisy and disrupted affair that night. We all sat around the table in the front room with lots of space to put the rationed meal before us. Mother had made good use of the butter and sugar with the flour she already had in her store cupboard. Using the last of her bottled fruit, we ate a huge crumble. It took rather longer than usual to eat our meal due to constant banging on the front door as neighbours kept on popping in to see me. *Have you seen our Kenneth on your travels? How about Bob? Are you keeping well? No nasty sergeant majors making your life hell …*

I'd smiled and nodded at each enquiry. I recalled my PT instructor who had made my life unbearable for a while, so I was able to agree with them about nasty sergeant majors. After a while the visitors began to fade away and we were left alone. I was exhausted from trying to give positive answers to all their questions. It wasn't a bed of roses in the forces, but at least we ate better than our families.

Father moved his chair back from the table and spread his hands. 'Son, you said you had changed tanks. What are they like? I saw the first ones in 1917, must say, didn't think they would last. But things change.'

'They're strong, well armoured tanks, Dad.' I answered him slowly and clearly; I wanted to reassure him I was safe. 'We've been put in an APT.'

Father frowned and cocked his head.

'They fire armour-piercing shells,' I said, by way of explanation. 'Hence armour piercing tanks – APT.' I found myself fiddling with the salt and pepper Mother hadn't yet cleared from the table.

'What?' said James, perking up in his chair. 'They can go through anything?'

I leant away, poking a finger around the ear he'd just shouted in. 'I hope so. Those German Tiger tanks are big and strong.' I coughed, I didn't want to worry them about the superiority of the German tanks over ours. 'Not as fast as our Shermans, but if the Tigers dig in we could be in trouble. That's why we have the APT.' I put the salt down but not before I'd spilt some. I took a pinch between finger and thumb and threw it over my left shoulder.

'How many are in the tank now, son?' said Father, ever curious. 'Are you still with your mates or have they split you up?'

I shook my head. 'Not done that yet, thank goodness. Just the four of us – Charley drives, Pete signals and Ian shoots the thing. Me, I just tell them where to go.'

I patted my arm with the stripes on it and smiled.

'Oh, that sounds dangerous, darling, you don't stand so your head is outside all the time, do you?' Mother gathered up the salt and pepper pots from my hands.

'No, Mum, we batten down the hatches at the first sign of the enemy. Gets a bit sweaty, I can tell you, and the engine fumes are awful.'

'You do wash regularly, don't you, darling?' Mother glared at me.

'Yes, Mum, we do.' I flashed her what I hoped was a convincing smile while she cleared the last of the dishes from the table.

I was getting weary of all the questions, all my reassurances that I was safe – would be safe. I couldn't take much more. I was scared myself.

I jumped to my feet. 'Come on, James, let's wash up and you can tell me about the girls at school.'

'Girls, what do I want with girls?' James snorted in derision but coloured slightly under his hair. Nevertheless, he followed my example and got up from the table and moved towards the doorway.

I saw my parents smile at my short exchange with James, and then they both spoke the same words in unison: 'He has been washing better recently.' Mother began to laugh, quickly joined by my father.

'Oh, Mum!' James bolted from the room to help me with the washing up. As I passed through the doorway, I glanced back to see our parents sat at the table holding hands, smiling at our brotherly banter.

Half an hour later I walked out of the front door, surreptitiously watched by Mother through the blackout curtains; I could just see her as I walked past the window. I brushed the front of my coat down and straightened my beret before beginning the short walk to Pamela's.

This time I stood back on the pavement after I had made the knocker reverberate in the house – and most of the street. As I waited I acknowledged the calls of friends and acquaintances, but mainly I stared along the road at the shell of the factory and wondered how many of the houses would still be standing at the end of the war if the bombing continued. I repositioned my beret a couple of times and nervously moved my heavily shod feet on the cobbles. At long last Pamela came to the door, calling out behind her.

'Bye, Mum, I won't be late.' Smiling at me she added, 'I have work in the morning.'

Arm in arm we went down the street together, happy in each other's company, the initial awkwardness of our reunion thankfully now faded away.

Gone with the Wind was showing so we watched that again.

I thought I could repeat the whole dialogue, I must have seen it ten times. Sitting in the third row from the back, surrounded by courting couples, we watched the film hand in hand, a clean white handkerchief folded in my pocket ready for tears at the final scene.

The walk to her home took longer than it should have as we frequently sheltered in shop doorways for a quick kiss and cuddle. We gave anxious looks up into the night at the bright lights criss-crossing the blackness, and listened for planes droning overhead. Somehow I felt content despite the loss of friends, I was happy with Pamela. She was the one, I was sure of it.

It was late when I got home. As I entered the hallway I saw the dining room light was still on and saw Father sitting at the table reading the paper. I stood in the doorway watching him.

'Hello, Dad,' I said. 'Thought you'd be in bed by now.'

'Hello, son,' said Dad, looking up suddenly as though he didn't know I was there. 'Thought I'd wait up for you.'

I took my coat off, threw it over the banisters and

came into the room. 'Any tea brewed?' I nodded towards the teapot on the table by Father.

'No, had my last cup over an hour ago. Cold by now, make yourself one, if you like.'

'I'm not that desperate for one. A glass of water will do me.' My hand ran through my hair and brushed it down again, then sneaked back to rub my head.

The paper rustled as my father carefully folded it and placed it down on the table. 'Son, how is it really going?' Father's voice was low, I could hardly hear what he was saying.

'Fine, Dad.' I knew I had to reassure him, but I craved some reassurance myself. 'Some of the men are not too good, got to watch your possessions, but on the main, we're all in it together.' I moved further into the room and stood opposite Father on the other side of the table, avoiding looking at him directly.

Father huffed. 'Yes you are, but some, well, we had those sorts in the first bash. You be careful of your stuff.' He stared at me, concern in his eyes.

I managed to look back at him, hoping that I exuded a confidence I didn't feel. 'Don't worry, I am careful with my stuff, some mates have had bits stolen. Some of the chaps come from wealthy backgrounds, usually made up in the ranks pretty quick. Others have only what they stand in.'

I sat down and now really looked at Father for the first time since I'd come home. I saw a man who had aged since I left, grey in the face – or had he always looked like that but I just hadn't noticed? He was a hard-working man, fighting the war on the home front, keeping his family safe in the house, working long hours but still finding time to plant the garden with vegetables – digging for victory, they called it.

'Your tank mates, are they dependable?' Father met my gaze.

'Yes, I think so,' I said, shifting in my chair.

'You think so?' Father's eyes questioned me intently.

'Yes, they are,' I replied in a firmer voice.

'You … Son, you need to be able to depend on the men around you.' Father moved the paper that was still on the table so it faced away from him, then he picked it up and folded it tightly. He didn't seem to know what to do with his hands while he talked to me.

'I know Dad, they're OK.' I looked away and thought about my comrades. 'Ian, not really sure where he comes from, but he's steady. Charley and Pete are Scottish – rib them a bit – Charley's a great driver, and Pete, he's a bit quiet, but fine.'

'You got your things in order for the final push, son?' Father picked up the newspaper again and opened it up, his hands shaking as he refolded it.

My stomach did a little growl. The final push, the invasion of Europe. 'Yes, Dad, all letters written and sealed for you should anything happen.' I reached out to the teapot and turned it around so the spout was facing me. I remembered the small teapot from when I was a little boy. I didn't want to look Father in the face. I knew there were things that should be said, and some left unsaid between us, but we would leave those for another day.

He spoke quietly to me. 'Your mother lies awake at night worrying, but that can't be avoided. Telephone me at the shop if you can. It works most of the time, though bomb blasts do sometimes pull the lines down. After the …' He looked at me; we both knew what he meant. The invasion. 'If you could find time to write, take some paper and envelopes with you. Some will get through. It would make her waiting for you to come home more bearable. It's the not knowing.'

'I'll try, Dad.' I rubbed the back of my neck. Maybe I could write more. 'Yes, I will.'

'Good lad, take these.' Father reached behind him and pulled out a pad of thin blue writing paper and some banded blue envelopes, 'Here, take them now.'

I stood and took them from his trembling hand. 'You OK, Dad, everything fine?'

'Yes, son, just a long day. Put them in your coat pocket now so you don't forget them in the morning.'

I did as I was told, putting them in my coat pocket, which I'd left at the bottom of the stairs, and then returned to the room. 'Dad, I am going up now. I'll be fine, you know. I will come home.'

'Make sure you do, lad, and no heroics. Come home safe … and, son?'

I paused at the doorway.

'Leave nothing undone before it starts. No regrets. Promise?'

'Yes, Dad, I promise.'

Chapter 3

See you soon, son. Come home safe. The words kept ringing in my mind as I walked into the smoky London station.

The kit bag bumped my legs as I walked along the concourse until I set it closely by my side. I slumped against a wall and slid wearily to the floor, wincing at the cold touch of the stone. I stretched my legs out and pulled a packet of cigarettes from my tunic pocket, lighting one and drawing heavily while looking around.

I was hoping to see another of my tank crew but I closed my eyes for a minute and again drew on the cigarette, thinking of Pamela, the lovely Pamela: nights down the dance hall, the pictures, how many times had we seen *Gone with the Wind*? I was glad I'd been able to bring some photographs of her with me. A smile flitted across my face. A golden-haired girl danced behind my eyelids. The one.

'Andrew! Wake up.' A heavy boot connected painfully with my thigh to reinforce the command. My eyes immediately flipped open. A figure loomed over me.

'Andrew. The train, you idiot.'

'Ian, where did you come from?' I looked up at the uniformed young man and, as I did so, scrunched the burning end of my cigarette until it no longer glowed, and tucked it safely in my pocket.

'I've been standing in front of you for a good minute,' said Ian, shaking his head. 'Daydreaming of some girl? Come on, we may still get a seat.'

I scrambled to my feet and grabbed the kit bag, holding it tightly to my chest. We sprinted towards what I hoped was the right train; announcements were a little unclear during the war, if there were any at all.

The station was heaving with people. I followed slightly behind Ian as he pushed his way through the throng. Two bodies were much better than one for forcing a way through the mass of travellers. After what seemed an age, our heavy boots clattering on the stone paving, we emerged on to the right platform, where the train was preparing to depart; the last open door was closing in front of our eyes.

'Hey,' shouted Ian. 'Wait on! Andrew – go for it!' Ian pushed me towards the train since I was nearer the last open door.

I followed my friend's order, making a grab for the brass handle on the door as it was halfway through its arc to close.

'Got you,' I muttered as my hand grasped the cold

handle.

'In you go, mate. Push,' groaned Andrew. 'Plenty of room in there for two of us.'

I felt a strong hand in the small of my back forcing me upwards, and then a hand from the train reached out and grabbed me. I was yanked up the step into the carriage, glancing off another soldier's stomach before falling on to the dirty floor.

'There we go,' said Ian. 'I told you we'd make it.' Behind me, Ian pushed his way into the carriage, having thrown his bag over my prostrate body. He reached down and hauled me to my feet. Straightening, I dusted some fluff from my uniform and looked at the soldier I'd fallen on to. I felt my face flush and my stomach tense.

'Sorry, sir,' I managed, saluting quickly. Oh hell, will a charge of some kind follow? Striking an officer or something? The thoughts ran quickly through my mind.

The regimental sergeant major raised his eyebrows at the sight of us and spoke in a deep voice. 'What do you think you're doing, lads? Circus acrobatics? Too long on leave, that's your problem.'

I gave a relieved smile at the officer. Yes! I'd got away with it.

The RSM huffed and moved away, swaying in time with the now moving train as it left the station. We watched him enter a compartment two down from the train doorway.

'Did he just get on?' I said to Ian.

'Don't think so, must have been watching us through the window as we were running to catch the train.'

We grinned at each other, finished dusting ourselves down, and picked the kit bags up from the floor.

Finding the carriage corridor surprisingly clear, we walked along the train, looking into each compartment. Towards the end of the carriage, there were seats free and, even better, we found our two tank mates. Ian and I exchanged greetings with the Scots pair, Charley and Pete. In the best Scottish tradition, they had a bottle of whisky, which they shared as the train swayed on its journey into the countryside.

Sitting down at last, luggage safely stowed, Ian and I each lit a cigarette, the smoke swirling upwards to join the fug inside our warm compartment. A poster advertising the benefits of a holiday in Cornwall looked down on us men going to war. I wondered if I would ever get the chance to go on holiday there with Pamela.

'Well mates,' Ian said, 'how long is this going to take?' He took a pack of cards from his top pocket and shuffled them professionally. 'Shall we?'

Groans emanated, but all took the challenge. A few hours went by surprisingly fast, and Ian, as was his luck, made a large profit. As a keen photographer, and with an eye for detail, I had quietly checked the cards on one occasion but could see no marks. Just luck, perhaps.

The charm of the cards ran out and slowly all the men succumbed to sleep, arms folded, heads on each other's shoulders. Occasional snores disturbed me; I still wasn't used to sleeping in the same room as other men.

The blinds had been tightly drawn down on the

guard's orders, and the long journey continued in the darkness until the train steamed into its final destination. Everyone in a khaki uniform transferred to the waiting transport, which was soon filled with tired but cheerful soldiers.

The lorries rumbled through the dead of night. A few lights were still visible in the countryside but they were quickly extinguished as the train approached, as though the noise reminded the owners of the strict blackout rules. Not that we cared; we were soon asleep, a jumble of arms and legs lying on the floor, or on seats and bags.

After the comforts of home, the barracks were cold and unwelcoming. But as the men arrived, their warm exchange of greetings and news from home soon enlivened the austere building. One man had got married the day before, and Ian joined in the ribald jokes made at his expense. I stood to one side avoiding the jollity. Ian glanced at me and came over.

'Come on, Andrew, he's just got married. We have to josh him a bit.'

'Not tonight, Ian, it doesn't seem right somehow.' I lightly punched Ian's arm and left, to talk to others.

I spotted a few men looking sad, sitting or standing alone, but they wouldn't talk to me or anyone else. A Dear John letter, or maybe family killed in the bombing raids. It wouldn't surprise me. Other men were regaling their mates with stories about their families and friends, and laughter spread around the barracks. After a while I felt fatigue coming over me after the adrenaline rush of reaching my destination. I guess the others felt it too, since the men broke up into ever smaller groups scattered around the room, and slowly the guys slipped away to their beds. I was yawning with the best of them and I felt a tiredness that came from deep within. I went to find my bed too.

The bareness of the barrack room with the serried ranks of bunks had become depressing. I found my bed next to Ian and stretched out on it. It was the first time we'd been alone to talk, albeit in a room full of men. Oddly, it was private despite the closeness of the beds. After acknowledging each other, men averted their eyes; we respected each other's space.

'Ian.'

'Yep.' Ian's voice was dozy with sleep.

'I saw my girl again.'

Ian sounded more alert. 'What girl would want to see you twice! Not a looker, I bet.'

I reached into my top pocket and produced a photo of the blonde girl of my dreams sitting on a park bench among daffodils. I leant over, the photograph suspended in the space between our beds.

Ian took it carefully from my fingers. 'Well I am surprised at that; sure it's not one of your photographic models you brag about?'

I grinned broadly in the half-light of the barracks.

'No, she's for real. You've heard me talk of her. Met her in the butcher's, leave before last. Friend of an old school friend. I'd met her once or twice while at school, pigtails and all that. Now, well, grown a bit.'

'I can see that. This is the Pamela?' Ian smiled his approval.

'I've got a few more. Want to see them?' My right hand began to rummage in a pocket.

'No thanks, mate,' Ian answered. 'I'll look in the morning. You need your beauty sleep or she won't look at you when this business is over.'

Ian turned, threw himself back down on to his bed and fell fast asleep, a slight snore and whistles the only sign he was still alive.

I took one long last look at the photograph, and then carefully put it back into a pocket and turned over to sleep.

The wake-up call came early and we all mustered on the parade ground, bleary-eyed but eager to return to work, despite the interrupted periods of sleep the night before. Mist rose from the breaths of the men standing in the cool morning air, waiting for the officers to arrive. Discreet blowing and rubbing of hands to keep them warm occurred as we stood in the cold of the morning.

The RSM from the train appeared, immaculately dressed as always, and looked at the men before him. He let out a sigh, pushed his shoulders back, and began.

'Well done, boys. All present and accounted for.' The fearsome soldier glared along the front rank. 'As much as I'd like to be rid of some of you layabouts, all are needed on this little war in which we are partaking.'

He handed a clipboard to a sergeant who then rattled off names and gave short orders to report to various blocks of buildings. Ian, myself, Charley and Pete were ordered

41

to report for further orders in Block C. On being dismissed we walked over the parade ground to the building and through the open doorway guarded by a soldier. The guard nodded us into an office that doubled as a waiting room. There were some chairs set against the wall, and we sat down, but seconds later a telephone rang and the sergeant motioned us into the inner office. We entered and stood in front of the large desk, saluting the man sat there. Then waited. He was new. I hadn't seen this officer before; he was so new there wasn't even a name plate on his desk. I studied his face: lines about his dark brown eyes, black smudges under his eyes and stained fingers from the cigarette he was smoking. I guessed he was younger than he looked.

'Right, gentlemen.' The officer looked up from the papers in his hands. 'You were the recon chappies, yes?'

'Yes, sir,' I quickly replied.

'Right, a bit of tweaking on those tanks to do before you move on to APTs. Important work. Report, do the necessary with Williams on recon, then pick up your APT and off to the Plain for a small exercise.

The officer glared at us. 'Any questions?'

I thought, Williams? But I didn't speak fast enough.

'Go, men, out of here now.' The officer returned to the stack of papers in front of him, dismissing us all physically and mentally.

We executed a sharp salute and left quickly. I was hungry; we all wanted breakfast, but we continued on to the large buildings which housed the tanks. The doors were wide open and going in we found a table with a welcome urn of tea and a plate of sandwiches. I poured a steaming cup of tea that was so hot I knew it would hurt my mouth if I tried to drink it straightaway. We all took our cups of tea and bit into the sandwiches hungrily while standing around the table.

'Where's this Williams fellow then?' Ian muttered through his sandwich. Pete and Charley looked around the hangar as they munched and drank.

A smallish man, not heavily built but looked useful to have around in a fight, got up from sitting in a chair just inside the hangar. He wandered over to us, wiping his hands on a dingy cloth. After slinging the cloth aside, he picked up a chipped enamel mug of tea.

'I'm George Williams, driver and mender of all things mechanical.' He had a deep Welsh-lilted voice.

I looked him up and down, gauging him quickly. His boots were clean, but his neatly pressed trousers showed oil and other stains, especially around the knees. He was a worker.

'Good to meet you, mate. Where you come from?' I asked, as I appeared to be the only one who had finished his sandwich. The others were chewing away or drinking the still hot tea.

'South-East Wales, near Abergavenny. On the land before this kicked off.' He took a swig of his tea. 'That's better – I've been trying out our transport since four a.m. Canteen's not open at that time. They expect us to work but nothing to help us out food-wise.'

'No, that's why we pack our own,' I said, laughing. 'You'll learn. Got a thermos about you?'

'Nope. Where can I get one?' he asked, slurping his tea.

Pete answered. 'Next trip into stores, see if they have one. Cost you, not regulation but the QM stocks them on his own behalf, if you know what I mean.' Pete tapped his nose and inclined his head at the man in front of him.

All four of us nodded in agreement and smiled at the new arrival finishing his tea.

I put my now empty mug down and stretched my arms out above my head. 'Well, gentlemen, shall we see what George has done to our tank then?'

The other men quickly drank the last of their tea and, still eating the remains of their sandwiches, joined George as he led the way towards the vehicle.

'What've you done then, George?' Ian enquired. 'She was running sweet when I left her. Not touched my Picture Post pictures have you? I meant to get them before we left, bit frightened they wouldn't be there when I got back.'

A broad grin came over George's face. 'No, lad, still there. Tidy looking girls. The photograph of a girl with plaits is a bit young for me, though.'

I thought Ian was going to hit him. 'My sister,' he said through tight lips. 'How did …?'

'Hey, Ian,' I said. 'You mean you have a photo of her and you haven't shown me?' I was a bit upset about this since I shared with him but, as usual, he hadn't shared with me.

Ian ignored me and spoke to George. 'Where was it?'

'Oh, it was under the seat. It must have fallen sometime.' George rubbed his face and left a smudge of oil behind. 'Bit bent but OK. I put it with the Picture Post cuttings.'

'Thanks. I'll get it.' Ian made a small apologetic face as if acknowledging his abrupt speech.

'Where is she then?' I wanted to see this sister and know a bit more.

'Who?' said Ian as though the last two minutes hadn't taken place.

'Your sister!'

'Oh, in London doing something. Not a lot of contact, she writes sometimes.'

'So those are the letters you keep close to your chest. I wondered why you kept them under wraps.' I tried to lighten the mood between us. 'I thought they were from a wife or someone.'

'Don't want your grubby paws on them,' he said, then more brightly, 'Come on lads, let's see what George has done.'

The cold steel tank stood waiting inside the garage building. It had been our first tank, a Honey tank we'd enjoyed driving until we were transferred to Shermans before leave.

'Where's the turret gone?' I said, gawping at her.

'Well they decided it should be a bit lighter.' George waved a hand at the vehicle. 'Get more speed out of it, less juice needed in the old tanks.'

'But we've got spare fuel tanks.' I didn't understand the loss of the turret, and I looked at the others, who seemed similarly nonplussed.

We had treasured the old girl before the transfer, coaxing extra miles out of the tank, learning its idio-syncrasies, how to turn quickly, how fast it could go in reverse.

'Yes, mate,' said George. 'You have the extra fuel tanks, but if you can make the tank lighter you can go even further. Don't want Jerry catching up with you on one of your little recon trips, do you? George made a gun motion with his hand. 'The top brass made the decision and I have to follow orders. Should make it quicker and capable of longer journeys without a top-up.'

George paused to draw breath. 'The fuel can's more secure, made a few modifications of my own. Real tidy now, even if I say so myself.'

George rubbed the armour plating with a grubby rag. Seeing a smudge, he rubbed it with the elbow of his shirt. He turned and wagged a finger at me.

'Had dirty spark plugs as well,' he said with a frown. 'When did you change them last? Anyway, running smooth as silk now.'

Ian and I climbed up into the tank and looked inside; it was even cleaner down there than when we'd left to go on leave.

'George, you've certainly been cleaning up in here,' I shouted.

Ian climbed down into the interior and started looking around; we all heard him muttering to himself. I moved to one side and watched Ian checking things.

George called up, 'Just a bit here and there when I needed access to bits and pieces. Nothing touched, still got your stashes secured.'

Ian stuck his head out of the top, 'You better have kept your hands off my stash.'

'Not touched it, don't smoke that much, much rather use it to exchange for other things, if you know what I mean.' A broad grin spread across George's face and he began to roll himself a cigarette.

Ian took another look at the Picture Post pictures stuck to the inside of the tank; the photograph of a girl with long plaits was there. Ian took it down carefully, smoothing a crease out. I watched as his fingers ran over the side of a building behind the girl, high pitched roofed houses in front of tall mountain peaks, then put it into his breast pocket.

'Is that your sister?' I asked him. 'Hey, let me have a proper look before you put it away again.'

'Later, don't want grease marks on it.' Ian avoided my eyes as he spoke.

George stuck his head through the opening. 'I thought she was a looker. Where was it taken, not in England was it?' His speech blew smoke downwards towards us.

'No,' said Ian. 'On holiday. We liked to walk the hills.' He forced a smile.

I noticed Ian hadn't said where they were, just that they were on holiday.

'Hills?' said George with surprise. 'Bloody big hills, mate, must have been creamed-crackered, as you London-ers say.' George withdrew his head and began whistling hymn tunes. I found myself singing along in my head to them.

Ian laughed, a short laugh that sounded barely convincing, and got out of the tank, forestalling any further discussion. We got to work on the tank, talking to George about what he had done. Hard work was making us forget about Ian's sister. I could see he liked that. Charley and Pete fretted about the small modifications George had made, and were not satisfied until he told them in more detail. He had even changed the angle of the seat to make it more comfortable. George then moved from tank to tank in the hanger, easily talking to the men working on them, exchanging ideas and information, helping, explaining. Time flew past and I realised I was hungry again. No officers had been near us, but many had been seen moving quickly to the adjacent hanger. I'd heard raised voices at times but they weren't near enough to discern what was being said.

'Time, I think, for lunch,' announced George, moving over to the side of the hanger to where we'd piled our tunics during the course of the morning. George searched through and found his at the bottom of the pile. As he began to put it on over his grease-spattered shirt, I saw the pips on the shoulders. George was a captain.

The men, who he had been working with all morning, started and stood to attention, giving a rather raggedy salute.

'Sorry, sir, we didn't realise, sir,' we all chorused.

'Not to worry about it, boys. Lunch, I'm hungry if you're not. After all, I was here well before you lot finished your beauty sleep.' Captain Williams shrugged himself fully into his uniform, leaving the buttons undone

48

and looking unlike any officer I'd seen before. Whistling louder than ever, he walked off towards the Nissen hut that housed the canteen. We stood staring after him, then turned to the other men working in the hangar.

'Don't look at us,' one said. 'He was here when I got here, stripped off working. He hasn't stopped.'

Ian looked at the back of Captain Williams striding across the field to the hut. 'I didn't realise. Come on, let's follow him, I could eat a horse.' He began to walk away, his tunic swinging from his hand.

I bent over to pick up my coat, it was the last one left on the floor. Something caught my eye and I stooped further to pick up a photograph.

'Well, she is pretty,' I said to myself. 'No wonder he keeps her under wraps.' I stared at the picture a little harder; the houses were not British, for sure. Maybe Ian's family had a little more money than he was letting on if they could afford holidays abroad.

Ian stopped dead and ran back. 'Give me that,' he shouted, snatching the photograph from my hand before I could react.

'Whoa, what's wrong with you?' I was shaken at his ferocity.

'It's the only one I have, bombs destroyed the rest.' Ian hurriedly put it into his pocket and this time buttoned it down securely.

Ian's eyes looked a little wild and his fists were clenched. I had to calm him down.

'Keep your hair on,' I said. 'Maybe I can bring my camera and do something about it next leave.'

Ian's voice was still raised, but less aggressive. 'No, it's OK.'

'Well, let me have it with me next leave and I'll get it copied,' I offered.

'Just leave it.' Ian was nearly shouting again.

'OK, OK, I will.' What was it with him and his sister?

Chapter 4

The rain, continuously falling, made me cold and wet; no one would think the New Forest was the place to spend a fun-filled holiday. I stood at the tent entrance and looked out at the puddles forming in the sodden grass that had been trampled by Army feet. Raindrops fell and made them bigger by the hour. I remember seeing photographs of this new idea of taking your home with you on holiday – camping holidays. A caravan might be preferable to a tent, at least you'd be off the ground; I could do with one of those now.

I turned and looked into my new home, a drab tent. The whole battalion had been moved down to the Forest in preparation for the invasion. That was an open secret, an invasion soon, but when? That was the big question. It was a closed camp; some had tried to get out for a visit to the local public house but had been caught. I smiled; at least I no longer had to take my turn cleaning the toilets, the miscreants had that job now.

Jerry would love to know when the invasion would be; we had lots of orders from officers to keep our mouths shut, even here on camp. No discussion of the invasion whatsoever. Yes, we knew it was coming but we had no idea when, so just shut up talking about it was the general consensus. We mainly kept our thoughts to ourselves, but sometimes, lying on our beds, we spoke in low tones about the coming fight.

Like everyone else in the Regiment, I had another twenty-four hour pass before the move to the Forest but had been unable to return home, it was too far away. But I had been able to speak to Pamela. I'd rung the local undertaker, who knew her family, well they knew everyone. They were very accommodating and arranged for Pamela to be in their office when I telephoned again. I didn't want Pamela to use Father's business phone, I had felt a little uneasy in making that request, but Mr Jenkins the undertaker wouldn't ask the awkward questions my father would. I was unsure about Pamela's true feelings towards me, and I didn't want to put her under any unnecessary pressure.

When the call came through I felt very awkward. 'Hello? Is that you, Pamela?'

'Yes it is, silly boy,' she laughed. 'You arranged it, or do you have another girl coming to speak to you?' Her voice sounded cheerful down the telephone line to my ears.

'Oh no, of course not.' I was flustered. 'I don't know anyone else like you, Pamela. I wanted to hear your voice

... I miss you.' The brown flex of the telephone receiver had snaked itself around my index finger.

'I miss you too. What's the weather like with you? It's really wet here. The rain just doesn't stop – and windy too.'

Her voice sounded bright, was it too bright and joyful? Had she found someone else to make her happy? My stomach ground uneasily and my finger began to tingle. I looked down, it was going red, as the snake wound even tighter around it.

'Raining here as well. It's no good in tents, I can tell you. How's your mother?' I tried to keep my voice cool.

'Very well thank you, she hasn't fainted for a few weeks. I saw your parents yesterday and they are well too. Have you spoken to them?'

'A little later,' I said, hoping she would appreciate the order of priority. 'After I speak to you.' I paused and swallowed hard. 'Pamela ...' The snake didn't give up its hold on my finger. I tried to wriggle it, just to see if it was still alive.

'Yes.'

'You know that I am awfully fond of you.' My tongue seemed to swell, filling my mouth, making it hard to talk. I struggled to hear her words over the wild rushing in my ears.

'I am of you too,' she said. 'I miss you ... I have always liked you, even when I was younger. You never noticed me though.'

My finger found a little relief from the snake as I started to unwind the cord. 'Oh, I did! I liked the pigtails you wore.'

'They were functional, kept my hair out of my eyes and schoolwork. I didn't think you'd noticed me.'

Pamela's voice had a slight whine to it. I hadn't noticed before.

'I did, but you're a girl.'

Pamela laughed. 'Yes,' she said. 'I know.'

'Boys don't notice girls, not at twelve.' My face burned, I was blushing. Why should my face turn red? Pamela couldn't see me. The snake fell from my finger.

I felt the collar at the back of my neck. I had started to sweat a little even in the chill caused by the incessant rain. 'Pamela?'

'Yes, Andrew.'

I paused, a tiny silence that sounded so loud. 'Pamela, would you consider being my wife?' There, I'd said it. The stomach did a somersault, my heart started to race, while I waited for the reply.

There was an intake of breath at the other end of the telephone line, then a little laugh came over the long wire.

'Oh, Andrew.'

'Pamela?' I felt a little exasperated. Will she or won't she? Why could she not just answer me?

'Yes, Andrew.'

'Yes? Yes what?

'Yes, I will.'

'Really?' Was that her answer, a yes? I didn't quite believe it.

'Yes.' Pamela sounded firmer that time.

'Oh. Yes,' I mumbled. 'Yes, oh good.' I fell silent, what do I say now? All I could hear was the sound of my racing heartbeat. I heard a door slam and men talking loudly, I looked around and saw two men glaring at me.

'Andrew, are you still there?'

'Pamela, I love you.' The words were out before I could think. I'd said it. Should I have said it? Of course I should have said it. I was being silly; I shook my head to clear my thoughts.

Pamela was talking. 'I know, Andrew, I love you too. Will you be able to come home soon?'

'No, I don't think so. I think you know what is about to happen before more leave is granted. I will try though, but it will have to be longer than twenty-four hours, unless we can meet in London or somewhere. Again, I nervously fingered the telephone cord; it began to wind its way up my finger again.

'That really depends on the time, I could pack a bag ready for your call, then I can leave straight away. I am so excited, Mummy will be so happy.'

Then Pamela's voice dropped. I could hardly hear what she said over the noise coming from the men in the room waiting to use the telephone. 'I wish Father was still alive.'

'I will write to your mother tonight.' I gave a little cough to clear my throat, it still felt a little constrained. 'I'll tell my parents today. They'll be pleased. Mother dropped a few hints while I was home.'

'So did mine,' Pamela agreed. 'I do miss you and want to hug you close.'

'I want to hug you too. I must go, Pamela, there are men queuing up to use the telephone. Please wait for me,

I love you. Bye.' I didn't wait for her reply. No sooner had the receiver rattled on to its cradle than the next lovesick soldier grabbed it up.

I hated goodbyes. I knew there was a chance it may be the last one with Pamela, ever. I wiped the back of my hand over moist eyes and gave a big sigh. It was done.

I could remember every word of our conversation and how each word made me feel. But was I right in asking her to marry me? I didn't know the answer, but one thing I did know: I hated this damned rain.

Chapter 5

The weather was foul. A few days ago the weather had been beautiful. Why had our commanders not decided to go then? I sighed and meandered back into the tent I shared with fellow tank crew members. Ian lay on his bed reading a book; he always found a book to read. I shook my head. It was books or cards to pass the time, though card playing had decreased once the chaps realised they lost more often than they won. I was bored, but anxious about what was to come, I couldn't settle down to read a book or play cards.

The tanks had been checked and rechecked, nothing left to chance. I breathed in, the tent smelt warm and stuffy, damp grass, beginning to decompose, pervading the air, it made my nose itch and, some days, I sneezed constantly.

'Well,' I announced to no one in particular, 'we're not going anywhere soon, not with this weather.'

Ian looked up from his book. 'Now then, Andrew, we're not meant to say anything are we?' He gave me a disapproving look. 'But I tend to agree with you. They've collected our wills and letters home, so it may be close.'

'Nah, not in this weather.' I wrinkled my nose. 'God, I hope not, I get sick on the boating pond at home.' I sat on my bed and contemplated my mud-spattered boots on the end of my outstretched legs.

Ian grinned. 'Not a sailor then? Good job you're not on a Navy.'

'Oh no, the very thought turns my stomach, shut up and read your book.'

Ian laughed and was soon immersed in reading again.

I looked at Ian with envy at how he seemed to be able to relax in any circumstances. I rubbed the back of my neck, it felt damp all the time – and the wind, I hated the wind. I prayed quietly to myself that the invasion wouldn't be launched in this weather, but then again, Jerry wouldn't expect us in this. If it were beautiful weather they would really be on the lookout.

We were all confused about when was the best time to go, there had been various opinions aired when we'd had our covert conversations late at night. They must know we were coming, the thousands of men all congregating in the south of England and God knows where else. Service men and women all over the place were practising the landings. I'd heard on the grapevine some poor lads had been killed in a horrible training accident in the South West. But then I smiled to myself, remembering our experiences in the swimming pool. All because some boffin said we could float the tanks over to the continent. Basically, just canvas around the bottom of the tanks; very simple, and those ideas often did work. I'd been sceptical, but when I saw it, I was convinced, much better than some of the other ideas they'd come up with. So, they wanted to make sure some of us could swim, but Charley couldn't swim and he wouldn't take his foot off the bottom of the pool. He stayed at the shallow end and waved his arms around whilst hopping along; the sergeant had seen the deception and gave him a right rollicking and threw Charley in at the deep end. I smiled even more broadly at the memory of the Scotsman flying through the air into the water. Charley still couldn't swim but at least now he wouldn't sink or panic if he had his life preserver on. I gave a sigh, when were we going?

Thankfully all my mates were OK, but for how much longer? I moved my feet closer to the bed and rested my head down into my hands. I felt sick again at the thought of the coming invasion or as I had heard some say, the battle of battles, it wouldn't be over in one day. How could it?

I looked down and studied the laces on my boot, tied tight and strong. I closed my eyes. My mind still raced with questions. How long would it take to push the Jerries out of the bit of France we were going to? Would it actually be France or maybe a bit further east to the Low Countries? Definitely not south to northern Spain through the Bay of Biscay, much too far to sail and the weather there was even worse than the Channel. I had to stop thinking about it so I opened my eyes and inspected my laces again.

Ian's head jerked up. 'What's that noise?'

'I didn't hear anything.' I stood up and peered out of the damp tent. 'Officers coming our way. How did you hear them?' I withdrew my head from the fresh air and picked up the beret I'd thrown down earlier on to my bed. As I put the headgear on and straightened my uniform, Ian joined me at the doorway, and we both went outside to hear our orders.

Captain Williams came along to our line of tents, stopped and shouted, 'Right, men.' He stood waiting for us with what looked like a forced smile on his face.

Weary men came out of their damp tents where we'd spent the last forty-eight hours sheltering from the rain. We formed a circle around Captain Williams and waited. A little action now, even in this horrible wet and windy weather, would be welcome. We had prepped our tanks. Jerry cans filled to the brim with fuel, ammunition strapped everywhere possible, the little extras stowed in the cockpit. Individuals no longer counted; we were with the rest of the company now, dependent upon each other to watch our backs. Big Sherman tanks, the Swimming Sherman, with the canvas collar that enabled it to float on water. And some of the tanks, like ours, had the armour-piercing shells. We were as prepared as we would ever be. I'd heard a whistle – no, a rattle – something from the tracks on our tank the last time we'd moved, but the engineers couldn't find it, a stone maybe. Otherwise, it was running smooth. We were as ready as we could be for what we found across the sea. I wiped my face, then ran my hand around to the back of my neck and felt the moisture of the rain mixed with nervous sweat. I was ready to fight now, but was I ready to fight and kill? I knew I had to, I had no choice; it was what I was trained for. I tuned in to what the captain was saying.

'We're on the move, men. Pack up and report to your vehicles.' It seemed to me that Captain Williams's voice got stronger as he talked. 'Some will be loaded today, others first thing tomorrow. Right, jump to it.' The captain looked at the men surrounding him. 'We're off!'

A buzz went through the rank of men at these orders. The invasion was on.

'Where to this time, Captain?' A voice came from the middle of the group of men encompassing the well-liked officer. He had always told us what he could, not like some of the others who thought the rank and file had no need to know what was going on. I liked the captain. I heard a slight murmur of anticipation and trepidation going through the crowd of soldiers milling around Captain Williams.

'You are going on a little boat trip, lad.' Captain Williams looked at the men standing about him, all shapes and sizes; the war had slimmed us all down but the height and build of the men varied immensely. I had heard the captain wondering to some of his fellow officers how the bigger ones got into their tanks at all. I understood what he meant: some of my mates were well over six feet tall.

We all set to, picking up our few personal belongings,

and some of us finishing that last letter. If it really was the invasion, letters would arrive long after it started, the censors had to run their pencil through them first. How many letters had been written with love and longing, only to be read by a faceless official before it reached its recipient? We were unusually quiet as we packed the last of our possessions away. It had stopped raining, but I noticed no birds sang. As I filled my kit bag I thought of the letter I'd written to Pamela.

My Darling Pamela,

Words cannot describe how I feel that you have agreed to be my wife. I walk around doing my duties with a big smile on my face, even after 12 hours straight on working I still keep beaming. My face aches with all the smiling. My mates probably think I have gone a bit strange.

I want to be with you so much. If I get leave again can we marry straight away? I do feel bad in asking this, you will surely want a wedding dress and all the trimmings we can get on rations.

We are working hard preparing for the big push, it is not said but the whole country knows it will come. We are told very little, and I cannot tell you the little I do know. I may not see you again before it all starts, but I have your photograph with me always. The one in the park, on our bench, surrounded by the daffodils.

Now you are an engaged woman you must

keep away from the Americans. We work with them and I do not like the way some talk about our British girls. Most are fine, but others with their nylons and chocolate think they can take anything they want. I am sorry, my love, to say that to you but I feel I must warn you.

When I come home on leave I will buy you a ring, until then I send this washer to show my unending devotion to you. I have polished it every moment I can so it shines like the best diamonds money can buy. I cannot buy the diamonds you deserve but when this cursed war is over I will do everything in my power to make you happy and content as my wife. How strange that sounds, my wife. One day you will be my wife and I look forward to that moment with all my heart.

Your adoring Andrew

The vehicles were now loaded on to the transport; all had been backed on so they could be driven off, no turning in four feet of seawater with shells landing all around. Not such a good idea, the sergeant had shouted at us, but maybe not in such polite terms.

We were all tired and dirty but, for once, not hungry. The breaking of waves on the boats caused constant movement of the landing craft, banging against one another, and the wind, the never-ending wind, made the thought of food unthinkable for most of us.

It was the night of the 4 June, the wind had grown

even stronger. The boats, tied so close together, groaned and rocked, men were sick everywhere. I thought I would die there and then. How on earth were we going to launch an invasion in this weather? Half the men would surely be at the bottom of the Channel within an hour of leaving Gosport. I had, at last, worked out where we were.

The port was so full of ships of all sizes, I saw men jumping from deck to deck with ease to get to the right one. Huge barrage balloons loomed overhead to prevent the German planes from dive-bombing the gathered fleet. They were straining at their ties as though anxious to be off too. At long last, I stood alone in the open air. For some reason I remembered English lessons, the endless reciting of Shakespeare for my teacher Miss Priest, and as I returned to my place in the boat, I repeated the words 'To sleep, perchance to dream.' But I didn't sleep and dream and nor did many of my fellow soldiers.

June 5 came; the boats still rolled in the wind and swell of the sea. We looked at one another, are we leaving today? The cards appeared, were played with and put away, and then re-appeared. Anything and everything possible was done, and done again, to take our minds off what was happening to our stomachs and what was to come. We waited all day and then the order came. The boats cast off; some towed, others under their own steam, all ventured out in to the Channel. The English Channel, cold and unwelcoming; the final defence of our island was the first obstacle to overcome in reclaiming freedom for Europe.

The full moon sometimes came out from its cloak of

cloud, a welcome low cloud that wrapped the fleet, protecting it from German reconnaissance planes patrolling the Channel. In the greyness of dawn, Ian and I looked out at the fleet about 5.00 a.m. We hadn't slept much, the rolling had eased but now the adrenaline kicked in. I looked about me, over the grey swelling sea, and saw the boats surrounding us, many more than in port.

'Where did they all come from?' I couldn't count the number of craft on the sea, the sight filled me with pride at what we had accomplished, but also a deep dread of what was to come.

Ian's gaze followed mine. 'Where indeed?' He grabbed the cold grey steel of the landing craft's walkway. 'All those ships, men, equipment. God help us all.' Ian ran a hand over his close-cropped hair. 'We are definitely not alone in this.'

'No we're not. We'll lose a few.' I paused, unsure of what to say, then changed the subject. 'I've asked Pamela to marry me.'

Ian's head snapped round. 'You sly one. You kept that quiet. When did you ask her, last leave?' Ian pulled a packet of cigarettes and matches out of his pocket, took a cigarette out, then he struck a match, shielding the flame from the wind.

'No, I telephoned her whilst on pass out.' I clung to the side of the rocking boat while watching my friend.

'I take it she said yes?' Ian held the match up to the wind and it immediately blew the flame out. He dropped it overboard.

'Yes, she did, but did I do the right thing, what with

all this going on?' I began to stare down at the waves, but I wouldn't find an answer there. 'Was I fair to her? Anything might happen. I may come home blind or maimed. It isn't fair to keep her to her answer, is it?'

I shook my head; it didn't clear my thoughts. I was confused about everything going on in my life. I looked up into the brightening sky. 'I know I do love her though, and don't want to lose her, but if I come back like some you see … That isn't fair, is it? Have I been selfish?'

Ian stood beside me and put a hand on my shoulder, squeezing it hard. 'You are no different from hundreds of men who have done the same thing on their last leave. Some won't come home, others will be wounded, but they have let the ones they love know that they are loved. Isn't that better than not declaring your love?' He paused and cleared his throat. 'I know I would want to know that someone loved me enough to marry me.' He gave a little laugh. 'Mind you, I'm better looking than you, so it isn't such an issue.'

I laughed back at Ian. Maybe I laughed a little too hard. 'I suppose you're right, not about the better looking, though.'

The first shells flying overhead made us duck, but we both regained our composure and we silently began to watch the massed power of the Allies driving through the water towards France. We continued to watch until the command came to go to collect our breakfast. Charley and Pete didn't eat the corned beef sandwiches or drink a noggin of rum; their stomachs couldn't stand it. They carefully re-wrapped the bread slices up ready to eat later. Pete joked about his childhood, getting sand in his jam sandwiches at the seaside.

'Who will be my mum and wipe it out for me?' He also wanted a bottle of pop. 'You can play marbles with the glass stoppers later.' It lightened the mood as stories were then swapped about marble-playing in the schoolyard.

I managed to eat my sandwich, I was not sure how. But I gave my rum away.

The boats ahead of us moved closer to the smoke-shrouded shore. Shells pounded the beach defences, the noise and smell of the explosions carried to us while we watched. Ian stood next to me and I saw his hands clenching and unclenching while he stared at the billowing smoke and explosions. They were getting closer and louder, beginning to numb my ears.

I shouted, 'Well, we're nearly there.'

'That's obvious,' snapped Ian.

'Have you ever been to France, Ian?' Hell, I'm doing well! We're about to go to war and I'm discussing holidays. I couldn't help it though. I mentally kicked myself.

'How do you know it's France?' shouted Ian about the din of shellfire. 'Might be northern Spain.'

I could hardly hear him. Ian didn't seem too sure of himself now.

I gave him a glance; he was pale, as I supposed I was. 'Got here too quick for it to be Spain. Looks like France on the map they've given me.' I tried to make light of the situation but my heart wasn't really in it. 'I'm assuming the Navy have got it right.' I turned to fully face my friend.

'Ian. Good luck.' I put out a hand, which was gripped tightly and shook long and slow. We shared a tank but what was to come we had no idea. Either one of us could die and leave the other unscathed in the same vehicle. We simply didn't know what the day and days ahead would bring, but I didn't feel afraid any more, just numb.

I looked into Ian's eyes; did I know him that well? Ian surprised me with little snippets of information about himself every now and then. His sister – I had only seen the photo once – he never spoke of her. Maybe it was just a privacy thing with him, but I thought he would've told me more. Father had told me to be careful and, whilst I trusted Ian, there was still something about him I couldn't put my finger on.

We made our way to colleagues and the tank, which seemed to be getting smaller as the time went on. Shells began raining down on the advancing fleet. The Germans had seen us and our boat was now in range. I kept thinking of 'Cry "Havoc", and let slip the dogs of war.' Miss Priest would have been proud of my recollection of the school's production of Julius Caesar, but I just looked out on the havoc of war and saw no dogs.

The boat stopped. Now wallowing on the sea, it prompted more sickness from those who had eaten and drunk the earlier breakfast. More shells rained down around us, we were sitting ducks – or should that be dogs? What was happening? I checked my watch; we had been waiting a good five minutes, though it seemed much longer. I said out loud what everyone must have been thinking.

'This is hell.'

No one spoke.

I rubbed my head, and looked at my crewmates. 'Now what? We're not going to retreat, are we? Men are already on the beaches.' I looked out across the grey water at the scene playing out before us.

Some boats continued on towards the beach, a few didn't make it. Shells landed on their targets and large explosions rent the air as fire found fuel and ammunition. Others managed to let down their ramps, and soldiers ran forward into the sea and on to the beach. I saw bodies floating around the transport and halfway up the beach, tossing in the surf like rag dolls.

'Do you think we're landing, what—'

Crump-crump-crump. The Germans pounded our men as they ran up the beach. We watched them run and die. Crump-crump—

An ear-shattering boom obliterated the machine gun fire. The big guns from our destroyers were retuning fire. Some emplacements on the French shore had been knocked out already, but not enough to stop the rain of shells on the soldiers who had got a small foothold on the beach. It would soon be our turn and we waited with many others for the order to come to disembark. It had started.

Julia Sutherland

Chapter 6

The sea came up the ramp to meet us. Cold, grey and menacing, the waves hurled themselves at the advancing ships, lapping at our feet as we jostled to be first off the boat. All the while the crump-crump-crump ... pause ... crump-crump-crump of shells whizzing as small bullets pinged off the sides and structure of our boats. The noise was overwhelming. I tried to focus on the chatter in the tank – Charley, Pete and Ian occasionally talking to one another. Sailors ducked and kept low as they went about their business to get us as near to the beach as they could. I could smell the sea over the increasing stench of diesel and petrol as the engines roared into life.

How strange the simplest of ideas would work, I thought, as I guided the tank down the ramp into the sea. The collars of canvas had kept the tanks afloat on exercises but some had sunk. I held my breath; the water was cold and hostile, now it had a sheen of oil that glistened as the waves broke. The huge tank reached the cold, dark Channel, we floated free, I exhaled slowly, the prop exploded into action, surging us forward towards the beach – and the fighting. Tanks exploded in front of us. The screams of men caught by the flames and flying metal were muffled by the louder sounds of more shells landing. All the sounds merged into one ear-pounding mess.

I saw officers urging their men on to the beach. It was then the months of training took over and hoards of soldiers followed orders without thought. Some didn't make it to the beach. I could imagine what it was like for them, rifles held high above heads, the sea sweeping into their eyes and mouths, up their nostrils, so they couldn't breathe. I saw the sea break over the top of men as they scrambled for a foothold on the seabed. They had no choice but to go on.

Caltrops and barbed wire conspired to catch the soldiers as they waded through the water and on to the sand. Equipment from those who didn't complete the race to the beach impeded the journey of those still going. Bodies moved with the surge of the waves breaking on the beach. Huge concrete walls at the head of the beach stopped the Allied invaders leaving the sand. All the while the bang and whizz of enemy fire flew through the air. I swallowed hard as I concentrated on living.

No time now for sandwiches to be unwrapped and for the sand to get in, they would have to wait until later, if we felt like eating after this day's work was done.

Men were flung into the air from the blast of shells

falling. Shrapnel catching those unwary enough to venture out of what little cover there was of broken tanks, impact holes and even dead bodies. Shells from our Destroyers continued to whistle overhead, the German shells still persistently coming in reply. I cried out to myself, God preserve us. All the while the crump-crump of guns battered my ears.

The beaches were becoming more and more crowded as soldiers landed and supplies were ferried on to the beaches. We should have been long gone by now. We had to get off the beach. Maybe take out one of the many gun emplacements strafing the beach. Help save a few lives.

I no longer smelt the sea nor the seaweed that had lain rotting on the seashore at the beginning of the day. Now it was the cordite from shells blackening my nostrils and filling my head. A smell a hundred times stronger than any Guy Fawkes Night. I smelt burning – engine fumes, cordite – it overwhelmed me. My smoke-filled eyes began to run with tears, and through them I saw tanks driving up the beaches, breaking through the barbed wire, some with flails to clear the minefields. Crump-crump-crump. I began to laugh, what was I doing here? It was unreal. I caught myself.

Eyes glanced left and right, I became increasingly desperate; I needed to get off the beach, anything to get off this beach that was rapidly filling with the dead and dying. But shells kept on coming. We answered fire, not quite sure what we were aiming at. Black, billowing smoke filled the air, visibility reduced to a few yards.

I was confused.

The sound was overwhelming.

I was terrified.

In the chaos I had lost our troop of tanks. We had come off the transporter one after the other, but somehow we'd parted company. Shells fell constantly all around, scattering the bodies of men into the air. Vehicles burst into flames, cremating the unlucky inhabitants. I realised now why they called the flaming tanks 'Ronson Lighters'. The crews didn't stand a chance.

My hand found its way to the back of my neck again, rubbing it sore as I had done so often in the last forty-eight hours. The boys had even stopped laughing at my habit now, they accepted it, they had their own habits: drumming fingers, coughing, shaking, we all knew the reason why.

I shouted above the roar of the engine and constant crump-crump-crump, 'Ian. Can you see a way through?'

'Just drive straight up the beach,' Ian shouted back.

'Jesus! How? Concrete, mines.' Uncertainty sounded in my voice, I could hear it, my training slipping away. 'Which way?'

'Follow some tracks!' Ian screamed. 'Go for it, let's get out of here.'

He was right. I had to show the way out of this living hell we were in.

'Go two o'clock.' I gave the order.

The engine raced, and we floundered through the sand tracks of other vehicles, onwards, upwards out of the chaos. Guns fired repeatedly around us. Small arms fire bounced off the sides of our tank, making our ears ring. Sand flew up into the air, choking men and machinery. Smoke billowed out of engines and craters; my eyes smarted with smoke and grit. Rubbing them to tears failed to help clear my vision, but I thought I spotted a gap in the concrete barrier ahead.

Machine gun fire pinged and whizzed off our armour, soldiers followed behind using our tank's bulk as a shield. I guided Ian through the gap and finally we were up and over the dunes. And then the fields opened out in front of us. I looked ahead and saw the dead cows and sheep and, among them, the bodies of soldiers who had gone before us.

Ian stopped the tank. The turret ranged over the grass in front of us but I could see no danger. I sighed. No crump-crump-crump of shells trying to blow us up, that was behind us. It was quiet in the field. I watched the infantry step out of the relative safety of the tank and deploy into the greenery, searching for cover wherever they could, stopping to fire at ghosts. Onwards the soldiers moved. The noise around me fell away until the rhythmic throb of the engine was the only thing I could hear. I just sat in the tank, numb, looking over the dead bodies, and waited.

Julia Sutherland

Chapter 7

The silence in the tank was broken by Charley shouting, 'Where the hell are we?'

Ian snapped back equally as loud, 'France!'

'OK, wise guy,' said Charley. 'Where in France?'

My eyes frantically searched the fields. I looked at my hands and clasped them together to stop them trembling, but my voice was still controlled. 'Well, we're a few miles off point, result of the beach chaos. Can you see the others?'

Pete answered quickly. 'No, and I can't use the radio to call them, it's been shaken up something bad, will take a bit of time to sort'.

Ian chimed in. 'Let's go inland, a village over there, there's no gunfire that way, we may be lucky, they could have withdrawn.' He was shouting over the noise of shells, now exploding all around. Sandy soil was thrown up into the air, blowing into every cranny of the tank, even though the hatches were closed.

I couldn't work out where the shells were coming from; what should I do? I made up my mind.

'Right, go to the village, there it is.' I pointed, although the others couldn't see what I was looking at. 'Keep an eye open for the others, they were to our left on the beach.'

I gave the quick concise orders needed and the tank reversed slightly, and began to drive slowly down a small road towards the village. Enclosed by hedges on both sides, it was eerily quiet; the soldiers that had followed us up from the beach had melted into the countryside. Guns continued to fire, the shells falling short as we trundled along. As we travelled further away from the beach the gunfire faded a little, but I could still hear the crump-crump-crump behind me, a constant reminder I was now at war.

'I don't like this one bit,' shouted Pete. 'It's much too quiet.'

I gave a little snort. 'I agree, watch for mines. This is really odd.'

Ian then asked the question I was asking myself. 'Um, where have the soldiers gone?'

My eyes scanned the horizon for something to fix on. 'I'm more worried about where I am. Where the hell are the other tanks? It's not right. We should be in the thick of it.'

Ian called out, 'I am not complaining, just drive on, mate, and worry about it later.'

The lane continued to wind towards the distant village, the tank eating the miles up slowly and purposefully; all the while the boom and crack of guns invaded the once peaceful countryside. Banked hedges precluded a good view of the fields and the animals, but I could hear the panicked lowing of the cows in between the boom of the louder gunfire.

'Stop!' I'd seen something.

The tank screeched to a halt, swinging as it did so. A gate stood ajar to my right as the tank came to rest in the lane.

Pete screamed out, 'Hey! Steady on, there are others in this tank, you know.'

Before I could say anything, Charley shouted back, 'When he shouts stop, I stop. Get used to it.'

I exhaled long and hard, keeping my temper. 'Here's a gate, get inside a field, see what's around. The land rises over there, we should be able to get a view of what's happening.'

I explained my order to the guys, but why do that? I shouldn't have to explain myself; their lives could depend on my decision-making. 'Just do it, Charley.' My voice was harsh.

'Right-ho, here goes.'

The tank swung and went into the field, brushing the wooden gate aside in a rush.

'Whoa, that was great,' shouted Charley. There was a trace of hysteria in his voice that I chose to ignore. I was just keeping it together myself, no time to sort others.

'Focus,' I muttered to myself.

Smashed wooden palings from the gate crunched under the tracks as it barged into the field. Mud flew up, hitting the sides, banging and thumping, making us all jump.

'Where?' Charley called out.

'Up, Charley, up,' I shouted. 'Up.'

The tank bucked and jumped over the earth as it sped up the hill, engine racing.

Pete yelled anxiously, 'Listen! It's that noise again.'

I felt a flash of exasperation. 'Ignore it, Pete, we're moving. That chopping sound, it's the crunching of the gate caught underneath.'

'I know,' shouted Pete, 'but that's not what's worrying me.'

'We didn't find anything,' said Charley before I could argue further. 'Ignore it.'

'Look,' I shouted over the revving of the engine straining to get up the long incline of the hill.

Alongside the hedges, men slowly became visible, moving singly along the line of the hedge towards the brow of the hill and the village.

'There they are,' I said. 'Wondered where they'd got to.'

'Not seen them before.' Ian peered out of the tank.

'Stop!' I barked. 'Don't move, we could draw attention to them. Back off slowly down the hill.' I anxiously scanned around the field and beyond. 'Can you see Jerry anywhere?'

'Too late,' said Ian. 'Look.'

The far hedge had come alive. German soldiers slowly emerged in a tight formation through a hole they'd cut in the thick hedge. They quickly broke into small groups.

I ducked down inside the tank, slamming the hatches shut. 'Bring the gun up, let's go.'

Charley glanced at me and shouted above the engines, 'If they have some artillery, we're sitting ducks.'

'Do it!' I snapped. 'We're here to fight, not skulk around.' I was beginning to get exasperated at my orders being questioned. It hadn't been like this on exercises, being second-guessed all the time.

I heard Pete muttering, 'OK, I know we are here to find the enemy but this is a bit close for comfort.'

The soldiers exchanged fire. Shocked at the pain and release of death, men fell where they stood. Ringing noises bounced off the skin of the tank, I suddenly realised it sounded much louder in France than on the firing ranges back in England. And then a brief silence.

I was shocked, even after the carnage of the landing. It was different in real life than on the training fields. Nothing could prepare me for the sight of dead and dying men lying alongside the hedgerow. And I'd helped cause their deaths.

A banging on the side of the tank made me jump, then a muffled English voice penetrated the armour. 'Hey, in there. Where did you come from, any more of you?'

Ian shouted back, 'No, just us. Got separated on the beach, trying to find where we are.'

I glared at Ian. 'Shush!' I raised the hatch and emerged into the fresh air, looking down at an army officer leaning against my tank. A distinctly grubby face looked back. Definitely English with a small moustache and an air of command about him.

'Right,' he said. 'You can come on to the village with us. We have to clear it.' The officer indicated the hole the Germans had come through.

I shook my head. 'We need to go along the road. I can't go through the hedges in this, they're too big and steep.' I pointed to the seemingly impenetrable greenery surrounding them. 'That's a real problem for us.'

'Fair enough,' he said, removing his cap and wiping his brow. 'Head for the church over there – see it? Mines, look out for those off-road, not had much time to do roads, but verges are dangerous.'

The officer pushed himself off the side of the tank and consulted with a sergeant who had run up to him. He pointed at the cut in the hedge and men began moving through it.

I called down to the officer, 'Mines. Yes, we were briefed on them, much resistance, do you think?'

There was a slight pause as the officer appeared to contemplate his answer. 'No, not too much at the moment, maybe we're lucky and they're on leave.' The officer laughed. 'I could do with a nice French holiday, wine, sun and no bloody rain.'

I called orders down to Charley, and the tank turned and left the field, crunching again over the remains of the gate. This time some soldiers followed, guns ready, trying not to trip on the churned-up surface as they jogged to keep up with the cover given by our tank.

The lane wound its way down toward the village. No Germans came out to fight. It was eerie, almost as if they hadn't planned for this day at all. Hitler must have soldiers stationed here to resist the invasion, but maybe not in this area, I thought. We kept motoring onward to the village, hoping our luck held.

I found myself saying a little prayer. I had hated Sunday school. Where did that thought come from? And then I took out a photograph of Pamela, I brushed it carefully with a finger and replaced it in my pocket. I had no time for thoughts of England; I was in Normandy on the biggest invasion ever seen. Concentrate. The invasion would be talked about for years, whichever side won. God willing, I'll survive and the Allies will win. Then I remembered the commander in chief's address that we'd received before embarking. What had he said? I reached into another pocket and took out a folded piece of paper and read it slowly.

'To us is given the honour of striking a blow for freedom which will live in history; and in the better days that lie ahead men will speak with pride of our doings.'

I refolded the paper and put it back in my pocket, and I returned to my 'doings'.

A small house heralded the beginning of the village. Closed windows gave the house a blind look, and no movement could be heard behind its blue shuttered windows.

The tank moved on its tracks, rattling seemingly ever more loudly as it passed the silent house. Soldiers ran up to the doorway, obeying their officer's arm-motioned orders; around the back they reconnoitred, but they found no sign of life. They moved on.

More houses began to line the road, again all shut-tered up tightly. Then we all heard the distinctive sound of a bicycle bell, ringing gaily, coming towards us. The small convoy stopped and the soldiers deployed to either side of the road, taking up positions in doorways and gates. A bicycle – what was that doing here? I scratched my head; of course, I'd seen them being loaded at embarkation. Horses were still being used to pull guns; mechanisation had not completely taken over the art of war. I hated the thought of the horses in battle, the animals lying in the fields near the beaches had upset me, but I'd covered my feelings. I suddenly remembered the rag-and-bone man's two horses that I had fed carrots to as a young boy. The younger horse had been taken at the beginning of the war, leaving the recently retired older horse to pull the cart around the streets alone. I could almost hear the noise made when the hooves hit the cobbles as it passed along the street. But I snapped back into the present – it was the tracks of the tank crunching over stones on the road that I could hear.

The bend we had stopped on had revealed the end of the road where it entered the village square. As I watched, a large man came into view, riding a bicycle. He held a flag above his head, intermittently lowering the white cloth to ring a bell on the handlebars.

'*Bonjour bonjour*,' he called out. 'Welcome, welcome.' His bike stuttered to a halt immediately in front of the tank and he laid his machine carefully on the ground. The man adjusted the brightly coloured sash he wore. His face beamed out at the soldiers. I suspected they thought, as I did, he was truly a mad Frenchman.

'I, Mayor,' shouted the Frenchman in a deep voice. 'Welcome. No Germans here. Come.'

I looked on in amazement. Ian muttered just loud enough for me to hear, 'What the hell is he doing here?'

I waited for the officer commanding the soldiers to cross the street to the Mayor; I didn't want to try and talk to him. As I waited, more people appeared, some out of the houses, others just seemed to materialise in the road. Cautiously, and then with growing confidence, they moved towards us.

'Welcome, welcome.' The man's voice seemed more joyous every time he spoke.

A long piece of bread was pushed at one young soldier as he attempted to keep the crowd away from the tank and the officer, now standing with the mayor. Cheese was brought on plates and offered. Wine bottles were proffered to the young men now watching in disbelief. Despite preferring whisky, Charley and Pete accepted gladly. Glugs of wine were taken and brought back up. Some stomachs couldn't cope with the unexpected glut of food and drink mixed with the acid produced by the fear of war. The older soldiers grinned at the young men retching in the gutter. They respectfully took a small sip of wine and handed the bottles back; I guessed they wanted to live through the day, and be sober enough to stay alive. A voice boomed out with orders.

'Right, men,' shouted the officer. 'Into the village, take position in the square on the entrances, up into the bell tower. See what you can.'

The officer turned his head left and right. 'The odd Jerry will still be around. Keep an eye out for snipers.' He looked directly at me. 'You boys in the tank, this village should give you bearings to find the rest of your company. Thanks for your help.' The officer's hand patted the tank, then he turned to walk away.

'What help?' said Ian above the clamour of French and English voices. 'We've done nothing.'

The officer turned back. 'Oh, on the contrary. The Germans saw your tank on the hill and decided to draw back. Expect they thought you were the first of many – you saved a few lives.'

The officer touched the fingers of his hand to his cap and nodded. 'Take the furthest road out of the square and keep going, you should meet up with the rest of your chaps along there. Tanks are meant to be supporting the bridge-taking. Watch out for the snipers, keep your head down. At the last report they're in the trees or high up in towers and chateau attics.'

A soldier ran up and, despite panting hard, managed to report. 'Sir … the church … we can't get up into the tower … no stairs … anywhere.'

'What? Of course there are stairs.'

'We can't find them, and there's a sniper up there, pinning us down in the road opposite. No way up to him, sir.' The soldier leaned on my tank catching his breath.

'We need your guns for this one,' the officer said. 'Blow the whole thing up. I would have preferred to put my man up there, good vantage point.' The officer looked up at the turret, smiling broadly. I took the hint; we would have to stay around for a little longer before finding our troop.

'Pete,' I shouted. 'How's that radio doing?' I was getting exasperated at the failure of the radio, and harried Pete all the time. I felt a bit guilty doing it, but we needed that radio to work properly.

'Not so well,' he grunted, shaking his head. 'I'm getting feedback now, which is progress, I suppose.'

I turned my attention to the problem of the bell tower. We manoeuvred the tank to the light gravelled square. As we entered, I saw the church at the end of the open space, and immediately, a series of pings hit the side of the tank.

'Whoa, that felt close,' said Ian, ducking instinctively. 'A sniper, eh? Nice church.'

Pete snorted. 'No stairs or doorway? What's that cretin saying – look!'

I looked at the square tower. At the base there was nothing, just substantial blocks of stonework. 'Nothing on this side, I assume no entrance outside. The stairs must be inside the tower.'

A snort came again. 'No, look higher,' Pete insisted. 'On the right side.'

Ian agreed with me. 'Where?' He couldn't see a staircase or doorway either.

'Higher. Twenty foot up.' Pete's patience had never been his strong suit and I could hear the exasperation in his voice.

I then saw the stairs and doorway. 'Good God! How

do they get up, jump?' The entrance was the same shape as the arched windows on all four sides of the tower so it blended in. I had to look hard to spot the doorway; a glance wouldn't reveal the entrance.

Ian was clearly exasperated. 'You imbecile! A ladder, they need a ladder. Drive up to the tower, right up close.'

The tank trundled up the square to the church tower, which was set back from the roadway that ran around the open space.

'Go to the side, under the stairway,' said Ian, sharp and clear. 'Yes, that's it.'

Ian was ordering the movement of the tank. I glared at him, and then I realised what Ian was thinking. Use the tank to climb up. Why hadn't I thought of that?

Bullets zinged past and pinged on the tank until we were too close under the tower to be a target. The infantry then realised what we were doing. They too had spotted the stairs starting halfway up the wall and the door a few steps up. Men scrambled on to the tank and made a pyramid to reach the bottom stair and began pulling themselves up on to it. Others kept firing at the sniper, keeping him pinned down so he was unable to shoot at the men on the tank.

'There they go, up, up.' Ian cheered them on. The door crashed open, surprisingly it hadn't been barricaded. There was a round of machine gun fire, then silence. I backed the tank off and sat surveying the whole square, the engine chugging quietly away.

Pete broke the moment. 'Hey, how will they get

down?'

'Look over there.' I pointed to the left.

A long ladder lay barely concealed by a house wall, a tarpaulin thrown over it. As we watched, two soldiers ran over and picked it up, returning to the church tower to allow the soldiers down from their eyrie. Two men remained in the tower, watching the village and surrounding countryside for danger.

'We should find the rest of the company now, come on let's go.' I pointed to a road we'd passed earlier. 'That's the road, biggest one, leads to the river and that bridge he was talking about. You can just hear the guns. It is so quiet here.'

We backed up to the end and turned to move off towards the road which ran through the rest of the village. The square and roads now had even more people coming out to see the soldiers and wave at the passing tank. Small boys ran alongside, causing me to swear under my breath, frightened at the closeness of the little legs running by the rapidly moving tracks.

The road beckoned us across the gravelled square and then we were out and motoring along, flanked by shuttered houses. We had gratefully taken our share of fresh bread and some rather smelly cheese, and we'd stowed a bottle of red wine safely away. Munching on the fresh food, we drove away from the village, eyes and ears open for German soldiers left behind.

Julia Sutherland

Chapter 8

'Can you hear that?' I called down.

'Yes,' agreed Pete, 'sounds like we're getting nearer. The Bosch are putting up a fight here.'

The noise of guns grew louder as I stood looking out of the speeding tank. I ran my hand over my face and felt the grit scratch my reddened cheeks. I was tired but we had to go on.

Charley drove the tank hard along the road; he wanted to get started with the war, the doings, I could just hear Charley muttering, 'Keep going, son, keep going.' The beach felt a long time ago, we had seen what war could do with its bombs, destroying machine and man so easily, throwing them into the air like twigs. The chaos, the death, all in the name of liberation. I felt sure that whenever Charley and the others shut their eyes they saw the same, men flying through the air or as flotsam on the water's edge, as I did.

I swallowed hard. I had to enter the war proper or I would lose my nerve. I hadn't frozen yet, but I was close: soldiers who sat staring wide-eyed looking at nothing; wild firing from guns, just firing, not aiming, just firing. I had to start the war, the doings, or I would stare into nothing too. My hand snuck around the back of my head and rubbed; I didn't want to think of what I was going to have to do. I would survive, but there was always the chance I wouldn't. A telegram being delivered to Mother was more than I could bear to think of. I would come home safe. 'Yes, Mum, I will.' I rubbed my neck again.

The tank shuddered to a halt at the side of the road by a wall for protection while we surveyed the scene. The bridge stood in front of us. Charley kept the engine ticking over as we waited.

Spanning the river, the bridge was a doorway further into France. A few Germans, dug in on the other side, were keeping the infantry pinned down. A stalemate. Perhaps our tank would be the deciding factor.

We waited for orders from someone; what did they want the tank to do? A bang on the side answered my unspoken question, a sergeant bearing orders.

'My boss wants you to fire a few rounds at Jerry, but don't take the bridge down.'

I looked down at the sergeant; a bit of ginger hair peeped out from his helmet as he strained his head up to see me.

'Then advance,' he continued. 'We'll follow through, grenades should finish them off. Remember, don't damage the bridge. We don't think it is rigged to blow, they would have blown it by now if they had.' He laughed and gave a thumbs up.

'Yes, Sergeant, will do,' I replied clearly and confidently, and then, under my breath, 'We don't think it is rigged to blow, let's hope that's right.'

I looked down into the tank's interior. 'Off we go then, across the bridge, boys.' I tried to sound cheerful, but I was shaking.

A roar as the engine gunned into action heralded our movement from behind the wall, and we released a few rounds as we advanced across the bridge.

Vibrations came up through the tracks, I could feel them in my feet. Explosions rattled our ears as the infantry threw grenades at the enemy. I heard the pinging of the bullets bouncing off the tank skin, the zinging as they passed at speed; they sounded like bumblebees.

Despite the security of the steel hull we still ducked at the frenzy of bullets as we made a final push to secure the bridge. Bullets seemed to come upwards and all ways at us as we traversed the bridge. German soldiers were under the spans of the bridge; it looked like they were planting demolition charges. We'd arrived just in time.

The tank approached the far bank and mounted the sandbags surrounding the German machine gun post. We tried to block our ears to the screams of men crushed underneath as we moved forward. The tank couldn't stop now; we had to secure the bridge so more soldiers – ours and theirs – weren't killed. One sacrifice to save many others, I kept reminding myself. It was suddenly quiet in the tank.

'We did it, boys,' shouted Ian. 'We did it.'

No one answered him. For a few minutes, silence reigned in the tank, then I flung open the turret with a clang and we heard the clear shouts and cries of the soldiers as they checked the bridge was intact and secure.

Ian and I dropped down from the tank. The ground felt strange under my feet. It rocked a little, but was secure. I kept a hand on the side of the tank to keep my balance. Looking around, I tried to avoid staring at the bodies of the Germans lying outstretched on the ground. Charles and Pete got out too, stretching to ease themselves from the confines of the tank. After a quick look round, Pete returned to the safety of the tank, but Charley was still outside. He was looking around on the ground for something. Then he stooped and picked up a metal object. He waved it in the air, a bullet dropped by our soldiers, then he picked another one up.

'Hey, get back in,' I said. 'We may need to move quick.'

Charley silently eased himself back into the confines of the tank and waited.

Soldiers rushed around, checking the bodies, making sure they were really dead and not faking so they could rise up and start shooting at us again. They had their assigned duties and they were doing them in a well-rehearsed action. Checkpoints and vantage positions, so recently vacated, were taken over, our men settling in quickly and easily. Even before the men were entrenched in their positions more soldiers poured over the bridge and on into the small village and countryside.

'Where did they come from?' Ian nodded towards

an advancing company of men.

'No idea,' I said, frowning. 'They were hidden from view somewhere. Amazing! How many, do you think?'

I moved away from the tank, looking for the officer commanding the infantry. I stiffened, almost retching on the spot. Before me a body lay stretched over the side of a parapet. The head flopped backwards, helmet swinging loose on its strap around the neck. I saw ginger hair move slightly in the cooling breeze, a breeze that gently dispersed the remains of the smoke from the short battle.

Taking the few steps up to the body, I put a hand out tentatively to the face, touching it. The wind would not need to cool the sergeant any more.

I gently closed the staring eyes and then shut mine in a moment of reflection at the sudden loss of the man who had been alive just minutes ago. I hadn't even known his name, and yet I felt an emptiness at the stupidity of this whole thing. I felt myself beginning to shake and put a hand out on to the bridgework for support. I kept my eyes tightly shut to block out the sights, but I still saw the body of the sergeant.

'OK, mate, let me have him.'

Two soldiers suddenly appeared behind me. I was moved aside in one movement and they took hold of the ginger-haired soldier and gently laid him on the ground.

'No, he's gone,' said one of the soldiers. A quick motion and he was lifted on to the man's shoulder and taken away.

I didn't know where he was going and didn't feel inclined to ask. I shook my head to clear it and turned to look at my little home – the tank, still standing where I'd left it, ready to go on with the invasion. I saw an officer by the tank, looking at me. I didn't move – I didn't feel I could move. I felt a coldness throughout my body, freezing me to the spot. The officer came to me. When he spoke, it seemed as if he were far, far away, a muted sound in my ears.

'Right, go on into the town, you'll find more tanks there, muster with them and get your orders. We're here until relieved. Thanks for your help.' He paused and put a hand on my cold forearm. 'Keep going, son.'

He wasn't much older than me, and he called me son. In some ways he *was* much older than me; he had been in battles before and had the wisdom that brought. The officer then left me on the bridge, he was on to other things now, collating weapons and ammunition he had at his disposal to defend the bridge until he too had to move on.

I shivered slightly and the cold began to fade. I joined Ian at the tank and lowered myself in; the heat and smell were almost welcome, and it felt strangely secure.

'Pete, got that radio going yet?' I asked.

'What a stupid question,' Pete snapped. 'I would have told you, wouldn't I?'

Revving the engine, we moved away from the bridge. A few soldiers waved as we passed, glad we'd been there otherwise the loss of life might have been greater among their comrades. Slowly we wound up the road from the bridge, no sign yet of the German soldiers who had run from the battle. They'd be out there somewhere, but perhaps they hadn't yet regrouped under a capable officer. There would be one soon, sure enough, to bring them back into a fighting unit.

As the tank got nearer the next village, we heard, then came upon, two tanks: Shermans. They were firing into some buildings. Almost immediately, heavy gunfire rained down on us and we stopped some way behind one tank and waited. I looked for the main source of fire; a few grenades were thrown by the enemy but fell short. I could really use that radio. An anti-tank gun took out the first of our Shermans in a huge explosion and blaze. No one climbed out. Charley hurriedly backed up the tank beside a large wall, and we all began scanning the buildings for the weapon that could destroy us too.

I made a decision. 'Look,' I yelled. 'If we go left down that alleyway, with luck we should come up behind the buildings.'

I looked down into the interior and nodded my head to convince the guys. 'That yellow one, with the blown-out windows. They're around there somewhere. Get a clear shot, we can take them out. Go on.'

The tank manoeuvred clumsily down the alley, scattering pots, grinding sunny flowers and herbs under the treads, releasing the oils on to the stones; every now and then I smelt herbs over the stink of diesel fumes.

Eventually we reached the end of the alleyway and came into a wider street; the yellow house was to our left. Machine gun fire rang off the tank. Bringing our gun to bear, we fired. The vibrations made my teeth jar and my ears pound as the house began to fall to the ground. The gunfire stopped. We had killed the soldiers hiding in the yellow house, but a machine gun started up from another house further away. As our gun turned to its next target, the door opened. A man and two children rushed out, running from the cover of the house, scampering along the street towards the tank. A woman quickly followed them, holding a bundle of clothes or food. I didn't know which, but it seemed precious to her. Gunfire shook the air. The woman slid on the cobbled street, stopped, fell to her knees, then staggered up again. She managed two or three steps, faltered and slumped to the ground. The man had stopped in the middle of the street. He looked at the woman, surely his wife. He looked at the children, their children, and then he looked wildly around, before dashing for a doorway. Finding shelter, he wrapped himself around the children.

'Where the hell did they come from?' Ian shouted out above the sound of gunfire.

'The house,' I shouted back.

'They'll be mown down. The bastards are firing at them.'

I screamed, 'Move, Charley!' I didn't have to tell him where.

The tank surged forward. In his little refuge, rooted to the spot, the man clutched the hand of each crying child. I realised he couldn't go back; his house was under fire, disintegrating behind him piece by piece. He couldn't go forward and he couldn't go back. The man looked around like a trapped fox, searching for an escape. On the corner of the alley a café stood with a forecourt for tables and chairs. He needed to get there somehow, then down the alley, but the Germans were firing around it.

'Run, you idiot, run,' I urged.

The tank swayed in its haste as it rumbled over the cobbled street, engine gunning. Charley placed it between the man and the houses where the gunfire was coming from.

'Run, you idiot, run,' I yelled.

Suddenly, it appeared the man realised he would be safe behind the tank. He ran, dragging the children with him so their feet hardly touched the cobbles. He gained the relative safety of the corner and plunged down the alleyway we had just come up.

But we had placed ourselves in danger. The gunfire was now directed at us. Any moment the anti-tank gun would find us. We had to leave the area.

'Let's get out of here now!'

'Too bloody right,' Charley shouted.

Reversing, black plumes of smoke came from the exhaust; a horrible burning smell seeped into my nostrils. Back we went to the café corner and the tanks commenced firing together. Within hours no house stood in the village. Piles of rubble showed where people had once made their homes. The man and his children were nowhere to be seen. Our tanks rumbled on to the next village, then the next.

I leant against the tank, my sweaty head resting on folded arms. I was trying not to give in to the tears I felt forming behind my eyelids. I was tired, so tired, a tiredness deeper than I'd felt before. All of us were exhausted. I stirred and lifted my head at the sound of shouting behind. I rubbed my eyes with the heel of my hands in an effort to wake, and to cover any tears that may have escaped.

Charley was lying beside the tank, trying to sleep; he hadn't slept for days like the rest of us, but he clearly couldn't rest. He had told me he still saw D-Day every time he closed his eyes, and all the things that had happened since, I think we all did. He also offered me the second bullet he had picked up saying if I had a bullet with my name on it I was safe. I declined the offer.

'What's up?' Charley asked as he rolled on to his front and raised himself on his forearms. He tried to get a better look at a group of men shouting some yards away beside another tank resting up.

'Dunno.' Ian's voice came from the front of the tank where he was shaving.

I strolled round the tank to stand next to Ian; Charley rose and stood, watching too. Pete stuck his head out of the tank and grunted, 'Shut them up, trying to sleep.' And then he disappeared again into the depths of the tank.

We three men stood and watched some soldiers, I couldn't count how many, who were standing in a circle around something. As we looked on, a sergeant walked up to the group and it parted so he could see what the centre of attention was. We started to walk towards the group and saw that a man was on his knees in the centre of the circle. Intrigued, and by common unspoken assent, we continued to walk over to the gathered soldiers. We heard clearer voices now, mainly English but a little German too.

Through a gap in the circle I saw the man kneeling. He had grey trousers on but nothing else to suggest he was a soldier, or even an officer. As I got nearer I saw his face, streaming with tears. He wasn't a man, he was a boy, maybe sixteen years old or younger. Blond hair, matted with dirt, his eyes blue and wild. He was terrified.

The sergeant questioned the men in the circle. 'Where did he come from?'

'Sarge, I went over there for a piss, he was in a drainage ditch. Whimpering.'

The sergeant stood and looked at the boy. 'Any more of you?'

Looking at the boy I realised he was about the same age as my brother. The boy just sobbed as he knelt before the men.

'Any more?' The sergeant addressed the man who had told him where the boy had been found.

'Not live ones.' The soldier blanched and shook his head. 'Two or three, dead, really dead …'

'And?' the sergeant prompted.

The soldier blinked. 'No uniforms,' he said, 'just like him, no guns either. He was hiding under them. Wouldn't have seen him but for the crying.'

'Deserters,' the sergeant said under his breath.

The boy knelt in front of them, tears streaming down his face, but he no longer made a sound as he cried.

'He's only a kid,' I said to Charley and Ian. 'Just like my little brother, James. How can they make them fight at this age?'

'War,' Charley sighed. 'Just war.'

I could no longer look at the crying boy so I left the soldiers to their prisoner and returned to the tank. Charley and Ian followed. We all lay down to sleep, but, despite our deep tiredness, I found sleep impossible. As I closed my eyes, I saw a tear-stained boy on his knees. I had no doubt Charley and Ian did too.

Chapter 9

The rain lashed down on our solitary tank as it rumbled along a road still lined with the high hedges that stopped us taking shelter in the fields. Occasional fire came from the wooded edges of the road, pinging harmlessly off the tank's skin. By returning fire we often quickly dealt with the source of the shots; other times it took a little longer.

At long last the rain and high winds ceased and I opened up the hatch to relieve the musty, fuggy air in the steel shell. The sun came out and faint whispers of steam came off the cobbled road as puddles slowly shrank during the day. An occasional shell fell close by to break the monotony, but the real firing lay ahead. The doings were now quiet, save for the odd ping, buzz and rumble as we progressed through the countryside. We had a specific target: a house in a valley, Chateau les Fleuve, according to the map we'd been given. The tank troop we were following got further and further away.

The tank seemed to be losing power; I'd reported our problems to the troop leader and we'd received orders to try to keep up, but they were advancing with or without us.

'Wait on!' I cried. 'That looks a little deep.' I saw an expanse of water I wasn't happy with.

The tank shuddered to a halt; a ford lay in our way. The ripples on the surface bounced the sun's reflections around like fireflies.

'Look out for mines,' shouted Pete above the sound of the engine.

'No, I don't think so,' I said. 'We can go through safely, the others did.' We all looked at the racing ford. For some reason my guts were telling me it was wrong to try and cross the ford. Had they mined it?

I felt my hand going to the back of my neck again. 'Pete, got that radio working yet?'

'Intermittent,' he said. 'Can't get a signal all the time, boss.'

'Right,' I muttered. 'No help there then.' I took a deep breath and made a decision. 'Can you see tracks through it? I can't. I'm not chancing it, looks really deep. If we back up a bit there was a track going east. We can take that.' I glanced back down the road we'd just come up.

'Are you kidding?' shouted Ian. 'We have to keep pushing on.'

I was annoyed; Ian was countering my orders again. 'We can't push on if we break down in a deep ford. We go back to that track.'

I glared at Ian, then at the other guys. 'We've fallen

behind anyway. The column knows where we are, and we are not AWOL. We are taking out stragglers, not taking point.'

'I say go on,' Ian insisted.

'No!' Saliva shot from my lips as I barked at Ian. 'Back a little way and take that other track.' My authority was being undermined and I could feel a tenseness in my shoulders.

'Fine, have it your way.' There was a distinct huff in Ian's voice.

The tank's steel tracks screeched as it twisted into the entrance to an unmade lane. Moist earth was squashed underneath the weight as the tank began moving along, snapping small branches off trees that littered the passageway, trees that had been blown down by the recent storm. Crunching, squeaking, sucking at the mud, the tank edged slowly up the narrowing lane that curved up a large, long hill. The incline made the engine work harder to pull the tracks from the squelching mud. We crested the rise and saw some farm buildings and a large yellow house with turrets on the corner, nestling in the valley below.

'Hey, look there,' I said. 'One of their small castles – mansions – whatever they call them.'

'Chateau,' Ian muttered.

'Really?' said Pete. 'I thought that was a cake.' A short round of laughter came from Charley and Ian.

'No,' Ian said, punching Pete on the arm.

I joined in the laughter. 'Well it looks the right colour for a cake. Very pretty.' The laughter had replaced the lingering sullenness at my order not to go through the ford, and then I stopped and properly looked down at the chateau.

We all sat for a few seconds taking in the view. The Chateau stood in a small valley. A river, now swollen with the rain, rushed down past it, partially surrounding the castle like a moat. Outbuildings stood some way from the main house. It looked deserted, save for some red and black Nazi flags still flying from a pole on the roof and out of two windows. As I watched, the flag on the roof was hurriedly pulled down. Then, as we continued to gaze down the valley, the window flags were dragged up. One caught on a drainpipe. A pair of arms wrestled to pull it free and then the person trying to retrieve it let go. The banner sank slowly to the ground, a remnant of wind caught it, throwing the symbol up into the air and then down. Swirling, it danced on the air until it reached the gushing river. A fallen branch caught an edge of the flag and dragged it down into the water, disappearing from view.

Small uniformed figures came out of the house, a car drew up, boxes, large and small, were put into the back and then they all got into the car and drove away. Another car arrived, more people emerged from the house, a lorry rumbled up and parked behind the car. We were too far away to do anything constructive to hinder their departure so we gazed on. The black figures put more boxes, and what I thought must be pictures, into the vehicles before they climbed aboard themselves and drove hurriedly away.

'The Germans have left it a bit late to do all that,' said Ian. 'Our main force must be well ahead of us by now, they are sure to run into them.'

'Yep.' I hit the side of the tank and Charley put it into gear, driving slowly down the incline to the house and buildings. It screamed and clanked down the narrow roadway that now widened as it neared the buildings. The well-kept road withstood the tank tracks as we made our way down towards the chateau and outbuildings.

Charley spoke, a little worry in his voice. 'There's that noise again, what is it?'

I was concerned too but didn't want them to know. 'If I knew I'd have fixed it.' We seemed to be getting slower and slower, the power coming and going. 'I have no idea.' I found myself shouting over the sound of tank tracks crunching on the stone lane.

'We must stop it somehow,' said Pete. 'You can hear us coming for miles.'

I thought Pete sounded concerned too. 'I know,' I agreed, testily. Pete, I felt, was stating the obvious and it was getting rather annoying. I began looking for cover for the tank so we could have another attempt at working out what the problem was without being rained on.

I saw our haven for the night. 'Pull in there. That must be the cow byre. The Germans have left, we saw them go.'

'Fair enough.' Charley carefully steered the large vehicle off the track. The tank rumbled and coughed – everything it shouldn't do – until it reached the barn.

'In you go, my dear little tank,' said Charley.

A loud bang came from under the tracks. 'What the hell … what was that?' Pete shouted.

A shudder went through the tank and then another bang. The tank finally juddered to a halt just after we entered the large open double doorway. We came to rest under the loft, facing towards the Chateau.

'Gentlemen,' said Charley, 'we've stopped, and I don't think we're going anywhere fast.'

I ignored Charley. 'Is the radio working now, Pete? We must tell them where we are, what has happened.' I was frightened; we were vulnerable if the Germans had not all gone from the chateau but were still in the area regrouping.

There was a frantic twiddling of knobs as screeching sounds emanated from the radio set as Pete attempted to get a signal.

I dropped down to the ground, partly to stretch my legs but also to get away from the sounds of the radio failing to connect to a signal. No sound of human contact came over the airways.

Ian snapped is head around. 'Charles! Pete! Make that damn thing work for a change, will you.'

'No reception here,' said Pete with a whine. 'Maybe at the top of the hill. We're too sheltered here.'

'It's nothing to do with reception,' barked Ian. 'Make it work.'

I could hear Ian was also becoming more frustrated at every second of radio failure.

'It's not my fault – the wires keep coming out.' The whine in Pete's voice rose as he set to, trying to make the radio work, the screeching worse than ever.

I wanted to change the subject before a fight began. 'Do you think that's the right house, the one we were looking for?' I consulted my map with a frown on my face.

'We can ask,' snapped Ian.

'How's your French?' I asked, peering at him, wondering why he was so irritated.

Ian huffed. 'Not too bad, holidays abroad before the war.'

I shook my head. What was Ian up to? One moment he denied leaving Britain, the next he was holidaying abroad. I continued to study the map and, after a moment, made up my mind. 'I think it's the chateau we were meant to be looking out for. But where are the rest of the boys? They were ahead of us.'

'No idea,' answered Ian as he climbed out of the tank. 'Maybe we found the shortcut with that lane, or they met some resistance on the way. I doubt they'll be long getting here.' Ian flexed his legs and groaned when he stood next to me.

My legs and body were also sore from being in the tank, I'd found myself standing too stiffly and it was taking its toll. 'Let's take a walk down to the chateau,' I suggested.

The ground outside the barn was soggy from the rain, but not too slippery. Our army boots coped well with the mud and grass, and then we stepped on to the well-kept roadway that meandered downwards to the chateau. Charley and Pete stayed at the tank; the radio was now in pieces and they were arguing noisily about how it should be put back together. I could still hear them from outside the barn. I just hoped there were no Germans left around to hear them too.

'Do you think anyone else is there?' Ian asked as we walked down the hill.

I saw our feet were now in step with each other. 'Not sure, maybe local housekeeping staff, that sort of thing. It's a big house. Um, glad I have the revolver though.' I gave a weak smile at my companion.

'Don't panic, the French want us here,' Ian said, giving me a smile of his own.

'It's not the French I'm worried about, although we have had more wars against them than against the Germans,' I muttered.

Ian laughed. 'History was not my subject at school.'

'Well, we had a hundred years war for a start.' My eyes were casting around the chateau and outer buildings as I walked. Did I see a bit of movement alongside the house? Then Ian's answer broke into my thoughts.

'OK, point taken. So who won?'

'Do we speak French?' I said wearily.

'Fair enough.' Ian looked a little sheepish as he now turned his attention to the chateau partially surrounded by the rushing water.

As we reached the end of the roadway, which was a few yards from a bridge over the river, I motioned Ian to stop and be quiet. We stood, listening. I wanted to make sure that all Germans had left.

'What's that noise?' whispered Ian.

'A pig wanting his food, by the sounds of it,' I said,

matching Ian's whisper.

'It sounds almost human.' Ian's voice faltered.

'That was a scream. A woman's.' I started at the repeat of the sound. 'But where? The chateau, come on!'

We both broke into a run, feet scrunching on the gravel that surrounded the entrance to the small bridge leading to the chateau terraces. We clattered across and paused. I was uncertain where to go, the front or the back of the chateau? Or had it come from further away?

Another scream; it definitely came from the chateau. We rushed towards the large yellow fairy-tale building where I thought the scream had come from. Boots scrunched on the gravel, heralding our arrival, but the person screaming seemed unaware of our presence. Now we heard words.

'Papa! Papa!' A female voice sounded frantic. 'Papa!'

We skidded to a halt by the large wooden door. As we froze, I sensed someone behind. I tried to turn but fell into a blackness.

Julia Sutherland

Chapter 10

My head hurt as it had never hurt before. Sharp gravel dug into my skin as I lay on the ground, the pain running around the inside of my skull. My eyes wouldn't open. I moaned and my legs kicked out, hitting something, which yelped.

The pain subsided slightly and I managed to open my eyes. But the sunlight seemed so bright and I shut them again. As I did so a dark figure loomed over me. I tried to get up but couldn't.

'He's coming round,' said a man's voice, a booming voice that made my ears drum.

A soft hand caressed my face, a slight scent of flowers. I'd smelt them before, but couldn't remember what they were called. The smell reassured me that everything was going to be all right.

'No, miss,' said the booming voice. 'Leave him to come to, slow like.' A firm hand pushed my shoulder down on to the ground. That didn't smell of flowers. 'Take it slow, mate, amongst friends.' The hand kept me down.

'Wait a moment or two, sonny, we gave you a big wallop.'

I tensed, unable to remember anything. What had happened? Where was I, and who was that talking to me? Was the tank OK – had they taken a shell? No! What about my crew? My mind whirled.

My hands rose to my pain-racked head. 'Oh, God … my head.' I held it for a moment then rolled sideways on to my front, moving unsteadily on to my hands and knees, then I vomited hard.

'Ah, he'll be OK now,' said the man's voice, still booming. 'Take it easy, fella, no rush. Germans have gone, only us lot. Sorry about the head, not sure who was coming down.'

I turned my head to where the voice was coming from, this time with my eyes open, and saw a pair of army boots beside me.

'What the hell hit me?' I managed to say.

A soft feminine voice murmured something, French, yes, I was in France. I remembered that – a house.

'Give me a second,' I said. 'What … where …? Oh boy.' I was sick again.

'Take it easy,' the man said, a little softer now, still insistent, but softer.

'What happened?'

I crawled away from the vomit and rolled into a sitting position on the gravel. I looked around through slitted eyes, the daylight hurt too much to open them properly. I peered at a large doorway: Ian, soldiers, an older man, a woman – no, two women, one older – all gazing down at me.

'What happened?' I asked again.

A soldier with pips on his shoulder spoke. 'You ran down to the chateau just as we were entering. We found the Mademoiselle, and her father. He was waving a gun around, so took him down.' The soldier turned and addressed the young woman, 'He was carrying a gun, so we had to deal with it, then ask questions later, miss.'

The young woman glared at me then took a few steps forward to where I was still sitting, in a heap on the gravel. 'Are you alright?'

I squinted up at the woman who was silhouetted against the sky.

'Not too bad, give me a minute.' I felt light-headed, but the pain wasn't running around my head like a train anymore. Now it was quietly chuffing, and the wheels were spinning only now and then. It was coming to a stop and would soon be gone. I rubbed my neck. I remembered: I had come down the hill – screams, the doorway, then bang, blackness, something had hit me, hard, very hard. The young woman had spoken in English, accented, but English. That or my French had improved immensely from when I was a schoolboy. I peered up at a man's figure now looming over me.

'Come on, son, up you get, come inside, sit down, coffee, brandy.'

Immediately his suggestion was countermanded by the young woman. '*Non, de l'eau*, only water', then she said, 'Do you not agree, Madame?'

I was helped to my feet and led inside the coolness of the chateau into a room with fine, light furniture; it didn't look strong enough to sit on, but I was guided to an armchair and told to sit. Obediently I did so, I was too weak to do anything else. I looked around; things were slightly out of focus, but getting sharper by the minute. The room was elegantly furnished, although sparsely so, blanks on the walls where the paint was lighter, where pictures once hung. A huge picture of a man on horseback remained on one wall opposite the elaborate fireplace; a stepladder was next to it.

The two women saw me looking at it and seemed to read my thoughts. The younger one spoke.

'They tried to get it down, is screwed to the wall, it kept falling down a year or two ago, so they nail it up. Halfway through taking it down they realised they had no time, so it stays.' There was a Gallic shrug of the shoulders.

'Oh, you mean the Germans?' I muttered.

Madame replied, 'Yes, the Germans.' The answer was almost spat out.

'We saw them leave,' Ian said from somewhere behind me.

A happy voice came from the young woman. '*Dieu merci*. Those were the final ones, they clear up papers, a huge bonfire yesterday. Most left then, a few left over in case you did not advance this far.'

'I see.' I didn't really, my head was spinning, my eyes hurt. I rubbed them but it didn't do any good. 'Any chance of some water?' I asked.

'Certainly,' said Madame, and walked to the doorway. 'Armande? Armande, have you got the water?' The sound of her voice reverberated around my head, causing the throbbing to resume, even more intensely. Madame then moved silently across the floor and sat watching me from beside the fireplace.

I sat and waited, my head pounding and the figures in the room coming and going out of focus.

After a minute or two an elderly male figure came bustling into the room with a tray, glasses and a water jug. He placed the tray on a small table by the fireplace and poured me a large glass. I took it, but saw my hands were trembling. Using both hands, I put the glass to my lips and drank deeply. Unfortunately, I couldn't keep the ice-cold water down, and was violently sick. I heard Madame tut-tutting. I felt wretched with the pain in my head, and the embarrassment of spoiling her polished wooden floor.

Madame spoke. 'I think you are worse than you look, lay down for a few hours is best treatment. Let the body heal itself.' She stood up and moved towards me. 'Anneke, the blue bedroom I think is best.'

I peered at the girl. Who is she? Who is Anneke? My head thumped again, and I sank once more into a cold dark place as I slowly slid from the chair to the cool wooden floor.

Julia Sutherland

Chapter 11

'Hello, how's the head?'

I heard Ian's voice; he really didn't need to shout. I slowly opened my eyes and saw a high ceiling above me.

I answered in a whisper. 'Fair, I think. Stop shouting, you're just next to me.' I felt the softness of the pillow under my head. Slowly, I moved so I could see Ian standing next to me.

'Shouting? I'm not shouting, Andrew.'

'Yes you are,' I argued.

Ian gave a small laugh that reverberated through my brain. 'No I wasn't! Get up, you lazy man. You've been asleep hours while the rest of us have been working.'

'Have I?' I raised myself up on to an elbow on the very comfortable bed I was lying on. I had no recollection of going to bed; the room was unfamiliar, nice furniture, not to my taste, a bit overdone with the blue, but I thought it very expensive and old. 'How did we get here?' I whispered. Speaking made my head pound.

'Not remember anything?' There was concern in his voice.

I shook my head slowly and muttered, trying to recall. 'The hill, chateau in a valley, oh the tank bust, then nothing really, a bridge over water, a flag in the river.'

Ian sat down on the bed next to me and explained. 'We came down the hill, heard a woman screaming, so you rush on doing your Errol Flynn to the rescue, headlong into some of our boys clearing the last of the Germans out. They weren't sure what was flying towards them so one of them bonked you – rather hard I must say – on the head. Now here you are in a very nice bedroom in the said yellow chateau.'

I moved on the bed, easing my aching body. 'Oh.'

Ian gave a little snort. 'Oh? Is that all you can say? They've had me moving filing cabinets, jemmying them open, raking through an enormous bonfire for bits of papers, I got absolutely filthy.' Ian stood up from the bed and walked to the window where he looked out. 'Just like the coal mines, if I'd ever been down one. Glad I wasn't a Bevin boy, wouldn't have liked the black stuff, it gets everywhere.'

Ian hated being untidy or dirty. 'The tank?' I asked.

He shook his head. 'Not been up to her yet, no time. These boys' radio works so got a message through. We're to sit tight. When they can spare some tank support people, they'll let us know. The other tanks came and have gone on. Otherwise, we just help these guys to search the place.' Ian stayed by the window, looking at me.

I'd managed to lever myself upright and was now sitting on the edge of the bed. 'What are they looking for?' I raised a questioning eyebrow at Ian.

Ian sighed. 'No idea, but I've been looking for whatever it is.'

I made a move to get up from the bed. 'Oh! That was interesting.' I rubbed the back of my neck. 'I still have one hell of a headache.'

'Take it easy, mate, no rush. They have a bathroom through that door, very posh here, no queuing for some. Soap, smelly stuff, all in there, the young lady brought it up especially for you. I'm going to lie down on your bed and have a snooze whilst I wait.' Ian walked around the bed and stood next to me. 'They're going to feed us as well. Jerry didn't take all his rations with him.'

'Fine.' I managed to stand, swayed then stiffened, determined not to fall. With Ian's steadying hand on my arm, I got my balance then shook him free and walked determinedly across the room to a door that was slightly ajar. I pushed it open and went into the huge bathroom. I saw a toilet, a hand basin on the opposite wall – a small basin type thing was next to the toilet – and a bath with a shower over. The shower was all brass, gleaming bright; the water would surround anyone standing underneath the large nozzle. I'd never seen one in real life, only in newspapers and magazines. A chair stood next to the bath and I sat down. The room swayed and then settled. I stood again and turned the basin taps on; cool, clear water ran into the washbasin and I splashed water on to my face. With water dripping from my nose

I looked up into a mirror and saw a man with a leaner face than I remembered, a hairy chin, not quite a beard, and eyes that stared back at me, deep with the memory of the doings.

'I think I'll try and have a shower,' I called out.

Ian's weary voice came through the doorway. 'Take all the time you want, leave the door ajar, call if you need a hand, but shout loud, I'm going to have forty winks.'

I smiled at the reflection in the mirror and then I turned to investigate the workings of the shower. Slowly I began to take off shirt and trousers. I realised I didn't know where my jacket was; I would find that later and check the photographs were still there.

The water began to steam and hiss. With some difficulty I mixed the hot and cold water till it ran at a tolerable temperature. I managed to climb over the lip of the bath and stand under the shower nozzle, letting the warm water wash away the aches and pains. When I finished I could hear a gentle snore coming from next door: Ian had indeed fallen asleep. Emerging from the bathroom into the bedroom I felt refreshed and my head didn't ache quite so much. I realised I felt clean for the first time since before D-Day. I approached the bed and touched Ian's shoulder as he slept.

'Ian,' I whispered.

'*Schnell*! Hurry.'

I blinked and took a small step back. 'What are you saying?'

Ian sat up quickly. 'What? Oh, dreaming … guarding POWs,' he said, glancing around. 'Gave me a start, you did. I've told you not to wake me suddenly.'

'Come on, sleepy head, let's go down – in my case slowly – see what's what, get up to date orders, see to the tank.'

'Yes sir, whatever you say, sir.' Ian gave me a mock salute and swung his legs from the bed, slipping his boots on and tying them quickly. 'Let's be off.'

The bedroom door led on to a wide passageway with the occasional side table and chair, just like the one's I'd seen in Mother's one and only copy of Country Life. She had bought it as it had an article on the big house near where she'd grown up. Mum had never been inside it, save for the kitchen, and she was so pleased to see what it really looked like. Now I was walking down similar highly polished wood boards in big army boots. At least the mud had dried and wasn't staining the sheen. The passageway led past three more doors, bedrooms I thought, to the top of a fairly impressive staircase. I ran my fingers lightly over the polished wooden rail, and marvelled at the sight of the marble stairs and ironwork balustrades. Ian joined me at the top of the stairs and put a hand on my shoulder.

'You OK, mate, need a hand down?'

'No thanks, just a headache,' I said, with a weak smile. 'Not too bad, the legs have stopped shaking now. No brass bands to herald my arrival, I couldn't stand that.'

'No band?' Ian grinned. 'They did leave a gramophone player though – heavy music, Wagner, want some of that instead?'

I pulled a face that I hoped said no thanks.

'The old woman had it playing for a while,' said Ian. 'Then she took them off and smashed every single one. Madame put some other stuff on which was a lot easier on the ear.'

I shook my head, which made me wince. 'I'll pass on the music.' I took a few tentative steps and then, with more confidence, strode down the stairs, watching each step carefully in case I did slip. I held on to the banister rail firmly.

'Monsieur! Oh you do look better.' A softly accented voice wafted up the stairs to my ears. I looked down the stairs to see a woman standing in the sunlight, the open doorway framed her so I couldn't see her face, just the fine outline of her figure.

'Yes, thank you, Madame,' I answered as confidently as I could.

'No, please call me Anneke, I am not Madame.'

Once I reached the bottom step of the stairs the woman walked towards me with an outstretched hand. I wasn't sure whether it was to steady me or to shake hands. I dithered.

'Please come into the dining room.' Anneke changed the outstretched hand to indicate the way to go, and she took my arm. My heart was thumping, and then I smelt the flowers again. I should have known what it was; Mother grew them in our small garden. Every year they filled the garden with scent and bees came to rest on the long blue stalks. Lavender, that was it, Mum used it too.

We all walked across the hallway into a large room where a table was set with numerous places, but the table wasn't full; there was room for more to sit. I'd never seen a table so big, bigger than even the one we had at home. The wooden surface gleamed in the sunlight that was pouring through the open windows. I could hear the gurgling of the river as it took away the last of the rainfall. I wandered over to the windows and looked out on to the gravel terrace in front of the house.

'Thank you, Mademoiselle,' I said to my guide. 'I'm sorry to have caused you trouble.'

'Please call me Anneke,' she said, smiling at me. 'It has been no trouble. You ran to my aid, after all, and were hurt. It was a quite traumatic time. The Germans had just left and then your soldiers came, we were not expecting anyone soon.'

'Sit down, son.' The voice I recalled from the doorway sounded from behind me. I turned and saw an army captain looking at me, concern on his face. I gave a shaky salute.

'Captain Myers,' he said, with a curt nod of his head. 'Sit down before you fall down.' The officer pulled a chair out and pushed me into it. Ian sat next to me and smiled encouragingly; I felt awful and suspected I didn't look too good.

The captain inclined his head at me. 'The food is wonderful. The Germans kept a good table.'

'Our food, young man.' Madame's voice boomed from the end of the table where she was sitting. 'They did not get everything. We managed to clear the cellar of most of the good wine and cognac before they came and it has been kept well hidden. The food was more difficult, but we managed.'

I looked along the table: fresh bread, the warm yeasty smell reminded me of home. I didn't really like the hard, long loaves the French had given us, but when freshly baked, the centre was soft and lovely. Butter, fresh and yellow, next to it. A steaming tureen was placed on the table by an elderly gentleman who disappeared through a small doorway set in the wall behind the older woman. I was sure I'd seen him before, in a big room, with a picture. I shut my eyes and tried to remember.

'Now help yourself,' said Anneke. 'Armande will return with some legumes.'

I looked around the table as Anneke spoke but couldn't see Pete or Charley; they must still be with the tank.

We all eagerly began to follow the invitation and reached for the fragrant food. My mouth watered as I used the spoon to ladle rabbit stew on to my plate. It was a welcome change to the rations we'd brought with us, and the army food offered in camp.

Armande, as promised, delivered some steaming bowls of vegetables and then began to pour wine, leaving opened bottles on the table. It was strange having someone wait upon me at the table, the closest I'd come was Mother. Then I remembered Armande had brought me water.

'Not too much, lads,' said Captain Myers. 'We still have work to do.'

The officer raised his voice to give the order as the men grinned and tried the wine with gusto, but they soon came to their senses and poured glasses of water to drink with their food too. I filled my glass with water, and ran the coldness of the glass across my forehead when no one was looking at me.

'Captain Myers?' said Anneke, softly. She played with her fork, pushing it into vegetables and moving them around her plate. 'I do not think we can help you much more. The Germans, they either burnt the papers or took them with them.'

Captain Myers swallowed a mouthful of food. 'Thank you, Miss Anneke, we have a few things of interest still, and your father ... well, he is the most important thing. I have come to secure his safety and take him to England.'

Myers nodded at the distinguished man sitting beside the older woman at the top of the table. I realised then who the gentleman was: Anneke's father.

'Papa, did you hear that? Your work must be still known in Britain too,' Anneke called down the table to her father.

I followed her look along the table and saw the gentleman's head nod slowly as he replied, 'Yes, I think it is.'

Captain Myers looked at the man with an expression I couldn't read.

'Certainly, that is our mission, Miss Anneke, to bring your father safely to Britain.'

The old man's words rang out. 'Oh no, Captain, I am not leaving here. If I go anywhere, I will return to my home, nowhere else.' His answer had a firmness I hadn't expected.

Captain Myers cleared his throat and in an equally firm tone said, 'Those are my orders, sir. Once I get more information on the situation at the Channel, we will be leaving—'

A loud bang made me jump; my head snapped around to look at the old man, who was holding a large silver serving spoon.

'I am not going!'

I saw him bounce the large serving spoon down on to the polished surface of the table, and realised that was what had made the sound.

The older man continued, not shouting now. 'Pardon, Madame.' A head was inclined towards Madame, whose mouth lifted slightly at the corners in reply as she acknowledged the apology. All eyes now looked at the older man's reddening face.

The captain ignored the outburst and smiled. 'We can talk about the arrangements later, Mr Verdonk, I don't want to spoil this delicious meal.' The captain made a slight bow of his head towards Madame at the top of the table and fell to eating his meal without further comment.

I looked to Ian and raised a quizzical eyebrow, but then I too began to eat and enjoy the fine meal before me. No wine passed my lips, only fresh, cool water, the best I had tasted for a long time.

Madame spoke as Armande cleared the plates and re-laid the table with smaller plates. 'We have some cheeses but no fruit at the moment. Raspberries are growing but still not ready to eat. We will have a good crop this year so long as the sun shines to ripen them.'

Armande brought in the cheese, the smell met my nose and I felt myself gag. I rose unsteadily from my chair.

'If you will excuse me, Madame,' I said in a low voice. 'I think I need some fresh air to clear my head.'

'*Certainement*,' she said. 'Anneke, take him into the garden.' Madame inclined her head towards the younger woman.

Anneke smiled at Madame and pushed her chair back. 'I would be glad to.'

I was pleased she was to join me, even with my head pounding she would be good company. I waited for the girl as she rounded the table towards me. I hadn't really had a good look at her yet, seated as she was, beyond the captain. Anneke was wearing a sage-green belted dress, finishing below her knee. No stockings, but clad in a good pair of black tie-up shoes, sensible shoes for walking in. Her hair was curled to shoulder-length and the darkest black I had ever seen, which swung as she walked, just showing her small ears pierced with gold-coloured earrings.

'Thank you,' I managed to say, 'but it really isn't necessary.'

'Do come. I do not like the smelly cheeses either.' She didn't wait for my answer and moved ahead of me in an easy stride, out through the open French window on to the crunchy gravel and on toward the river.

I gathered myself and followed. The headache was now a dull throb, and I could see clearly. I thought with luck it might be completely gone by the morning. I should be clear-thinking enough to consider repairing the tank, or at least try before the tank engineers turned up. I didn't want to leave the tank here; I'd become surprisingly fond of it.

The gravel felt familiar under my boots as I stepped

129

through the window. I squinted in the sunlight and then rubbed the back of my neck, I felt sure I could still feel an indentation there.

I saw Anneke now stood on the grass by the river; it rushed and gushed past her. I walked slowly over to stand next to her and I too watched the water running past. A tree branch was stuck into the side of the bank and a piece of cloth tugged and bucked to get away.

'I saw that come down.' I pointed at the red and black material swirling at their feet. 'It danced in the air before being caught.'

Anneke looked up from the flag. 'I wish the Germans had been caught.'

'A hard time?' I looked into her eyes; they were so deep; dark pools of brown that also seemed to twinkle. 'You seemed quite well set up here.'

Anneke laughed. 'It takes more than food and a house to make you happy. The Germans were strict, we had a job to do and it was a war. Germans threaten us, because ... they watch us all the time, pestered Papa all the time, complete this, do that, or ...'

'I'm sorry, Anneke. I don't understand what happened here. Who is your father, what does he do?' I moved slightly away from her and waited.

Anneke looked up into my eyes; she paused a second or two, then she looked away down at the river.

'Papa is an engineer. We had a small firm in the Netherlands before the invasion. It was overrun and they brought us here.'

'I'm sorry. Many I know have lost their homes to

bombs, I have been lucky so far, but …' I put my hands in my pockets, and tugged at a small piece of thread I found there.

'It is fine. We take the important things, we are ready to move all the time.'

We stood side-by-side just looking at the river and the hills that formed the valley, listening to the quiet.

I again pointed out the flag waving in the water, trying to free itself. As we stood and watched, the material began to give, tearing a large rent down the side of the flag until, at last, the swastika broke away and fled down the river, leaving the blood-red of the rest still swirling in the water.

'I burnt the others,' said Anneke. 'I do not want to see them ever again.'

'I can understand that.' I thought I did, but I was not quite sure. The Union flag was displayed everywhere at home, and I would not want to see another country's flag flying in its place, or a different language spoken in the streets and shops. I shuddered. The reasons for the war were making more sense now I was in France. The war was becoming more and more personal.

Anneke continued. 'They have taken so much from Madame. The house had some wonderful things, furniture, pictures.'

'Maybe the boys will stop them and she'll get them back.'

'Oh. They were not in the lorries that have just left, they packed them up months ago and sent them to Berlin.' Anneke sighed. 'It seemed that every senior officer who was here took something as a souvenir. I hope she hid some possessions before the invasion, she managed the wine cellar quite well.'

I grinned at her. 'I suspect she did, she seems more than capable of holding her own. Reminds me of my grandmother. The wine she saved, maybe I can sample something tomorrow, but I'm more of a beer man myself, only ever had sherry before and the stuff the people have been giving us, we British are not great wine drinkers.' Why had I said that? I was talking for the sake of it. I must stop talking.

We continued to stand side-by-side in the sunshine watching the remnants of the blood-red flag flounder and jig in the rushing water, together but alone.

Chapter 12

The sun was setting and Anneke shivered. I noticed the small movement out of the corner of my eye. 'Oh I'm sorry, you're getting cold. I was deep in thought, shall we go in?'

'No, it's pleasant here,' said Anneke. 'I'm not cold, I was thinking of the beginning of the war.'

I gazed at her, I couldn't help myself. 'The move to here, during the fighting, must have been hard? Leaving friends, relations.'

Anneke smiled at me. 'No, we are used to it I think, in the blood, we are Jews.'

That statement caught me off guard. 'I didn't know.' I moved from foot to foot. I knew that the Jews had been persecuted in Hitler's Germany, and some had managed to get to England before the outbreak. I'd heard of families that had settled near home, most of them had been welcomed quickly into the Jewish community – in the

Jewellery Quarter and outside it. I didn't know what to say next.

'Well, how could you know?' said Anneke. 'We are not wearing stars here.' Her voice was sharp, then it continued in a softer tone. 'I am sorry, you did not deserve that, we are the lucky ones, they wanted Father's engineering knowledge. I do his typing for him.' She stretched out her hands towards me and I saw the nails were well manicured.

I blanched, I still didn't know what to say. I coughed to clear my throat, which gave me a few seconds to gather my thoughts. 'That explains the captain and his men.'

'Yes, it seems to, although Father does not want to go anywhere, he wants to stay with Madame. Do you think they can make us go?' Anneke watched my face carefully, which was making me feel a little uneasy; she was asking questions I couldn't answer.

I considered her words carefully. 'I would think so, it's still not safe here, you know, the fighting could come back this way, we've only just landed. We came through villages and towns that were completely destroyed. The Channel ports are being fought over, it really isn't safe here.' I didn't want to admit to this woman that I'd helped destroy villages and kill people.

Anneke looked down at her shoes for a moment then straight up into my face again. 'I do not want to leave either. We only want to go home to Amsterdam, see our friends who have survived the camps.'

'Camps?' The query was out before I could think.

'Yes, work camps. A big one outside Amsterdam,

lots of Jews were taken there and then transferred into Germany, to work in the factories, rebuild the bombing. That is what the people were told. Put them to work to repay the harm they have done.' Anneke hugged herself.

I gabbled a reply. 'I didn't know there were work camps. We have prisoner of war camps, and so do the Bosch, my friend Arthur is in one. In the RAF, he is. His mum gets letters and she sends a parcel by the Red Cross.'

Anneke smiled up at me. 'I hope he comes home soon.'

I laughed. 'Despite the food not being good, Arthur seems to be having fun, football, concerts, he may not want to come back. He may be saying that for his mother of course.'

Anneke shook her head. 'I do not think the Jews have that sort of camp to live in.' Anneke shrugged her shoulders dismissively. 'Come down the river bank a little way, it is unspoilt, that is if you feel OK?'

I glanced back at the chateau. 'Are you sure? They'll be wondering where we are.'

Anneke had started to walk away from the chateau, but she turned to me and, laughing, said, 'Of course they wonder, but they will not come out until the fromage and wine are finished.'

I looked back at the building again, at the sentry standing on one corner; he was watching us, but then he turned and walked from view.

I stared after Anneke. A walk by the riverbank – granted it was a fine evening, but no girl I knew would walk with a man she had just met. What if a German soldier was still lurking nearby? I had better go with her. I broke into a fast walk and made my way up a lightly marked path that ran alongside the swirling river. I slipped a little but the army boots found grip and I caught myself from falling.

Anneke must have heard me take a slight intake of breath as I slipped. She called to me, glancing back over her shoulder, 'Careful, are you well?'

'Oh yes, a slight headache but the fresh air is helping. The constant burbling of conversation at the meal didn't help, but it's clearing now.'

'Good,' she said. 'Look, you can see the trout by the river bank, we catch those a lot, I shall be glad to eat something else.'

'I don't think I have ever had trout. Cod and haddock … and a nice bit of plaice if the housekeeping could stretch.' My face felt hot; the girl was well read, had money – that was obvious – and had an air of sophistication I hadn't experienced before. I was talking too much again.

Anneke didn't seem to notice my embarrassment. 'Yes, I know the problem, we had the German rations, but it was not all fine dining.'

The path meandered by the river, a little stony in places, mud puddles still draining away after the heavy rain. We walked in companionable silence for a few minutes, just enjoying the peace. I could hear no guns down in the valley or beyond; the war could have been a world away. The odd aircraft, circling some miles away, was the only unnatural sound breaking the silence of the countryside.

I asked something which had crossed my mind earlier. 'How come you speak such good English?' I thought I ought to start a conversation; the silence was beginning to be a little awkward.

'I had an English governess,' she said. 'Papa worked in London for a couple of years before the war, I went too with Mama.' Anneke hesitated. 'She died there.'

'I'm so sorry. I still have my mother, but I can't imagine how that must feel, I have lost some close friends in the war, but...' I put my size-twelve-booted feet carefully down on the ground feeling I had put one of them in my mouth. I must have upset her by saying that; nothing one compares to one's own mother.

Anneke didn't seem to realise I'd spoken. 'A few years have gone by and much has happened. We stayed outside London with family. I have wonderful memories of the two summers, and the daisy chains we made when sitting on the lawn and on walks in the countryside. I loved the yellow of the daffodils. It was a happy time.'

Daffodils, I thought, yes daffodils. Pamela. I glanced around and came back to the moment with Anneke. 'It's lovely here too.'

We continued on our way; the river ran fast beside us as we walked, rushing down to the sea and the continuing carnage of war at the Channel.

'Shush, look.' I reached out and touched Anneke's arm, then I caught it firmly. She started.

'It's OK, look over there,' I said in hushed tones. As I did so, I raised my right arm slowly and I pointed to the far bank, to a flash of blue, then two flashes. 'Just there, by the tree trunk suspended over the water.'

Our eyes focused on two blue birds fishing in the late evening sun. Two independent splashes, but only one fish appeared in a beak.

'Oh, how wonderful,' said Anneke, nodding. 'I saw them last year. I hoped they would be here again. Look, you can see the hole of their nest.'

My hand remained on Anneke's arm. I slid it slowly down to her hand and pulled her down on to the damp grass. At first she resisted, but then sank gracefully down.

'Let's watch, they may do it again,' I whispered.

Anneke now sat upright next to me. Not too close. Her eyes firmly fixed on the antics of the birds.

'I—'

'Shush!' The sound came softly from Anneke's lips. 'Watch, they may go if we make much noise.'

I glanced at the girl beside me; her hair hung down to her shoulders, catching the light as she moved. I felt … I wasn't sure what I felt, but I knew I wanted to make sure she was safe. I turned my eyes to the birds and watched them dart around the river in the setting sun, oblivious to the world around us.

The little blue birds continued to catch fish, take them to their nest and then return for more fishing, sitting on twigs above the running water, watching it sweep past. We watched the river too.

I broke the silence. 'Well, I'm getting a little damp, maybe we should go in.'

'Yes, you are right. I do hope I do not have a wet skirt,' Anneke giggled.

Anneke moved her hands to her side and began to lever herself up. I leapt up like an eager puppy and immediately lost my footing and, like a fool, fell on her feet.

'Ouch!' Anneke made a little squeak of pain and fell back down to the ground again.

I rolled off her feet, red-faced and confused, and got to my knees. I could hardly talk I was so embarrassed. 'I'm sorry, did I hurt you? Can you move your feet?'

Anneke pulled her feet up one by one and rubbed them. 'Yes I think so, I am not used to men falling at my feet.'

I moved to one knee and then rose carefully to both, brushing the mud off my trousers. 'Please let me help you get up. I'm OK now I'm upright.'

Anneke offered up her hands to me and I pulled her carefully to her feet.

'There you are. No harm done, I trust.' I spoke so softly I wasn't sure Anneke could hear me. I felt silly at falling.

Anneke looked at me and I saw her eyes shining. She looked kind and considerate, not at all angry at my failings.

'Thank you,' she said. 'No harm.'

'Here, take my arm, it's a little slippery here.' I tentatively offered my arm, which she took straight away.

'I find if you fall once on a walk you fall again,' she said. 'All to do with confidence I think, don't you?'

I beamed at her, relieved that there was no harm done and she'd forgiven me. 'So do I. Bit accident-prone at times, I'm afraid. I'll try not to do it again.'

'Oh I don't mind nice men falling at my feet, no girl would.' A tinge of colour had crept up Anneke's cheeks, and I thought it made her eyes sparkle even more.

My smile got broader, and Anneke patted my hand lightly and led us forward towards the house.

'I shall try not to do it again,' I said, with more confidence than I felt.

Anneke gently dropped my arm as we walked back along the riverbank. The sun was setting faster now; it had fallen behind the top of the trees in the few minutes since I last looked. I turned round to scan the countryside thinking I'd heard something. I moved my head to one side, then smiled at the action: our dog used to do that when he was listening. I missed Scamp. He had died a few years ago; we hadn't bought another dog, not that any could replace him, because the war had just started. I wondered if the head-tilting really did help you hear things.

Anneke looked sideways at me. 'Did you hear something?'

'Um, not sure.'

'I thought I heard a bang of some kind.' She motioned towards a green hill behind us.

My mind was made up. I had heard something. 'So it wasn't just me, then. We must get back as fast as we can to the house.' I was glad my hearing hadn't been affected long-term by the blow to the head.

'I don't think I can go much faster without running, you have been fast walking, you know.' Anneke was getting a little breathless and her voice was becoming husky.

I wasn't really listening to her. 'Sorry, have I?' I half turned to look up the hill. I'd noticed the different shades of green of the trees earlier; now I scanned for the browns and blacks of camouflage or even the glint of something that wasn't natural. 'Right, in front of me, as quick as you can – what is it you say, toot sweet?'

Anneke laughed, her smile lighting up her face. 'Close enough, my British Tommy.'

I gave a little snort. 'Tommy? Not quite. Tank crew are different, we try not to walk that much.' I cast my eyes around the landscape again. I felt as if we were being watched.

I took Anneke firmly by the arm and quite roughly moved her in front of me, then I gave her a push on the back between her shoulder blades. 'Walk as fast as you can, quickly now.'

'*Oui*. I am. Please, Andrew do not push.'

Anneke sped up, breaking into a trot where the ground wasn't slippery.

Perhaps I had been a bit rough but I ignored her plea and kept a steady hand at her back, urging her on all the time. It seemed a longer walk to return to the chateau. Once in a while I glanced over my shoulder towards the hill; no more sound came but once I thought I saw a glint of light reflecting off glass. The chateau suddenly came close and we crunched over the gravel to the still-open dining room window. I urged Anneke through the opening and closed the window immediately behind me. Pulling Anneke away from the window, I called out to Captain

Myers who was talking to his sergeant by the fireplace.

Captain Myers walked across to the table and placed a map on top, which he and the sergeant now studied intently.

'Captain, I think they're back, up on the hill.' I found myself almost stammering.

'What?' The captain looked up. 'Sergeant! Where are the patrols, what are they doing?'

'I have two boys up on the hill,' said the sergeant. He prodded his finger at a point on the map. 'Checked in half an hour ago.'

'Check again,' the captain snapped.

'Sir.' The sergeant turned and ran from the room, his boots skidding on the highly polished floor.

Captain Myers' attention turned to me. 'What did you see? How many?'

'Didn't see anything,' I told him. 'Heard something, and a glint of something, a gut feeling, sir.' I gave a shaky salute.

'Yes, I know that feeling. I'll go with that.' The captain consulted the map again, looking more closely at the ground shown around the chateau, his finger following the con tours drawn on the map.

I looked at Anneke. 'Did you hear anything else?'

'Non, no sorry, just a bang of some kind.' Anneke moved away, and stood looking out of the window.

'Come away from the window, miss,' Myers ordered crisply, momentarily looking up from his perusal of the map.

'Shall I close the shutters, sir?' I said.

'Yes, most of them, not all. I'd still like to see out at this stage.' He looked at the windows as if seeing them for the first time. 'Do the rest of the downstairs, lock the outside doors, there should be a man on each by now.' Captain Myers looked worried. 'I gave the order while you were out. I felt something was wrong too.'

I fell to the task of closing the shutters in the room; they were quite substantial, not flimsy as I had first thought. They were each held in place by a long, narrow metal rod fixed deeply into the ceiling and floor. On a couple of windows, I only unfurled the shutter from its cupboard so it could be closed in a hurry if needed. Once I'd finished I saw that Anneke had left the room and I heard the sound of windows in other rooms being shut and shutters closed.

'Sir, anything else?'

Captain Myers looked as if he was considering a few things before he answered. 'How is that tank of yours?'

I nodded furiously. 'Well, not going to drive any-where far, but still able to fire. Makes a terrible noise, something not right, but we haven't been able to find the problem yet—'

'Don't need a story, man,' he snapped. 'Can it fire?'

'Yes, sir.'

'Is it still up on the hill?'

'Yes. Opposite side of house, halfway down, just inside a barn.' I'd calmed myself down a little to reply properly.

'Not readily visible?'

'No, sir, we weren't sure who was down here when

we arrived, you must have heard us.'

Captain Myers gave a small smile before answering me. 'No, son, rounding up the stragglers of Germans running away, or so we thought.'

'Sir.'

Captain Myers began poring over his map again, marking it with a pencil. 'Collect your gear and get your mate, in here in five.'

'Sir.' I gave a quick salute and left the room. Running up the stairs I started shouting.

'Ian! Ian!' My voice reverberated around the chateau's hallways.

'Here, mate.' Ian's head appeared from a doorway on the ground floor. He shouted at me again. 'Down here.'

I stopped running up the stairs and I called out to him, 'Get your stuff and mine, in the dining room now. Trouble.' I turned around and ran back down again, but as I reached the bottom, the hallway swayed and I nearly fell. My head had begun to ache again, but I couldn't stop and rest now. I had to do what was necessary, my doings.

Ian came up to me and put a hand on my shoulder. 'You OK, mate? You don't look so good.'

'I'm OK.' I took a deep breath. 'What you doing in there?'

Ian gave me a little grin. 'Me? Just having a nosey, never been in a house like this before.'

I didn't have time to ask more; we had things to do. 'Right, in to the captain.' I led the way back to Captain Myers to receive our orders.

We clattered into the dining room where the captain

was still leaning over the map, a pencil in his hand, tap-tapping on the finely polished surface of the table. I noticed he left tiny traces of lead on the sheen as he did so – tiny indentations as it went tap-tap-tap.

Captain Myers looked up at us as we came into the room. We executed what I must say were rather sloppy salutes.

'Right, you two, get back to your tank. Don't move her at the moment, I may want her down here later, but she would be a sitting target down by the house, see the hills all around? Leave her where she is for the moment. Um, now where will they come from?' The captain seemed to be talking out loud to himself. He did, however, move the map to show us our position.

We stood looking at the con tours on the map that surrounded the house.

'With respect, sir,' I said, 'if we can move her a little out of the barn, or punch a hole through the wall, we can see down the hill to the house. The wall is wood, you know how they make the sides of boats, we should be able to get through that with a bit of brute strength.'

Captain Myers looked at me through half-closed eyes as if considering his options. 'Do that. I was expecting more men to come up today, arrive by nightfall at least, but we have another ten minutes of light left, if that. I reported all OK to HQ just before you fell through the window. So, we are on our own for tonight at least.' He gave a big final tap of his pencil on the table. 'Safest here in the house I think. Off you go, lads. Check in every fifteen minutes, see the sergeant for frequencies.'

'Sir.' Ian and I saluted and left, half-running from the room. Pausing to confirm frequencies, we left the house at a sprint. The hill was long and night was falling fast now. We didn't want to miss our footing in the dark running up to the tank so we slowed to a trot. The crunching gravel had never sounded so loud as we trod over it, passing through the gate and on to the small bridge again. The hill seemed longer and steeper than when we'd come down it. Slightly out of breath, we arrived at the barns, and the safety of the tank, and found them exactly as we had left it. The barn smelt musty. After throwing down our jackets I banged on the side of the tank. Pete stuck his head out of the turret.

'I heard you coming, what's up boys?' Pete asked.

'Germans, we think, up the hill,' Ian grunted.

Charley called out from the depths of the tank, 'You're kidding! I would be on my bike out of here if I was Jerry.'

I laughed out loud; it broke the moment before I began to think of the task ahead.

'Shall we get the wall sorted now?' asked Ian.

'Yes, not too much noise.'

'How the hell do you make a hole in something without making a lot of noise?'

I shook my head at him. 'OK, fair point, but as little noise as possible, maybe we can tear it back once we make the initial breakthrough. Let's have a look.'

Ian and I walked a few paces to the wall, which in theory should overlook the chateau. Overlapping planks of wood made up the wall, flimsy in themselves but strong when combined. The roughly planed wood still had bark along parts of the edges. I pulled at one of the planks but it didn't budge. I pulled again. Nothing came away.

'Um, bit stronger than I thought,' I said. 'Where's the spade? Anything else in here that could help us make a hole?'

We both looked around but the ground was bare; it seemed that if cattle had been housed here over winter, the place had been cleared afterwards. There were no signs of tools anywhere.

'Go behind the tank,' I told Ian. 'Look on the walls, check the loft too, might be something there.'

'Right.' Ian sauntered towards the back of the barn, scanning the walls as he did so.

Wood pins stuck out of the beams criss-crossing above his head, some holding pieces of a leather harness. It appeared to have been used on a regular basis, still shiny but had that old look of well used leather. I hadn't seen a horse around in the fields when we'd been outside of the chateau.

'Ian, seen any horses?'

'No, why?'

I continued to look at the horse leather. 'Just curious that's all.'

Ian continued to move back into the barn. 'There's a loft, no ladder ... hang on, there it is.' He walked to a ladder lying lengthwise along the wall, partially hidden by some old tarpaulins. Straw had built up on one end, making it appear shorter than it was.

'Ouch!' Ian had swung the ladder around and caught me on the shoulder.

'Quiet!'

'You hit me with it.'

'You try lifting this,' he said, breathlessly. 'It weighs a ton.'

The ladder continued its arc, coming to rest on the edge of the loft floor. Ian put one foot on the bottom rung and bounced, testing the strength; it seemed to be made of rock it was so steady. He paused. 'Here I go.'

'Get on with it,' I hissed.

'You do it! You know I don't like heights.'

'That's not high, climb up and have a look. Is there a window or opening up there we can see out of?'

Ian sighed. 'Fine, when I fall on you in a dead faint you'll be sorry.' Ian was still on the bottom rung looking at me.

'Just do it.' I was getting exasperated now.

Charley and Pete got down from the tank and watched Ian hesitating at the bottom of the ladder. I saw that they both had large grins on their faces as they urged Ian on.

Ian sighed again and took another step on to the ladder – both feet were off the ground. He climbed steadily and gingerly to the edge of the loft. His head rose above the floor level of the loft and he eased both his arms on to the hay-strewn surface. He held a gun in his right hand while he scanned the area slowly and carefully.

He called down, relief lifting his voice. 'No one up here.'

'That's the real reason you didn't want to go up.' I laughed out loud, Charley joined in.

Ian clearly wasn't that happy at our attitude. 'OK,

I admit it,' he snapped. 'There may have been someone hiding, got left behind, you know.'

Pete came and stood beside me. 'They would have taken off long ago. Though, if I were them, I'd have changed clothes and left my uniform.'

'Like the ones in front of me?' said Ian.

'You're kidding!' I said. It wasn't a question, I didn't believe him.

'Nope, fine set of officer's kit here,' said Ian. 'He kept the boots, so we just have to look for a peasant with shiny boots on his feet.'

I called up to Ian again. 'Will bear that in mind, anything we can use up there?'

'Hang on.' Ian hauled himself up on the loft floor and began walking around, kicking the hay, which caused dust to fly in the air and down to rain on those below.

Ian shouted down at me, 'Not sure why they say hay lofts are a good place for romance, makes you sneeze every time you move.'

I was trying to avoid the falling dust getting into my eyes and mouth. I tried to wave it away but failed and hay made its way on to my face. 'Forget women for one minute, will you, can you see anything?' I made no attempt to hide my exasperation.

'Hang on,' he said. 'Floor's clear here ... now, what is this?'

I shook my head. 'Show me, can we use it?'

Ian grunted as he picked something up. Footsteps came nearer and I heard Ian drop to his knees. Leaning over the side of the loft edge Ian moved his arm down with something in his hand.

'Here, what is it?' He waved it around in the air.

'That, my dear friend, is a scythe, a hand one, no handle by the look of it. That could do the job quite nicely, bring it down.'

Ian dropped the grass-cutting tool at my feet. It landed with a heavy thud as the point entered the floor, leaving the rust-encrusted scythe gently rocking back and forward.

'Whoa, that was close.'

'Stop whingeing, nowhere near,' shouted Ian.

I leant down and pulled the farm implement out of the ground, and weighed it in my hands, considering it carefully. I walked to the wall and inserted the point up under an overlap and heaved, long and hard. I heaved again and a sharp crack broke at the point of my exertion and I staggered back with the momentum. I put the blade in again, further this time, and heaved, another crack and the plank gave way.

'There, I've made a start. Let's make this bigger. Shall we get the muzzle out or not? Out I think. They'll know where we are when we start firing so why worry too much?'

We all set to work and made the opening big enough for us to bring the tank forward with the muzzle protruding. Darkness fell as we worked.

Ian yawned. 'OK, sleep, I think. Nothing will happen until the morning, surely?'

'No, shouldn't think so,' I said. 'But you can never be too sure with those blighters. I'll take first watch.'

A grin from Ian met my agreement and he walked a few paces away from us. He pulled a blanket off the supplies strapped to the tank's body and slung it over his shoulder. 'I'll go upstairs.'

Charley watched him go. 'Bloody dark now, watch your step.'

Ian grinned in the dim light. 'I have been, old chap. Night.'

I snorted and rubbed my head, it still ached, not as much as it did, but I didn't want to sleep yet. I felt restless; my mind whirred with images and thoughts. I picked up a blanket, threw it around my shoulders and began to pace the floor.

I walked outside and stopped, watching and listening. As I stood, my eyes became accustomed to the night and I could make out the shapes of trees and branches. Faint chinks of light escaped through the insecurely closed upper windows.

Then, as I watched quietly like a church mouse, I began to hear real mice behind me snuffling around the straw on the hunt for food. I could also hear snores coming from Ian, then a whoosh as a bat plunged past, swooping at prey, unseen and heard by me. Another bat joined the dance above my head; they dived and rose, circled and fell, hunting their tiny prey. A grey shape flew across my line of vision as I continued to look down on the buildings below. An owl hooted as it came to rest in the trees to the left. A branch snapped, making me stiffen. I stood even more silently – if that was possible – my breathing shallow, not a muscle moving. I didn't hear another branch break, only the bats' soft wings gliding over me, never hitting a hair on my head. I looked up to try and see the bats as they flew and saw the myriad of twinkling stars in the heavens. I couldn't recall ever seeing so many. The silence and the chill of the night made me feel more in tune with everything going on around than I'd ever been, although I was no part of it. I moved and the bats flew higher. I walked around the barn, stopping every few paces, listening to the countryside at night. Where was the war? Where were the doings I'd come to do? They would come tomorrow, I felt sure. But now I shivered in the cold and felt alone but strangely at peace.

Chapter 13

The early sun blazed out on to the chateau making the river twinkle as it rushed past. We were all standing looking down at the building as the sun began to warm our bodies from the cold of the night.

Ian coughed, clearing his throat of the dust from the barn. 'Well, where are they then?'

'I don't know, definitely something up there last night,' I replied slowly. 'I saw a few lights moving.'

Ian gave a little laugh. 'So unless a fox or rabbit has a torch, it's someone who shouldn't be up there.'

'Nope.'

Charley and Pete returned to the tank and I could hear them talking and moving things around behind me. I was enjoying the sunlight, the quiet and the view; I really didn't want to start doing anything just yet.

'Look,' said Ian, breaking my thoughts. 'Your lady friend is coming up, carrying a basket, breakfast maybe.'

He nodded down towards the chateau.

I smiled. 'That would be good, I was just debating where to light the stove so it wouldn't burn the barn down.' I looked at the woman walking up to us.

Anneke advanced up the hill with long-legged strides; she moved effortlessly with the ease of youth and fitness. Coming to a halt before us she smiled broadly.

'Bonjour, did you sleep well?'

'Thank you, miss, we did. Bit too quiet, if you ask me.' Ian managed to get a reply in before I could even open my mouth.

'Yes thank you, and you?' I managed to reply.

Anneke gave a little sigh. 'Madame and I played cards for a little while, the men were so noisy, running around the house, but later we sleep well.' Anneke pushed her hair behind her ear and offered up the wicker basket she was carrying. 'Breakfast, I have some bread, Armand is a good baker, some coffee, good?'

I just smiled at her; I was tongue-tied.

'Thank you, miss, much appreciated.' Ian again broke the silence.

Charley had come up behind us while we were talking to Anneke in the doorway. Charley now stood beside me. I knew he hadn't seen the young woman before and he looked suitably impressed.

Charley welcomed Anneke. 'Come on in, miss, have a sit down after your walk up here, we have blankets by the tank, we were just going to have a look at her again.'

As Charley spoke a head bobbed up from inside the tank. 'Morning, miss, nice to meet you.' Pete then disappeared again.

Anneke looked at the three of us standing by her side.

'Pete,' I said, 'he is fixing the radio, again.

I moved ahead and grabbed a blanket, shook it out and then spread it on the ground.

'Please sit, we have no chairs, or stools.' Was I being a bit too attentive? I decided not.

'Oh, non, I am not staying here.' She offered the large wicker basket to Ian to take from her.

'My father is unwell, I return straight away. If you bring the basket down later we have food for midday too. The captain, he says to stay working on the tank, and to keep watch.'

'Will do, miss.' Charley smiled at her, he clearly liked the Dutch woman and had moved to stand closer, all the while looking at Anneke with open admiration.

Ian put the basket down on the floor and looked at Anneke standing with me on the other side of the blanket. 'If you will excuse me a moment, I have to … go outside a second.' Ian quickly left the barn, going out into the warming air of a June morning, pulling a reluctant Charley with him.

I looked at the beautiful woman in front of me; she seemed even more so in the soft morning light filtered by the barn shadows. I started to talk, I didn't like the silence.

'I am glad you slept well. I don't think there is really anything to worry about – a stray soldier, a sniper maybe. If it was more we would have been under attack by now.'

Anneke nodded. 'I am so glad. I don't want to think of

fighting here. We have waited so long.' Her mouth broke into a tiny smile but then moved into a more serious line. 'If it is a sniper why does he not shoot me?'

I knew I had to reassure her, keep her safe. I spoke more confidently than I felt. 'He is after the soldiers, not beautiful women. Sorry, I shouldn't have said that. I think he is a little too far away and is maybe a bit nervous to start firing.' I then felt confused and looked down at the packed basket.

'So, we should be safe?' Anneke queried.

'Yes.' I coughed a little to clear my throat, which felt strangely constricted. 'Miss Anneke, I think you should return to your father. I hope he feels better soon.' I was still looking down and noticed my boots were very dusty, so I rubbed one on the back of a trouser leg.

Anneke didn't seem to notice my standing on one leg. 'I think the excitement of the Germans going leaves him, how do you say, dried out?'

I moved my feet and a small volcano of dust rose into the air, covering again the just dusted boot. 'I know what you mean. You should go back.'

Those eyes – I couldn't ignore her eyes any longer.

Anneke took a step nearer me and took my hand. I didn't know what to do.

'I enjoyed our walk yesterday. It was restful, thank you.' Anneke had leaned slightly forward when she'd taken my hand. She softly squeezed it, then suddenly she dropped it.

'I go now.' She moved away, but when she reached the barn door she turned towards me once more. 'Do you think they are still there, in the *bois*?'

'I don't know, Miss Anneke. Walk quickly and not in a straight line down the track just to be sure.' I assumed *bois* meant wood or something. I didn't move from beside the blanket.

'*Oui.*'

Ian and Charley appeared, smiling behind Anneke at the barn door. Charley hesitated and then moved past the woman into the barn towards the open basket. A faint aroma of freshly baked bread met my nose when Charley leaned down and took off the linen napkin covering the contents.

'That is so welcome,' said Charley. 'Ah, the smell of fresh bread, not had it so fresh you can smell it warm from the oven for a long time.'

I agreed with him. 'No, not the good stuff.' I remembered the bread we'd received from the villagers: hard, but still a welcome addition to our rations.

Anneke looked at Ian and smiled broadly. Taking a few steps towards him, she spoke in a confidential tone.

'I will see you later then at lunch, Ian?'

I just heard the low words and looked sharply at Anneke. My face sagged, I felt deflated.

Ian ignored me and smiled broadly at the beautiful woman. 'Oui, Mademoiselle, I will bring the basket down with me.'

Anneke acknowledged us all before she set off from the barn. We three watched her go down the hill. Taking my advice, she didn't walk in a straight line but meandered across the pathway at a brisk pace and was soon at the bridge, and safely ensconced in the chateau once more.

'Well, mate, you must have upset her somehow.' Ian clapped his hand on my shoulder and squeezed.

I shook my head. What had I done? We were getting on well, I thought. 'I don't know what, maybe she is like all women: fickle. Come on, let's have a look at this damn tank.' I rubbed the back of my neck as we walked over to the tank and made to climb up.

Ian clearly had other priorities. 'Hey, what about breakfast? Let's eat first and then take a better look.' He took a step away from me. 'Pete, breakfast, come and get it.'

Ian pulled the basket to him and began to unload the contents on to the bare blanket. 'Come on, mate, we'll work better with a full stomach. Afterwards I'll have a look around outside while you three sit here and contemplate the tank, see if you can finally work out where that infernal noise is coming from.'

We fell on the fresh breakfast, I ate quietly and didn't join in the banter between the other three. I kept looking at Ian, wondering what I had done or not done. The morning was spent between patrolling the small area around our hideaway barn and working on the tank, pulling parts off, inspecting intently and then replacing them. The sun was high in the sky when Ian packed all the linen napkins back into the basket and moved out of the barn doorway. He called back, seemingly to me in particular.

'Off to pick up lunch, see you in an hour.'

Pete shouted out, 'Hang on, Ian, I'll come too, you

told me the sergeant was a mechanic in a previous life, he may have some thoughts on this.'

Pete flung the cloth he was wiping his hands with back up on to the tank's side and jogged to catch up with Ian, who was already turning to walk away.

I looked up from the piece of metal I was puzzling over. 'Right, see you later. Keep your eyes open, I still feel that there's someone watching us out there.'

Ian turned back. 'Fair enough, old boy, I keep thinking I see something out of the corner of my eye. Could be nothing, but ... why not attack?'

I looked at Ian with a confused feeling. I didn't know why either. I answered him, though, more to clarify my thoughts than to inform him what I was thinking. 'Is the sniper connected to the chateau and Anneke's father? I shall try and raise HQ on the radio again, get up-to-date orders.'

Ian gave a mock salute to me. 'Yes, sir! See you later.' With that gesture, he and Pete marched briskly down the path, zig-zagging as they went.

'Hey, Charley,' I called. 'What you up to in there?'

His answer surprised me. 'I'm going to go down to the chateau and see if they have any parts for this radio, it works, just.' Charley swung down from the tank and quickly followed the other two men down the roadway. All three of them zig-zagging just in case a sniper did emerge and take a shot at them.

I sighed and turned to the tank, replacing the metal bit in the engine. I'd taken it out and now I had to put it back; it seemed perfectly all right to me. I rubbed the back of my head in confusion and frustration; all bits were working perfectly, not broken, but it made a horrendous noise. I climbed up into the cockpit and turned the radio on. After some twiddling and screeching I managed to connect with Brigade headquarters. I quietly and firmly informed the sergeant on the other end we were unable to move and were above the Chateau les Fleuve. Anneke had confirmed the name to me the previous night and I had found it on the map earlier. We were not exactly where we were meant to be by now, but hey, it was war and people got lost sometimes. I sat pondering in the cockpit whilst I waited for orders to come back to me.

I didn't know what I was thinking about but my eyes roamed around the insides of our tank. How did we manage to live for hours together in that confined space? My picture of Pamela was still stuck on the wall, in the spot where I could easily see it. That day seemed a lifetime away. The war was not over, but I'd already seen things I wouldn't want to tell her. I knew I would remember the sight of burning tanks and dying men for the rest of my life. And there'd be worse to come. I continued to look at the photograph of the girl with daffodils. My stomach contracted. Was I doing the right thing, marriage, children, debt, responsibility? The radio burst into life. I snatched up the mouthpiece and answered, then listened to the orders.

I couldn't believe it: wait where we were. Engineers would come and fix the tank, or take it apart for spares. Not today, though, there was a big battle taking place in Villers-Bocage. A few days at the most. Keep heads down. Protect the chateau.

Relief at knowing what was happening made my stomach relax and I shook my shoulders free of the tension I hadn't realised I'd been holding in. I stretched my arms as far as I could and then I took the picture from the wall and put it in my trouser pocket, buttoning it up safely. Easing myself up and out of the cockpit, I jumped down to the barn floor. Dust volcanoes erupted around me, making me sneeze. I heard another sneeze come from the doorway. I swung around alarmed, ready to fight or flee. A shadow I saw there was no threat.

'Anneke! You startled me.'

Anneke moved her head so her black hair bobbed in the sunlight. 'I am sorry.'

I coughed with the dust. 'I, no, I was not expecting you. The boys have gone down to get lunch.'

A large smile lit up her face. 'Armand is waiting for them, I thought I would bring your lunch up to you.'

I swallowed and felt my face turn red and hot so I turned my back to her, embarrassed to show such a reaction.

'I, um, thank you, you didn't have to,' I mumbled.

'But I wanted to, I enjoyed our talk yesterday. All the men are soldiers, I am tired of soldiers.' Anneke moved closer to me. 'Here, take the basket, it is heavy.'

The basket bumped into my leg and a hand came up and took mine, putting it around the handle of the large open top basket. The weight of it made my arm fall, I hadn't expected it to be so heavy and it took me by surprise. I gathered it up into two hands as I turned to face the woman.

Anneke chatted away. 'I see a blanket, I shall spread it here by the door, we can watch the roadway as we eat, non?'

I nodded. I felt lost, a blankness in my brain seemed to be growing. I took a few uncertain steps towards the woman as she spread the blanket I'd been sleeping under hours earlier.

'The captain said that he was expecting reinforcements today, so not to worry my head, *n'est ce pas?*' She made a little laugh. 'I shall not worry, the Germans are gone. The man in the wood I think may be a deserter from the Germans. He is afraid to fight now battle comes.'

'Maybe.' Somehow I managed to get the word out.

Anneke knelt down on the blanket, facing out of the barn overlooking the chateau and the sparkling river. She spoke softly and I had to strain a little to hear what she said.

'I feel liberated, we have come free now. Germans are gone, now we work to find our family, friends, a new life. Make new friends?' She looked up at me. 'We are friend, no?'

I looked down on the most beautiful face I had ever seen, my mind still a blank, swirling mess. 'Yes, I would like to be friends.'

I knelt down beside her and as I did so something in my leg pocket dug into me causing me to pause.

'Let me unpack the basket.' Anneke leant over me and I smelt the lavender I'd noticed when I was lying on the ground in front of the chateau. She began to pick up the linen bundles lying snugly in the wicker basket.

'We have some more bread,' she said. 'Baked this morning from Armand. Some hard cheese, we do not like the smelly soft cheese, do we?' She laughed. 'A sausage, Madame showed me how to make this last year and this is one of mine. Pork.'

I looked into her laughing eyes. Pork, did I hear right?

'I have some cordial and fresh water, there is a pump up here, I believe, but I was not sure it was sweet, so I carried some water, made it quite *lourde*, sorry, heavy.'

I just smiled at her.

'I do not have anything else. The fruit is not come yet.'

'I do not mind,' I said, finally finding some words. 'It's more than enough. You made the sausage, you say?'

'Oui. It was not hard once I got used to the meat. But it is war, so I make.' She reached into the basket and brought out a long knife and cut the bread into chunks, laying it on a napkin spread between us. The sausage was then picked up and she sliced it quickly. Anneke offered a piece to me on the point of the knife. 'Try it.'

I took the proffered sausage and placed it in my mouth, the whole while watching the face of the woman beside me. I could not take my eyes off her.

'Oh, spicy.' A fire hit me, my tongue exploded with sensations I had never felt before.

'Oui, it is the garlic. Now I must have some. Otherwise you will smell horrible to me.' The knife flashed and she put a piece into her mouth and began to chew.

I fleetingly thought that she always smelled nice to me and then I brushed the thought away.

163

Anneke swallowed her piece of sausage and then laughed. 'Yes, I put on a little too much? The Germans, if they come again, will smell you Tommies before they see you after eating this sausage. Still it is good.'

'It is very good, you are a fine cook. Do you cook much?'

'Before the war, no. Now I cook with Armand, preserve vegetables and fruits and hide them well.'

'I see. We have rationing in England. Not a lot of food but enough.' I took another piece of sausage and chewed.

We fell into silence and looked down at the chateau; the river still ran fast and I saw a lone figure walking up the hill towards us. Ian was returning.

'He will be mad at me.' Anneke nodded at Ian.

I gave a little laugh. 'No, just a misunderstanding because you cannot speak English so well.'

Anneke sighed. 'But you said … oh, I understand, you're teasing.' Anneke slapped my arm. 'I shall go, I leave the sausage for you. The bread is getting harder now in the heat, but will last if you cover till this evening. I will not see you later, I think the captain will send a man with your dinner.'

I nodded. 'Sure, tomorrow maybe.'

I stood and stretched out a hand to her so she could rise. Our hands intertwined smoothly and she rose up in front of me easily and eagerly. Anneke looked into my face as she came upright, her eyes darted around as if she was trying to read my mind. Her other hand came up and stroked my hair. I felt myself tremble.

'I …' My mouth dried up.

I took her hand from my head and kissed the back, I felt a little shock within myself. Where had that come from? I had never done that before in my life. Only princes in fairy tales kiss a lady's hand. The soft hand smelt of garlic with a hint of lavender in the background, an unusual combination but one I knew I would remember the rest of my life, however long that may be.

'Well, that was good exercise.' A man's voice broke the moment.

Ian stood a few feet from us. 'Did you leave me anything to eat?' He moved and threw himself on to the blanket, ignoring us both. Ian rummaged in the napkins on the blanket and picked up the sausage and knife. He sniffed the sausage and cut a piece to eat. 'Whoa, that is strong. It's that funny onion stuff, isn't it?'

Anneke answered. 'Yes it is, rather strong sorry.'

I found I was still holding Anneke's hand; I dropped it and took a step back and cleared my throat. 'You took your time, surprised you didn't see Anneke on the way down earlier.'

Ian looked up at me and smiled. 'Oh, we went in the back way, wanted to see Armand quick, find out if there were any goodies going.' Ian's eyes twinkled up at us before he went back to eating his sausage.

'I must go,' said Anneke. 'I will see you tomorrow. Goodbye, Andrew, goodbye, Ian.' Anneke quickly stepped out of the shelter of the barn doorway and started down the hill, I followed her outside, watching her retreating figure with questions in my racing mind. What had just happened between us? Did she really care for me? I came back into the barn to the recumbent figure and began explaining HQ orders.

Later, Ian asked for the umpteenth time, 'Are you positive they said wait?'

'For the umpteenth time, yes, wait here, people will come.'

'I feel a fraud. The boys are out there fighting and we're here, good food, running water, toilets even.'

'I know, but it will change.' I had to agree with him, but I didn't want to go on with the war, I wanted to stay here.

Charley and Pete eventually came back carrying more bread and sausage and I told them of our orders. Charley was clearly pleased, giving a whoop of joy and patting us all on the back.

We pottered around the barn, watching the chateau and wood, talking about nothing in particular. Pete stayed on his blanket by the tank, watching us more than joining in, despite our attempts to get him to join us sitting in the barn doorway later, watching the countryside quieten.

'We can sort better sleeping arrangements for tonight,' I announced. 'I'll do the first night watch.'

'All right.' Ian stomped off to the ladder and climbed noisily above the floor of the barn on to the loft floor. 'At least hay mixed with straw is more comfortable than those paillasse back at the barracks.'

Charley nodded his agreement as he too ventured up the ladder. 'Aye, much better. A feather mattress cannot be beaten for comfort though.'

Pete clambered up into the tank.

I called back over my shoulder to the two men now up in the loft. 'Too right, never slept on straw before joining up.' I was at the barn door and peered out. The sun had already gone down and the night was closing in fast. 'I haven't seen a light or movement on that hill since yesterday, maybe they've gone.'

'Hope so,' came Charley's soft Scottish burr from the loft. It was heavy with sleep already.

My eyes were darting up on to the hill and then downwards to the chateau. I saw the odd bit of light come glaring up as doors were opened and then shut. All the windows were shuttered and I could see some slivers of light creeping out into the night if I squinted. Otherwise you wouldn't know the chateau was there. The owls and bats were out hunting their prey and the odd bark of a fox and squeal of a caught rabbit rent the air, while I remained still as a statue. I wasn't sure what I waited for, but felt I had to stand at the door and look out into the dusk. It wasn't the Germans I looked for. I was no longer frightened as I stood, listened and waited.

My mind wandered back to D-Day and the coldness of the water: bodies floating, having failed to make the beach; the smell of the burning tanks, the diesel; the sound of engines racing to get up the sand on to the dunes; the cordite from the guns, firing, always firing; the sight of the frail tanks going up the beach, mines exploding.

I rubbed my face and felt the beginnings of a beard. My mind started again.

D-Day. Chaos, yes, it was organised chaos. Infantry beating the tanks on to the beaches, the tanks that were meant to force a way through for the men. I'd been lucky so far, but how long would that last? Would the engineers come tomorrow for the tank? What was happening at the front? Were they moving, stuck in some places? Caen? The Panzers must be coming; they were good, very good. One of their Tiger tanks embedded in a hedgerow were a formidable opponent. The Allied tanks were more manoeuvrable, faster, but they were outgunned and the Cromwell was a deathtrap. I sighed. Speed was not a great advantage in those lanes I'd seen, *bocage,* the French called it – small woods, high sided lanes, fields. A bloody nightmare, I called it. I waited.

More minutes passed as I cast my eyes round, watching and listening all the time. Nothing. But something was out there, I could feel it. I stiffened: a crack of a twig, to the left, I moved my head slowly. A fox trotted up with a rabbit in its mouth. It stopped and quite majestically turned its head to look at me. He shook its prey to get a better grip and then continued on its way, one rabbit leg forlornly dragging on the ground.

I exhaled with relief then shut my eyes and again rubbed my face with my right hand. I was tired and confused; life wasn't straightforward anymore. I started to walk around the barn again and again, I found comfort in the rhythm of my steps until it was time to wake Pete and hopefully find some peace in sleep myself.

'Wake up, time for work and breakfast.' The voice penetrated my deep sleep. Then I remembered, Anneke had brought breakfast for us yesterday, she may come again, and so I stood up quickly and stretched and looked out of the barn door towards the chateau.

Ian patted me on the back. 'Steady on, old chap, the sergeant brought it up while you were snoring your head off. None of that French stuff this morning, bacon and eggs no less.'

I gave a quick grin. 'Really, checking up on us?'

'Yup, no news on relief of the chateau, so another day, I suspect, kicking our heels.' Ian sounded quite happy with the situation.

'Fair enough, now where's that breakfast I can smell cooking? Not letting Pete burn the bacon?' I was not so pleased Anneke hadn't come up again, but I tried not to let it show.

Breakfast was devoured quickly and in silence. We were all still tired and becoming restless at the same time at not being able to do anything.

'I fancy a good wash,' said Ian, suddenly. 'You OK while I go and have one when I take the basket back?'

'What a great idea!' Pete said. 'You had a shower when we came, didn't you, Andrew?'

I saw an annoyed look flash across Ian's face at the want of a wash at the chateau by Pete and wondered what that meant. I nodded to Pete. 'What? Yes I did, in a huge shower contraption. You want one? No problem. While you're all doing that I'll try headquarters again for the ETA of help.'

Ian and Pete gathered their shaving gear together and sauntered down the hill, whistling as they went. Suddenly Charley ran past me shouting, 'Wait for me!'

It was like they were on a camping holiday, not involved in the biggest invasion ever seen. I watched them for a few minutes and then went to the radio. I got through the chatter of the many frequencies being used and found HQ and got the same answer: stay where we were. I sighed. OK, we were safe, but this is not what we were trained for. I was scared again at what was coming but I wanted to get on with it. Rather like the wait for the invasion, I knew it was coming but the waiting was nearly as bad as waiting for D-Day.

I began to wander around the barn, looking into boxes. I felt the worn horse leather and wondered at its suppleness. I shook out the blankets, checked the ammunition and diesel supplies, refilled the water containers. My clothes could do with a wash; the sea salt had made them crinkly and hard to my touch. I thought another wash was in order too – feeling my chin, it felt like a few days growth, maybe I would shave too. I got the paraffin cooker out and heated some water. As I waited for it to get up to a good temperature, I stood in what was becoming my favourite place, the doorway, and looked around. No one was to be seen, all quiet, although I could hear the occasional gunfire far in the distance. Planes high overhead, never troubling us, gave a buzzing sound.

An hour later and I was washed and shaved; it felt smooth and clean now as I ran my hands over my face. I packed my shaving gear carefully away and sat afterwards with my back to the barn door in the warm sun and dozed. I moved a leg and felt the crunch of the photograph in the pocket. Reaching in, I pulled it out slowly

– one quick look and I put it away. I waited for the return of the crew and tried not to think about home too much.

Ian threw himself on to the blanket spread out by the tank tread. 'That was wonderful, although got a bit sweaty coming up that hill.'

I looked at him. 'You do look a bit cleaner.'

'So do you, nice clean shave there, mate.'

I smoothed my chin. 'It feels a lot better, never knew I hated not shaving so much. Funny, at home on a Sunday I wouldn't shave and it felt great.'

'No church to get ready for?' Ian turned over on to his back raising his head on his hands to look at me.

'Nah. Mother drags me along Christmas, Easter, but … when I was small I had to go every week, Sunday school. Stays with you, mind.' I again brushed a hand over my now smooth face.

Ian smiled. 'I suppose it does.' He nodded at the tank. 'We're stuck here until relief comes, so if the tank is OK, let's see what we can do to help the Tommies.'

'They need no help. Just keep our heads down and protect the tank, she can still be useful. A stray Jerry tank could bombard the house quite easily.'

'Suppose so,' said Ian. 'So, stay here it is then.' He put his arms behind his head and fell asleep straight away, his snoring being the only thing breaking the silence of the French countryside.

Pete was in the tank; I heard a whistle from him every now and then. Charley was patrolling outside. I moved around the barn, scanning the hillside for move-

171

ment, then back into the barn and up into the loft. Moving things around, putting them back where I found them – I just couldn't keep still. Looking again down at the chateau, I saw Anneke come out of a doorway and start up the hill towards us. My heart skipped a beat, then my throat constricted. I coughed and Ian stirred but didn't wake.

I walked out of the barn down the track to meet the woman coming up to me.

'Hello, I am just going for a walk.' Anneke brushed her hair off her face as she looked at me. 'Father is sleeping and the captain is driving me, how you say? Insane. He wants us to leave, but Father is in no condition. He seems to have lost all his strength.'

'I'm sorry to hear that. Where are you going?'

'Up into the forest, I thought I would see if the traps Armande set have caught any rabbit. It will help him, he is so busy with the house full, and Madame is a stickler for how things must be done. Even the Germans let her have her way.'

I nodded. 'It is her house, so she should.'

Anneke laughed. 'Yes it is. But she is a terrible, hard taskmaster.'

My face broke into a broad grin.

Anneke for an instant looked troubled. 'Did I say something terrible?'

'No, nothing wrong. I will come up with you. We are still not sure if someone is up there or not.'

'That would be lovely. Come, I have my sack and a knife for the despatch.' She held it up for me to see.

'Ian, I am off up the hill for some rabbits.'

An answering grunt came from the depths.

We moved quickly, and I easily fell into step with her as we walked up the track. I noted the deep tank treads recording our earlier arrival. Anneke stumbled and I caught her right arm to stop her fall; it felt so natural for her to then tuck her arm into mine as we progressed up towards the multi-coloured green trees ahead. I suddenly realised I was really enjoying myself walking with Anneke, the war seemed a long way away.

Anneke broke the spell. 'Armande told me where he put them. I have been a few times with him. I had to get out of the way of the soldiers. It was a good excuse-me.'

'Excuse.'

'Pardon? Oh I see.' Anneke gave a little smile.

We came to the tree line and then we moved to the right into the wood and along a small dirt track that led deeper into the wood under the darkening trees. Small branches and twigs had fallen in the recent storms but the path was mainly clear. Cracking and crunching came from underfoot as we moved, one behind the other.

'We go left now, see the little track?' Anneke moved on to the narrow path, leading the way. I followed, my eyes adapting quickly to the subdued light under the trees.

'Oh yes, this is the first one over there.' Anneke pointed with the knife. 'You see the fallen trunk, the huge one? A warren house is there, we get many, they do not learn.'

'OK, I see, yes you have one.' I moved past her and led the way to the tree, lent against the trunk and looked down at the still body of the rabbit. Its neck was dark red against the smoky grey of the fur.

'Here, let me.' I picked the rabbit up by its back legs then, pulling firmly, wrenched the anchor out of the ground and laid it across the trunk of the fallen tree. Fiddling with the garrotte, I made the noose big once more and the rabbit slid from my grasp, falling to the ground.

'Oh, he is a big one.' Anneke immediately picked the rabbit up and then dropped the still body into the sack she carried. 'Do you know how to set again?'

'Yes, I did this at home with Father. We would walk into the countryside in my school holidays and find the warrens on the moors. Cold and hard work, but the rabbit pie or roast rabbit was delicious.'

Anneke pulled the sack top together as she spoke to me. 'I did not know until Armande show me. It was and is horrible, but I too now eat rabbit and enjoy.'

Anneke's English skills sometimes failed her, and this was one of those times. I smiled inwardly: my schoolboy French had no comparison – *oui*, *non* and *bonjour* were all the words I remembered. Who was I to correct her version of English?

I bent down and pushed the anchor into the ground, arranging the noose over a new rabbit hole. I was quite pleased with my work.

'This way, it is next to a lovely clearing.' Anneke pointed along the faint pathway.

'Fine, here give me the sack.' I took the proffered hessian bag and threw it over my shoulder and followed the young woman up the track.

'Do you get fed up with rabbit?' I asked to break the

silence between us.

'No, not when you are hungry. The Germans gave us food, but we get more and give to those who do not. Pie, stew, paté, roasted, potted, it all is eaten.'

I nodded even though she couldn't see me. 'I see. We have rationing, not a lot to eat but enough.'

Anneke stopped in front of me and I came up to stand beside her. 'Here is the clearing. Oh, the trap, she is empty, we always have one here, more than the tree trap.' Anneke ran across the clearing to where I could see the trap lying on the grass.

'It has been taken. Look, the noose open, who do this?'

I stood at the edge of the clearing and watched Anneke kneeling by the trap, then I swung the sack free from my shoulder. 'I don't know.'

A blow hit the side of my arm. The sack fell from my grasp as the pain hit my brain. I spun, hands raised in defence, as I'd been taught by that sadist of a PT instructor. Right fist struck out then my left; they both connected to something. Right fist again, into soft putty, now sticky, again and again as I had been taught. Instinct took over, my face and ear were hit but I swung and connected, swung and connected.

'Andrew!' A scream came through. 'Non!' The voice screamed again. I focused and saw what I was fighting: a man, wearing farming clothes. On his feet, once shiny but now muddy, were German officer boots. They slid on the grass, desperate to gain purchase from my onslaught. A broken branch lay to one side with a hessian bag draped over it, the thing that had hit me. I stood with fists raised and faced the German whose blood gushed from his crooked nose. The man staggered, righted then turned and fled.

'Andrew!'

Stupefied, I stood there, gazing after the retreating figure. 'I think he may be your thief.'

'Andrew, please look at me.' I heard Anneke say, I turned and looked at Anneke, her eyes seemed blurry, her whole face did. My knees no longer kept my legs straight and I crumpled to the close-cropped grass and sat just gazing down the track. It felt as if bits of broken branch were sticking into my leg and I reached down to move them, but I couldn't find any by my leg pocket.

'Andrew, please. You frighten me.'

'I'm alright,' I said, checking my limbs. 'Just hit me a bit harder than I first thought.' I rubbed the back of my neck and felt bits of bark and broken twigs down my shirt. I fished them out, looked at them and then threw them down on to the ground.

Anneke knelt by my side, her hand went tentatively to my face. 'He hit you.'

'I know he did, the head and arm definitely knows.'

With a handkerchief Anneke slowly and gently wiped my face. I put up a hand and stopped her. Softly squeezing her hand, I moved it towards my lips and kissed it. 'I'm all right, promise.'

'I … Andrew, I was so afraid.' Her face dropped on to my chest and I felt the rest of her body lean against me. It felt so natural to put my arms around her and to hold her against me as her crying began.

As I held her, a quietness descended on the glade and a rabbit popped its head out of a burrow to see if all was clear. It bounced its way across the sun-lit clearing and began to crop the grass. I didn't dare move; either it would frighten the rabbit or the beautiful woman in my arms.

After a few minutes she stopped crying. I guessed her tears weren't simply a reaction to me being attacked – they were too heavy for that alone. But I hoped she cared a little, because I realised I was caring a little too much about her than I should. She lifted her head up to me and I moved so our lips met.

Her lips were of a sweetness I had never tasted before. I felt as if I could eat her, my head moved against hers and my hands found their way up to hold her head more firmly against mine. She moaned ever so slightly, was it in pain or pleasure? I dropped my hands, releasing her so quickly her head fell again on to my chest. I dropped my head down on to hers and smelt the cleanliness of her hair.

'Anneke, I am so sorry, I don't know … please forgive me.' My voice was lost in the hair my face was buried in. I couldn't help myself from softly kissing her tresses as we rested under the trees together. What was I doing?

'Andrew.' A small muffled voice came up to my ears. I raised my head and Anneke raised hers too, our eyes meeting.

'Andrew, there is nothing to be sorry for. I have wanted to kiss you from the moment I saw you lying on the ground, my saviour twice.' She raised my left hand and kissed it. 'There, I kiss your hand too.'

A broad grin spread across my face; I was happy, I had kissed her, she was in my arms, but it wasn't sensible to stay where we were. 'Anneke, I don't know what to do or say. But it is not safe here, we must go back.'

'No, we have three more traps to check, you can walk, no? So we finish and then walk slowly back.'

I shook my head; it hurt more when it moved. 'I'm not sure.'

'Kurt, he has run, like most of the Germans have done, he is a coward, I recall him, he lurks and boom, he is there,' Anneke insisted.

'Anneke, I think we should go.'

'No, Andrew, I stay here. Either we go rabbit or I remain here in your arms on the wood floor.'

I felt a moment of indecision; the ground was soft under my body, and the body I still held was soft. I gave an inward sigh. 'We go rabbit.'

'I help you up.' Anneke untangled herself from my arms and stood, holding a hand out to me. 'Here.'

My legs now worked, albeit slowly, so I rose up from the grass. As I did so, Anneke dropped my hand and took my pounding head in her soft palms and kissed me hard on the lips. I could do nothing but return the hard eagerness of the kiss and then I broke the seal between us. 'No, please, Anneke, I shouldn't.'

Anneke took a step back from me. 'Andrew, I am sorry. Please forgive me.'

My legs began to feel unsure. Would they hold me

up any longer. I drew a long breath and steadied myself. I looked and found the hessian bag. Reaching down, I pulled it up towards me. 'Rabbiting we go. Which way now?'

'We go that way.' An unsteady finger pointed past the lone rabbit, which was now curiously watching us. Anneke walked further away from me, causing the rabbit to return to its home in alarm. I placed the bag across my shoulder and followed her, watching and listening for the lone German who had caused my heart some trouble.

Some while later we returned to the barn, the sack containing a few rabbits. I hadn't been happy walking in the woods but, at long last, Anneke had announced we had checked the last of the traps. I was concerned that there was no activity in the barn.

'Ian, where are you?' I rattled the barn door as I stood scanning the empty floor. 'Charley, Pete,' I shouted. Nobody slept by the tank tracks, no pot of water was warming on the small campfire ready for a cup of tea.

'Whoa, hang on, mate.' Ian's head emerged from the tank. 'Checking the radio still worked, keep your hair on.'

'You should be keeping an eye out, there's a bloody German up in the woods, maybe more. I don't know.' I was shouting again.

'Fair enough, told them at the house yet?'

'No!' I snapped at Ian. My head hurt, and I didn't know what I was doing anymore, I was confused about many things.

Anneke came and stood beside me and laid a hand on

my arm. I shrugged it off and strode fully into the barn.

'Andrew, please.' Anneke followed me inside.

'No, Anneke, there may be more.' I had to keep her safe, the crew safe, the chateau.

Anneke put her hand on my arm and began to try and talk to me. Again I shrugged her hand off.

'I have told you that was Kurt,' she said. 'He is a loner, popping up all over the place. He was meant to help father in his work, terrified he would be sent back to the front, Russia – somewhere. He tried to keep out of people's way. He is alone, I am sure.' Anneke was insistent, but I wasn't listening.

I glared at her. She hadn't seen my eyes narrow before as they did now. I think I scared her a little. 'How can you be sure? Go down to the house, here, take the rabbits, go, now. I will follow soon.'

Anneke fled.

Chapter 14

'Sir, I was attacked in the woods, one soldier, he fled.' I stood before Captain Myers.

'Yes, Anneke told me, gave a short description of the man and what he did here. A deserter. He'll keep his head down, when more men arrive we can have a sweep. Just be aware. Dismissed.'

I realised the captain felt a little relieved there weren't more men hiding on the hill. As I looked at him the captain gazed out of the window towards the woods and sighed.

I saluted and left the room. I hadn't seen Anneke on my arrival at the house. I wasn't sure what to do. My heart skipped a beat at the sound of an upstairs door closing, I didn't want to see Anneke and so, almost running, I left the house and returned to the barn. There, hopefully, I could think, clear my mind.

'Well you have messed things up haven't you, old

boy.' Ian chortled at me whilst he tidied away his sleeping blanket. 'One at home and one here.'

I looked aghast. Is that the reason I felt so confused?

'I saw the way she looked at you, mate, your reaction, hers when you snapped, clear as day, that was.' Ian smiled at me enquiringly. 'What are you going to do, or is it just a fling?'

'Fling? No fling, we haven't done anything,' I insisted.

'But you will, given half the chance. I've seen your face when you look at her. Didn't think you had it in you at first, but now, well, we'll see.'

I felt puzzled, and went up into the loft. I could think there, away from Ian and his prying, and I could safely gaze down on the chateau where Anneke was.

The sun rose early every day and we four men got into a routine. I hadn't been down to the house since I saw the captain; Ian had fetched food, checking, waiting for further orders. Charley and Pete were staying down at the chateau, being useful. Now Ian and I became restless. Prowling around the barn, staring up into the wood, checking to see if the soldier was within view, but we saw nothing. The chateau was quiet, although Armande went past to check his traps with a young soldier as company. As the sun was setting and we were just finishing our evening meal, we heard a cough from outside the barn.

'Can I enter in?' Anneke's head peered around the door.

Ian leapt up. 'Must do a round, be back soon.' He almost ran from the barn, leaving me still sitting, eating bread and drinking tea.

'Sure, come in,' I answered.

Anneke tentatively entered and put a basket down on the ground in front of me. 'I am sorry.'

'You have nothing to be sorry about,' I said. 'I shouted at you.' I still wanted to keep her safe.

'True, but I was a fool, knowing everything, but I know Kurt. I am sorry, I should have not been so …'

'It doesn't matter, you're safe. We haven't seen him again. Maybe he's moved on.' I wanted to reassure her, protect her. I felt warm inside when I looked at her.

'Yes, maybe.' Anneke seemed uncertain.

'Come and sit down, we still have some tea brewing if you want some.' I wanted her to stay and talk to me.

'No thanks, it is too strong for me.' She came and sat next to me on the blanket Ian and I had been using. 'I am sorry though, I was not right.'

I fiddled with my mug of tea. 'It's me? I shouldn't have kissed you.'

A tiny sigh came from the woman sat beside me. 'Why, it was so natural. I felt concern and it felt right.'

Anneke whispered so quietly I could hardly hear her. I moved closer to hear her better, and made a decision.

'So it did.' I put up a hand to her face. 'It did feel right, I want to do it again, may I?'

'Oui.'

So I kissed her and, as I did so, I heard Ian quietly close the barn door.

Julia Sutherland

Chapter 15

I awoke engulfed in a haze of straw and dust. I opened one eye then the next and looked around the barn. I hadn't dreamed it. Anneke lay beside me covered by an army blanket. In the dawn light I tried to look down at myself: I was naked. I had never slept naked before. I could feel little fleabites; I assumed they were fleas or maybe hay mites we had disturbed. I moved my arm that was resting on the recumbent body next to me; the slight movement made her move, but she didn't wake. I began looking about for my uniform. I found it neatly piled at the bottom of what had been our bed. I then remembered Anneke had insisted on folding them, she had apologised, laughing at herself as she told me: 'I have to, it is something I have done all my life. I must, I do not sleep well otherwise and I stay awake until I do it.'

I reached slowly for my uniform and stood. Quietly I moved away from the still sleeping body, and dressed, watching her breathe, the blanket slowly rising and falling. Peering at my watch, I saw it was early morning. I looked out of the doorway set high up for the receiving of hay and straw for storage, but could see nothing. I rubbed the back of my neck. What exactly had I done? I knew what I had done, but Pamela was waiting for me … but Anneke was so … I glanced back and looked at the young woman lying so peacefully asleep.

I was overcome with a feeling of utter peace and joy that I had met Anneke. A warmness within wanted to break out and I wanted to jump with sheer happiness. I needed to hold her in my arms and tell her I loved her and wanted to spend the rest of my life with her. I left her still sleeping and, moving carefully, I climbed down the ladder.

'Well hello, Valentino, is it? Or is it my mate Andrew I see before me?'

Ian was leaning against the barn door, his back to me, on guard.

'I …' It was all I could say.

'I know, mate.' Ian motioned for me to come and stand by him.

'Someone is definitely out there,' said Ian. 'Maybe it's that deserter, but I keep hearing things, and it wasn't you two upstairs either! Long after you two had finished.'

My face blazed, I could feel the heat, or was it only in my mind? I didn't reply.

'Oh, come on, mate, we have all done it.' He looked at me straight in the eyes. 'Hell! You hadn't. Welcome to the club.' Ian clapped me hard on the back.

I smiled wanly at Ian, but said nothing, what was there to say?

The early morning air was clear and still, an occasional bat flitted past and I heard an owl calling, but nothing else.

'Think you're hearing things mate,' I whispered. 'He's long gone.'

Ian snorted. 'Where has he to go? There are two armies between him and home. Spain? Still got to get past our lines. If he goes into occupied France he will be shot as a deserter, I reckon he is still around here.'

'So if he is here, what is he going to do? We have guns and a little thing called a tank, it can still fire, you know.'

'When you're murdered in your bed, sleeping, or too occupied doing other things to notice a German soldier coming to slice your throat with a nice long knife and your lady love's too.'

'OK, I get the picture.' I felt a chill in the morning air and at something else that Ian had said.

'I'll start a brew,' said Ian. 'You finish watch, least you've had some sleep, unlike me.' He stomped off to fill the can for tea and fire up the small camp stove.

I stared over the countryside as it began to brighten in the morning sun, and soon my hot tea and a piece of bread were put into my hands by Ian. I tried to take a bite into the bread.

'God, that's hard.'

'Dunk it in your tea like I do,' Ian advised. 'There's two sugars – had a small find in one of the containers, tastes a bit like fuel got in but it's fine.' Ian began to drink his steaming cup of tea and we both watched the morning sky.

We stood in companionable silence, sipping hot tea and chewing on hard French bread. As the sun rose fully we heard movement from the loft and shortly after, Anneke backed down the ladder. She smiled at us, hopefully more at me than Ian. I didn't know what to say, what did you say in these situations? Father's sex talk before I left on call-up hadn't covered the morning after.

Anneke busied herself brushing straw off her clothes. 'I have to go back to the chateau quickly before I am missed.' Then she began brushing through her hair with her fingers.

'Bit late for that, lass,' said Ian, grinning. 'No one came looking so I think you're OK. I'll leave you two lovebirds for a minute, nature calls.'

That was my opening. I took a step towards Anneke who was standing in front of me. I didn't know what I was going to say or even do, but I had to do something.

'No,' she said, beating me to it. 'I … we will talk later, I go now.' Anneke shook her head.

I reluctantly stood aside for her to leave the barn and, as she moved past, I caught the scent of her hair. I stood and watched her return to the chateau and then disappear into a side door.

'The sentries aren't very good, are they?' I said when Ian returned.

'Oh, come off it, mate, they're making themselves scarce. Look.' Ian motioned with his arm towards the chateau.

As we watched, the sentries moved into view and began walking on their rounds.

'They know,' I muttered.

'Of course they bloody know, grow up. It's gone on for centuries, how do you think you arrived, a cabbage patch, or a stork in your country?' Ian laughed at me.

I laughed back – I was embarrassed, what else could I do?

'That's better,' said Ian. 'Stop being so uptight! You're not the first squaddie and you'll not be the last.'

'I suppose you're right, but she's so special.' I felt warm inside, happy. I smiled but then a remembrance of Pamela took it away again.

'They're all special until you get married then you keep it firmly buttoned up save it for the wife, or your life will be hell, seen it so many times.' Ian sneezed. 'Damn dust, it's time we got more orders, get you away from temptation, my lad. Contact HQ and remind them we cannot stay here for the next year, no matter how much you want to.'

I didn't move. I didn't want to countenance the idea of leaving Anneke.

Ian continued talking. 'Come on, lad, the radio, it's still working, orders and quick. I want out of here, beginning to give me the heebie-jeebies. What was her father up to I wonder? They want him to go with them but he isn't having it. The corporal told me he's waiting for his assistant to return from the factory. He won't go until then. Staying in his bed, he says he needs him, and the "powers that be" seem to agree.' Ian sneezed again. 'God knows where this assistant is though. Still behind enemy lines, apparently, if not taken back to Germany, a bit of a genius.'

I caught the last of what Ian was saying and I frowned. 'Assistant?' I reluctantly went to the radio and it sprang into life. I made contact and noted the instructions: wait for further orders. Didn't they know there was a war on?

The morning broke fully and we watched, and waited for orders. I hoped for a visit from the chateau. Birds dived and rose on the wind, catching insects. Others dug amongst the grass and bushes. A fox, late home, barked up in the wood.

A crackle came through the radio. Orders.

Ian clearly wasn't too happy with the orders. 'So we are to wait for transport to HQ, disable the tank – don't they know it is broken? – and then we're off again to fight.'

'Yup,' I confirmed. 'Disable the tank so it can't be fired.'

'Fine, let's get to it.'

'No, not now, they aren't coming for a couple of days yet.' I was so pleased, a few more days at least with Anneke, but would she want to see me? I was getting confused, I thought she would want to see me but she hadn't come up again.

'Blimey, not that organised, are they?' said Ian. 'Four fine soldiers ready and willing to fight and they say wait.'

I laughed. 'We are not that good. We broke the King's tank, after all.'

'Got a point,' said Ian. 'A few days then, you had

better make the most of it, off to the castle and find your damsel. Hope she hasn't changed into an ugly sister down there.' Ian hit me on the shoulder. His habit was beginning to leave me with bruises.

'I'll go down. I must see her.'

Ian nodded down the slope. 'No need mate, here she comes with a basket of goodies.'

The figure of a young woman was coming up the hill carrying a large basket that hopefully contained our rations from the house. Anneke was not the only thing I would miss about staying at the chateau.

Ian hit me on the arm again. 'I'll make myself scarce. God knows when I'll get some decent kip with you two lovebirds to take care of. Just going to do a walk around, I'm still convinced that Jerry is lurking.' Ian rushed out of the barn so he didn't meet the woman walking towards us. I stood and waited for the beautiful Anneke to arrive.

Anneke came in the barn and put the heavy basket at my feet. I said nothing. She then reached up and took my face in her hands, looked into my eyes, then playfully kissed my nose.

'Oh!' I hadn't expected that.

'I am well, I was not missed last night.' Anneke stroked the top of my arms as she talked to me.

'Fine, I ...'

She put her fingers on my mouth to stop me speaking. 'Don't say anything, I, we, have little time.'

I looked into her blue eyes and found a sense of sadness there. 'What's wrong?'

'Nothing, we are two people caught up in things,

that is all, I just hope.' She looked around the barn. 'Now where is Ian? I have a treat for him from Armande.'

I nodded my head towards the countryside. 'He is outside, giving us space. Pete and Charley are doing something at the chateau.'

Anneke gave a little nod. 'I will see him later. Come, let us sit, I have some hot coffee for you.' Anneke sat on one of the blankets, patted the space beside her and waited for me to sit down.

We drank our coffee and then there was no time for words; we kissed again and again.

Night came. Anneke had been gone some hours and I was sitting in the barn doorway watching the countryside. Ian's voice came from behind me. I got up and joined him by the tank.

'Well I needed that.' Ian rubbed his sleep-stuck eyes. 'Nice to have a bit of kip that lasts more than two hours.'

'She's wonderful, do you think she'll marry me?' I mused, leaning against the tank.

'Good heavens, mate! What can you offer her? Her father is a professional, he wants something a bit better than a squaddie for a son in law. How come she isn't married already? They like to marry them off young on the continent – an older man all set up, then he looks for a wife, not just when he's starting out. Get something behind you to offer the lass, then look for a girl.'

I was a bit surprised at Ian's reaction. 'I hadn't thought of that ... we have the shop.' My mind was racing, surely I was a reasonable candidate for marriage. I knew I was considered a bit of a catch at home.

'Sorry, Andrew, I think Daddy wants a bit more than that for his daughter. A couple of shops and you might get away with it.' Ian was ruffling his hair to get the dust and straw out of it.

I stared open-eyed at Ian. 'You mean that?'

'I sure do. Enjoy it for the next few days and then both move on.'

I appreciated he was trying to help, but I didn't want to take his advice.

'I can't do that.' There, I had made a decision.

'Sorry, mate, the Army says otherwise and a man called Hitler isn't going to wait around. Well, actually he will, gives him time to reorganise while you swan around enjoying yourself.' Ian was looking at me with a serious face.

'I ...'

'It's a romance, a fling, nothing more. Think of Pamela,' Ian hissed at me.

'I am, I must write and tell her it's off.' I looked around, where was the letter paper? I had recently written to my parents, and left the paper somewhere outside the tank. I was storing letters up to send home; they would get them all at once.

Ian took me by the arm and held me back. 'Oh no you don't, let her live in happiness. You may get killed and she may never need to know.'

'Charming, wanting me dead.' I shook his arm off.

'Do you want to cause her unnecessary pain? I ain't telling if you pop your clogs. Some things best left unsaid.'

Ian spoke through clenched teeth.

'But …' I was getting confused. Ian was so determined to stop me writing to Pamela.

He was now standing in front of me staring. 'No buts, no letter. Enjoy the next few days, or as long as we have, and move on, see what happens. You can come back when this is all over. Enjoy the moment, don't worry about tomorrow as you may be dead.'

I nodded agreement but later went to find the writing paper once Ian had left the barn. I settled with my back to the barn wall and composed what I thought was the hardest thing I had ever written. I didn't know when I would be able to give it over to the Company HQ to go into the post but I must have it ready for that opportunity.

My Pamela,

> *Don't worry I'm safe, the tank broke down, and we have spent some days at a lovely chateau deep in the countryside away from the fighting. You would love the place, just like a fairy tale castle.*
>
> *Pamela, I do not think that I should hold you to our engagement. I have had my doubts that proposing was right and whether I would come back whole to you. I have seen so many men fall, I cannot allow you to wait when there may be another man you could marry, who would keep you safe and content and not have to look after an ex-army man, wounded in the war, for the rest of your*

life. So Pamela I am breaking our engagement, I
think it is for the best.

Your friend Andrew

'You're not writing to Pamela, are you?' Ian's voice boomed across the barn floor at me.

'I owe it to her.' I knew I was right.

'No you do not.' Ian was shouting at me again. 'Wait until this is over, then decide. A lot can happen in war. Don't post it.'

I sighed, nodded and stuffed the letter in my pocket.

I lived the next two days waiting for the radio call that the transport was on its way and spending hazy time with Anneke. We were watched by the soldiers from the chateau as we walked in the fields and gardens together, and by the river where the kingfisher dipped and dived for us. We collected flowers for the house, huge marguerites, daisies, I called them; I had never seen so many and so colourful. A large vase stood in the middle of the hallway table, filling the room with the yellow of its centre and the whiteness of the petals radiating from the sun. I gazed at them as if I had never seen a flower before. Sucking in every detail, storing it in my memory. If I died it would be the last thing I thought of: Anneke's laughing face as she picked them.

Pamela was a distant memory, not pricking my conscience. I was at peace and in love with the most wonderful girl in the world. I tried not to think of the inevitable radio message that would tell me when we were to leave. I was happy.

We were all in the barn telling tales of previous lives before the war, the characters we had met, dreams for the future once the fighting was over, anything to break the tedium of life waiting to hear we were off on our doings again. I kept silent about Anneke and Pamela; I knew Ian's opinion and I didn't want a row.

Pete said he felt secure in our tank, his own little room when we were out of it. He didn't have his own room or even bed at home. Charley laughed and said he was happy to get out of the tank and away from the smells. Pete was welcome to stay in it as long as he wanted.

For a moment Charley looked quite serious, then he said, 'I have no idea what I'll do when all this finishes. I suppose I'll go home to the village and hope the game-keeper will take me on as he promised. Somehow, I can't see that happening.'

We fell into a silence. I was considering what I could do to be more of a catch for Anneke – what I could do once the war was over – when the radio crackled. Pete answered it quickly. We stood expectantly around the tank waiting for the news.

Pete dropped the handset and looked up. 'Andrew, orders, tomorrow, early. The lorry will be here at 0600.'

I blinked a little as I took in the news; my hand rubbed the back of my head. 'I see.'

'Go and tell her,' Ian insisted.

Heavy feet took me down to the chateau. I found Anneke in the kitchen, helping Armande prepare veg-etables. She looked up, clearly surprised to see me.

'Yes, Andrew.'

I just blurted the orders, I couldn't keep them within me. 'We leave tomorrow, early.' I hadn't meant to tell her this way. I felt ashamed but I felt distraught at the thought of leaving her so soon.

The stunned silence was broken when a knife dropped to the floor. Armande leant over and retrieved it, placing it carefully on the table, then silently he left the room.

'Tomorrow?'

'Yes, tomorrow.'

'I thought, I hoped a few more days.' Anneke picked up the knife again and began cutting the green fronds off the top of a baby carrot.

'No, tomorrow.' I was just standing there looking at her. I felt I couldn't move.

'I shall miss you, I ...' Anneke put the knife down slowly and deliberately by the carrot peelings and began to wipe her hands on her pinafore.

I said the obvious. 'I shall miss you, Anneke. I want to ...' I took a step towards her.

'I know.' she shook her head slightly. 'I shall miss you. Please leave it at that.'

I walked the final few steps towards her as she remained bolt upright behind the large kitchen table. 'I cannot, I want to be with you.' I desperately wanted to take her in my arms.

'It is not possible to be with you. I have to be with ... Father. He needs me.' Anneke continued to wipe her hands on the floral pinafore.

I reached her and raised my arms. 'We cannot do

anything.' I enveloped her in my arms and hugged her tightly, feeling that I could never let her go. Anneke's face was buried in my shirt and I could feel it beginning to get damp from her tears.

Words said quietly into my chest filtered up to my ears. 'We have today. Let us not waste.'

Anneke took me by the hand and led me up the stairs to her room.

Chapter 16

'Right, boys time to go,' Sergeant Timpson shouted through the open door of the chateau. His parade ground voice reverberated around the hall and staircase until it reached our ears. Anneke and I were standing at the bedroom window looking out on to the river. We had seen the lorry arrive a little while ago but now it was time. I whispered in her ear; my breath misted the little gold studs she wore, the ones I'd noticed on our first meeting.

'I will come back, I promise.' I meant every word.

'Do not make promises you cannot keep.' Anneke took a step away from me. 'You may be killed. If you return it is so. But things change and I cannot promise I will be the same if you return. Perhaps it is best we say goodbye.' Anneke turned back to me, smiling, but with her eyes beginning to fill with tears.

'I will come back,' I insisted.

Anneke reached up and held my head in her hands and kissed my slightly peeling nose. 'I know you will come if you can.' She started to tidy my uniform, patting and pulling it into shape.

I took Anneke in my arms one last time and hugged hard so all her breath was pushed out. My head nuzzled into her hair, and I smelled her perfume that I had grown to love, then I sighed.

'I must go.' But I didn't let her go. We held each other for a few more seconds and then stood apart.

I left Anneke standing in the middle of her bedroom with her arms wrapped around herself as she watched me leave the room. She must have heard the sound of my army boots ring down the stairs accompanied by my shouts.

'Coming, Sarge.' I passed Madame on the stairs and I smartly gave her a salute in farewell, which she acknowledged with a nod and a smile. She had never had a lot of words for me. I'd seen her watching on many occasions when I was with Anneke. I heard her knock on the bedroom door and let herself in.

'Not a bloody chauffeur service at your convenience, son,' snarled the sergeant. 'Get in the back with the rest.'

Ian had told the waiting men I was saying goodbye to Anneke and they were a little sympathetic, but not a lot as the transport had to leave.

With a few jeers and shouts I was helped up into the back of the lorry that was to take us to headquarters and our new tank. Onward into battle again, the tug of war could not be denied by us. The crew made room for me and my kit bag, and we settled down for the journey as the engine sprung into life.

Dust spiralled up from the wheels of the truck as it began its drive away from the chateau. As I looked back up at Anneke's bedroom window I could see two women watching. One looked down stoney-faced, the other was crying. Madame lent down and I saw a flash of paper at the window. I checked my pocket; the letter was gone.

Ian hit me on the shoulder. 'Well, here we go again, at least we'll not be seasick this time.'

A smile flitted across my face. 'No. I just wish ...'

A voice came from the interior of the lorry. 'You are not the first, nor the last, boy in war to find someone and have to leave. Just be glad you found it. Some never did and they are lying in a foreign field now.'

'Aye, he has a point, boy.' Another voice agreed and then the conversation veered into remembrances of the women they had loved and left, or even hoped to find. I didn't join in the banter. I just sat and watched the chateau finally disappear from view.

The journey took six long hours and when we jumped down from the back we were tired, dusty, hungry and stiff from being bumped from the hard wooden-slatted seating. Kit bags were thrown down and retrieved.

The sergeant's booming voice penetrated our coma-tose minds. 'Right, off to the mess, see what delights they have for you. Clean yourselves up and get some sleep, tents over there, grab an empty space. Form up 0600 hours.' He left us to it, but shouted back as he marched away, 'Letters here for some of you, collect them now.'

A warm meal and a wash made us feel better – and finding empty campaign beds to sleep in. The sound of snoring soon filled the air. I opened a letter, I knew it was from Mother, all were well, the food was still being used, she had measured it out and had her own ration system. Another letter was in my hand and I opened it slowly. It was from Pamela.

My darling Andrew,

I received your letter after we heard the news on the wireless that the invasion had started. I cried and cried to think you were with those brave men risking and losing their lives so that we can sleep safe in our beds from those horrible Nazis. I popped into the local Roman Catholic church, please do not tell Mother, and lit a candle for you and your crew. I said a prayer too. The church was ablaze with candles. I saw Mrs Peabody there from the Methodist chapel but when she saw me she scuttled away. She has already lost one boy to this war, it is so sad.

I am ready to marry you as soon as you come home. I have some clothing coupons, I was going to get a new winter coat. Do not worry, my present one is fine, but I do have a stain on it, Mother says it is not noticeable, but I can see it. You always do, don't you, when you know it is there. So I will use those for a nice costume, I do

*not need a wedding dress, all frills and lace, so long
as I have you. You will look so handsome in your
uniform, you will wear your uniform won't you? I
do not have enough coupons for a suit for you too.
I will not buy the costume yet as I suspect we have
a few months before you return home on leave.
If it is a spring wedding I thought a nice lilac for
me if I can find the colour. I can ask Mrs Windsor
if she would make it for me, if I can find material
rather than a ready-made costume. I can sew of
course, you have no need to worry on that account,
but she is such a good seamstress and she has been
such a good friend to Mother I am sure she would
do it and not charge much. I will save as much as
I can to pay for it. It would look so much better if
she made it. If you do not like the lilac colour, what
would you prefer? May be a daffodil yellow? Now,
if it is the summer, I thought a cream with high-
lights of navy blue, what do you think?*

*Your parents have said we must live with
them, so has Mother. We will not be able to afford
our own place and you will most likely go back to
the army for a while anyway so really we do not
have to worry, but do you think I should move in
with your parents? I would rather not, Mother not
being well, but I do not want to upset your parents
by refusing, do you think they will mind? Mother
does not want people to know she is unwell. She
was so excited at the news, thinking of her costume too. No coupons, but she has a nice suit from*

before the war, she had just bought it when they invaded Poland. I do not think she has worn it yet. Keeping it for best. Our wedding is best isn't it, so she can wear that. I am going to have trouble with my shoes, only have 2 pairs now. If you do see some off-coupon can you buy a pair, size 5. Creamy colour if possible but I don't mind, but if they are cream they go with most things and maybe I could dye them, what do you think?

I must dash, Cynthia and I are going to the picture house tonight, she has a new beau. A nice American. I know you do not approve of them, but he is very nice, I am going with them. Her mother asked me to. Please keep safe my darling. Keep away from those nasty Germans and come home safe to me.

Your ever loving,

Pamela

Feeling confused, I folded it up neatly and put it back in the envelope and then into a trouser pocket. Going on a date? She was engaged! Where did she think I would find a shoe shop in the middle of a war? Shoes! I lay down to sleep and dreamed fitfully of daffodils and daisies in a field.

'You four! Tank for the use of. Try not to break this one.' This was one of several comments we received from the engineers. News of our troubles with the tank had got around the camp. No known reason for breaking down, at a beautiful chateau with a beautiful woman. Coincidence? The officers thought not, but maybe we could be given the benefit of the doubt.

'Orders, join the troop and follow orders, we're heading north.' I was glad I had received these orders, we were going to continue on our doings, and the other three seemed pleased as well.

We met our new troop and quickly bonded as we checked through the mechanics, inventory of food, fuel, armaments – we mustn't run low on bullets.

The days followed on from one another, sometimes meeting resistance as we travelled, other days going without meeting another living person. Sleeping by tanks, shaving and eating rations, sometimes supplemented by foraging and grateful local people we met. It was difficult to prevent the people giving us things, especially as it became obvious they had little enough of their own. German soldiers came out of hiding to surrender, and once we passed a stream of prisoners under escort. Their uniforms were hanging off them, pale young faces looked up at us as they marched south. A mixture of relief and resentment, but with a rueful smile they no longer had to fight. It was over for them.

Julia Sutherland

Chapter 17

Yet again we lounged by our vehicles, spread out over the countryside, baking in the summer heat. We were now outside Caen waiting for the offensive to start. Bodies dozed in the welcome shade of tarpaulins strung alongside tanks, artillery and lorries. No one slept under a vehicle anymore, especially tanks as they could sink into the ground whilst you slept and crush you. I'd seen it. Nothing could be done if that happened, you were dead. Snores, talking or even occasional laughter broke a silence of contemplation of what the day would bring.

Birds came seeking a crumb of food, and we heard cows, lowing as they were taken in to be milked. And everywhere, insects droned in the summer heat. I saw a bumblebee hunting nearby as I tried to doze by the tank. I closed my eyes and relaxed in the warmth of the day. Suddenly, I leapt to my feet, a whizzing noise in my ear.

'Sniper!' Shaking, I screamed out a warning.

'No, mate, a bee just landed on your head,' said Charley to reassure me. Ian and Charley laughed at me though; I'd heard bumblebees all summer and was beginning to loathe them. Charley muttered, 'You don't hear the one with your name on it.' He fished in his top pocket of his battle dress jacket that had been lying on the ground beside him. 'Look, I have the bullet with my name on it, see? If I have it, no one can shoot me, can they?' He looked beseechingly at us for confirmation.

I nodded. I'd heard from my dad that some men believed this in the first war; he said the old soldiers from India had started the belief. I didn't believe it, how could a bullet save your life?

'No, mate, they can't.' Ian patted him on the back.

'Another cup of tea, boys.' I broke the moment as Pete climbed down from the tank with his mug and joined us.

'Great, I'll be swimming in tea soon,' said Ian.

As we gathered our mugs we heard another sound above the insects, a heavier muffled drone, getter louder from somewhere high in the early evening sky. Bombers, in formation, were soon passing over our heads. We all stood, heads looking up. Lancaster and Halifax bombers filled the sky, their fuselages burning red in the glow of the setting sun. I had never seen anything like it. It was a beautiful sight, but I felt cold with the destruction they would bring.

German anti-aircraft fire opened up on the advancing planes, but still they flew on through the curtain of white flak smoke. British and Canadian artillery opened up in reply, an attempt to help our aircraft survive the sweep across the city. The different sounds of guns firing, crump-crump, aircraft droning with the effort of keeping their heavy loads airborne penetrated our heads as the bombing started. We felt the percussion coming up through our boots as the explosions reverberated through the ground.

After the planes dropped their dreadful payloads, I thought they seemed to leap up into the air like huge flattened rabbits. A few paid the terrible price of war. I watched the smoke trails hang in the sky as planes fell to earth, or the lucky residents of Caen limping away from the broken city. Men around me stared at the fires flickering above the rooftops. Many just stared at the scene unfolding before them, some turned away unable to watch anymore. Then another wave of bombers came to unload their cargo on to the burning city.

'Jesus, I don't think the Germans are going to survive this.' I kept gazing at the fires and the wave of bombers flying towards the burning city. I wanted to stop, but I couldn't help but watch the horror unfold in front of us all.

Ian gave a deep sigh. 'I'm more worried how we're going to get into the city if it's bombed to hell and back. The roads will be blocked with fallen buildings. Will there be anything left to take after all that?' Ian gestured with his head upwards at another wave of planes droning overhead.

'Monty knows what he's doing,' I said.

'Does he?' muttered Ian. 'I do wonder sometimes.'

Some of the men stayed up all night, watching the fires burn like all hell had opened up. I tried to sleep, but it was impossible.

Tanks roared into life in the early morning and I saw crews waving optimistically to each other before they started the short drive to the battered outskirts of Caen. Our crew joined in the exchanges, but I felt apprehensive over what we would find and was quiet for the most part.

'I've had a few warnings from the captain during the briefing, we could find some surprises left by the Germans and to watch out for snipers.' I relayed the message to my crew as we drove towards the battered, smoking city.

There was silence for a moment before Charley spoke up. 'I heard that the infantry found some snipers tied to the trees so they don't fall out. They died up there too, but soldiers keep shooting them as they think they're still alive.' His voice changed so I could hardly hear him say, 'Creepy.'

As we advanced, dust flew up around the tanks. Any remaining Germans would easily see us coming. But then we saw the woods.

'Christ! What did they do here?' I was aghast at what was around me, I had never seen anything like it.

The trees had been reduced to stumps, splintered branches filled craters, smoke rose from the burning wood.

'Looks like those pictures of the Western Front,' whispered Ian. 'Absolutely nothing left.'

'Why bomb a wood like that?' I said, also lowering my voice to a whisper. 'No emplacements I can see.'

We pressed on into the city. Buildings blocked the roadways, but we pushed slowly through and over the mounds of rubble. We passed houses that had been partially demolished, just a wall or two standing. Some houses had lost their frontage, and I could see the tables and chairs standing where their owners had left them. It was eerily quiet. Occasional bursts of gunfire punctuated our progress through the shattered town. Onwards towards the river and the canal, that was the aim of the thrust into Caen. Secure any bridges still intact, and the canal port too. I shook my head, searching around for some landmark to get my bearings. But there was none left.

'Where the hell are we?'

'I have no idea,' said Ian. 'Just keep on this so-called road. Must lead somewhere.'

'Keep going—'

A loud ping stopped me mid-sentence. 'Snipers!'

I ducked down, my hand holding on to my helmet. 'Keep down!'

'Will do,' Charley said over the intercom.

The turret swung around, and a burst of gunfire persuading the sniper to keep his head down too.

Ian called out, 'Let's find this bridge over the Orne, then we can get the hell out of here.'

We made our way through the town, moving, firing, moving, firing, until we were so tired we could hardly keep our eyes open. But still we kept moving and firing, on through and out of Caen.

Julia Sutherland

Chapter 18

I threw back the turret cover and drew in a deep breath of air, air that was, for once, not tainted with diesel, urine or unwashed bodies. It felt good.

'Come on, boys, let's go,' I said as I swung my legs over and dropped to the ground. I untied a shovel from the side of the tank and hurried over to the roadside. A ditch confronted me; I dropped down into it, my legs not working well after being confined in the tank for so long. I stiffly climbed up the other side, legs easing as I did so. A small clump of bushes gave me some privacy. The relief I felt after emptying my bowels was just a little short of euphoric, and I sauntered back to the ditch with a smile on my face. I drove the shovel into the ground and then came back over the ditch back to the tank.

'Thanks!' Ian gasped as he ran to the ditch. On the other side he pulled the shovel out in one movement and then also disappeared.

I began to look over the outside of the tank whilst Charley, watching me, began to hop from one leg to the other.

'Strange,' he said, doing some kind of jig. 'You know how you can bottle it up for literally days and then when the opportunity comes, bam! You can't wait a second longer. Hurry up, Ian! Others here.'

'Heck! Forget the spade,' yelled Pete, looking at Charley. They both suddenly sprinted to the ditch, fingers fumbling at their trousers as they went. I laughed as they scrambled over the ditch and up the other side, their descending trousers hampering every movement.

'Hang on a minute!' said Pete, stopping dead. 'What about the mines?'

'Bit late now,' said Ian as he met them coming back.

'I saw some large dogs running around here as we drew up,' I said. 'So I figured it was safe enough.'

As we stood watching the arrival of other tank crews, we lit cigarettes and inhaled deeply, the smoke masking the smell of burning flesh that hung in the air. I looked in distaste at the burning stick in my hand. I hadn't smoked before the war, well not properly, but now it helped.

I threw the half-smoked cigarette away and looked at Ian. 'Let's brew up, but first, Ian, renew some of the camouflage, some of those blasts were a bit close for comfort.'

'Yep, will do.' Ian produced his favoured tool for cutting branches from trees: a blade he kept sharp each evening with a wet tool he had found. He wandered off over the ditch and began cutting, the sharp noises reverberating around the silent countryside as he hacked at the branches.

Charley and Pete returned to the tank, retied the shovel to the side and began helping me to rearrange and secure the remaining foliage we were using as camouflage, while we waited for Ian to bring a fresh supply.

Once the majority of it was secure, I brought down the primus stove and splashed water into a can to start a brew. 'Getting a bit low on water, lads, keep your eye out for a fresh supply.'

I stood and looked around again, acknowledging the wave of another tank commander who had also stopped on the road. Our position was exposed but we couldn't pass the ditches on either side of the road for fear of mines, and we were now some way behind the new front line. A village lay in ruins behind us where our tanks had blasted their way through, destroying everything as they did so. A few German soldiers had made a last stand, mining the road and buildings in an attempt to stop our advance. The main force had gone round but we and two other tanks had been ordered to push through the village clustered around the small church, and take out the entrenched soldiers. I rubbed my face; I could still feel the blast from one tank as it had blown. It had lived up to its nickname 'Ronson Lighter'.

'What's up, mate?' Ian made me start as he clapped me on the shoulder.

I gave him an answer I didn't believe. 'I'm fine.'

Ian turned away and looked back over the ditch to where he'd been working. 'Right, give us a hand with your trees.'

Together we went back over the ditch and manhandled the foliage over to the tank and then began covering it once more. Once we'd camouflaged the tank I clapped my hands together and turned to the men.

'Tea, gentlemen, get the rations out,' I said. 'Anything left of that cheese we liberated?'

With food and hot tea in our bellies, we lay down beneath a tarpaulin and all began to fall asleep. I was grateful to be able to stretch out and sleep in fairly peaceful and secure surroundings. I was just drifting off when Pete jumped up, waking us as he clambered noisily up the side of the tank.

'I will just have a look at the radio,' he said, disappearing from view.

'How does the tank smell now?' said Charley, sleepily.

'No different,' said Pete, his voice muffled from inside the tank.

We could hear him quietly singing to himself as we three outside began to settle again.

How different we were: Pete preferring the safety of the steel tank, the others staying outside as long as we could. I'd felt ill the first thirty-six hours we'd stayed locked down: the aromas of the men, combined with the diesel and cordite, had once made me vomit.

Unable to settle, my mind continued to race. 'I'm looking forward to having a good wash later,' I said. 'You could do with one too.' I nodded at Ian beside me.

'Me? I'm sweet as the day's long!'

We lay there enjoying the moment, then it came to me. 'I'm grateful that I don't carry the wooden crosses for the burials.'

'Yep,' agreed Ian. 'The padre has my admiration.'

I turned away and wiped my face. Moisture had crept into my eyes at the thought of the padre who accompanied the infantry and how he had dealt with the Ronson tanks. I couldn't forget the image of the burning tank and the man falling from the blazing turret as he tried to escape the inferno. There was nothing we could have done. It wasn't a new experience to see a tank burn but we'd never been that close before. We'd all heard the screams of the man as he lay writhing on the ground. The crew inside hadn't stood a chance. We drove on; we still had a job to do and it took our minds off the sight we had just seen.

Much later our tank had returned to the site; the blackened body still lay by the remains of the Sherman and I saw the padre praying beside him. As we all watched, the padre straightened, adjusted a pair of gloves and then tried to enter the tank. We saw him pull the wizened black twigs of bodies from the tank and lay them reverently on the ground. Infantry members helped him lay them down and stood to attention as he said a few words over them. We didn't move, in silence we watched.

'How can he do that day after day?' I said to no one in particular after the padre stopped praying.

'It's his calling,' said Ian. 'Not mine, his.'

'I don't want a calling like that,' said Charley.

'Did you go to church, Charley?' Ian asked quietly.

Charley sighed a little. 'When I was little, my mam clipped my ear if I missed, but when I got as big as her she stopped. Only little is my mam.' A smile came over the man's face as he spoke of his mother.

We continued to watch the horrifying but familiar tableau until it broke up with soldiers carrying the bodies over to a field where they were laid out and left for burial.

Often I had seen the padre bury the fallen straight away, but not today. In a book he noted the rank and number of every man who died, together with details of where he had died and been buried. He always refused help from the tank crews, telling us he didn't want us to be involved. I was grateful for that refusal.

Orders came from HQ: we were to stay where we were overnight and go forward at 0400 hours. Men secured tarpaulins and laid blankets out to sleep even though it wasn't fully dark. We were weary and needed rest as and when we could get it. I slept fitfully, waking each time an infantry unit marched past us.

It was nearly dawn, the hot tea was welcome, and we managed to use a tin can filled with earth and sprinkled with diesel to cook the bacon and eggs we'd bartered a few days ago. A quick and easy way to start a cooking fire. It heated our frying pan in what seemed like a minute and the soil was easy to dispose of when we'd finished. Pete had cared for the eggs like the chicken might have done. There wasn't even a hairline crack on any of the shells.

The engines fired up just before 0400 and our two

tanks moved off down the road the infantry had taken in the night.

After some thirty minutes or so, I heard shooting and, as we progressed along the road, I saw the bodies of our soldiers, lying where they had fallen. A horse and cart had been pushed off the road, the dead horse lying on the roadside with just enough room for the traffic to pass. All of it was now a familiar sight.

'Eyes open,' I said. 'Snipers, anti-tank guns, anything.' I didn't really have to remind them of that, but I did.

Grunts came back in acknowledgement; they were already watching.

We finally arrived at the cluster of houses that represented the village; the infantry had penetrated halfway along the street towards the church, which appeared to be in the centre of the small square. The tanks rumbled on down the road, infantry fell in behind and beside, a few jumped on board watching with guns ready at the houses, houses that were already showing the signs of battle. A shell fell some way ahead of us.

'Over to the right!' yelled someone nearby. 'Two o'clock, the house with green shutters.'

'They all have green shutters,' Charley muttered.

'Fire!' I commanded.

As our shells hit, bricks and wood tumbled to the road. The bodies of three Germans fell from the second floor as it collapsed.

'Got the bastards,' I said, then louder, 'Keep on.'

Sporadic gunfire kept the infantry busy as they pushed through; some wouldn't return home, but others had the luxury of suffering only minor wounds that would allow them to return to dressing stations and remain out of action for a few days. I noticed some even looked a little cheerful when inspecting their bloody bandages.

We emerged from yet another village, having driven along narrow lanes between the buildings, which we could hardly traverse. At one stage we couldn't turn left, the three-point turn to get into the lane causing some ribald humour from the soldiers waiting for us to enter and take out a machine post half way down. I made a note of their faces. When they wanted a lift, some would have an easier ride than others.

It was nearing midday when we stopped at a cross-roads at the edge of a village. A small barn stood in ruins on one side, the roof now reaching the ground, resting on the stones that had been its supporting wall. The farmhouse opposite was relatively intact and the soldiers had just cleared it through. The roof was nearly gone but the walls were still standing. It had a court-yard where soldiers milled around; cows lowed in their fields waiting to be brought in to be milked. I watched the farmer and his wife appear warily from the cellar and cautiously move into the courtyard where the soldiers greeted them warmly. I saw much hand-shaking and hugging taking place. Broad smiles of relief crossed the elderly couple's faces. Despite the damage to their home, they didn't seem to mind, even after they'd gazed around them at the damage in the farmyard.

'Do we continue to push on?' Charley queried.

I thought we needed a rest, even a short one. 'No,

wait,' I said. 'The infantry are exhausted, looks as if they have orders to fall out, take a rest. We can give support here then push on with them in an hour or two. They're sweeping again, making sure no Germans are left. Takes time.' I coughed from another cigarette I had lit. I looked at it; why did I keep smoking? I didn't enjoy it but the smells of war were hidden for a few minutes while I smoked. 'The bastards hide in the attics, shooting down at our men. So they start at the top of the houses and work down, not up. They've lost too many men that way.'

I consulted my map. 'Now where would you put a gun emplacement around here?'

We waited, hearing gunfire and the odd explosion of a hand grenade, but not close by. I was relieved the fighting seemed to be getting further away. As we waited we saw a group of German soldiers walk towards our tank with their hands held high.

'God, some are so young,' I said.

'No younger than you, mate,' said Ian, nudging my elbow.

'I suppose so.' They looked relieved to be surrendering.

Infantry appeared and took them away behind the lines. They would be picked up and held for the rest of the war. It was over for them, I felt a little envious.

A whistle blew, piercing my thoughts – must be the all-clear. I sighed in relief, we could all relax.

'Right-ho, time for a brew,' said Pete. Pete loved his tea, even the all-in-one they drank, which I found hard to swallow at times.

Ian waved the water container in the air. 'Fresh water needed. We used the last this morning, pass me the can.'

Charley volunteered. 'I'll get some, saw a village pump at the crossroads.' He started taking his battle dress off and placed it on the side of the tank. 'Bit hot, I am.'

'It's my turn,' said Ian. 'You did it last time.' He made to pick up the can from where he'd dropped it by the side of the tank.

Charley got there first. 'It's OK, I want to stretch my legs.'

Charley took the can and started to walk the short way to the pump by the barn, whistling as he went.

I saw him join the infantry, lounging around the pump filling their bottles, running the cool water over their faces and heads to clear the dust. Much-needed long drinks of water were taken. They hadn't stopped since the early hours of the morning, and the determined resistance had taken them a little by surprise. Now the village had been cleared, I supposed they anticipated a long walk to the next one.

Charley held his can while another soldier pumped the water up. The two tired soldiers exchanged jokes and stories, lighting cigarettes and puffing away like old friends. I watched Charley nod his thanks and stagger back the few yards to the tank with the heavy water can. Charley dropped the can by the tank's side and stretched his arms up to the sky and groaned. He seemed happy enough. I was looking forward to a warm cup of tea too.

That noise again! I ducked and waved my hand around my face. 'Damn bumblebees!'

'Sniper!'

I stopped waving my arms and looked around, unsure. Another zing went past my ear. Charley jerked, and his head exploded over his battle jacket.

Julia Sutherland

Chapter 19

Our column of tanks had been rumbling along the gravel track next to the meandering river for a couple of hours, occasionally passing over wooden bridges which creaked ominously as we drove across. Sunshine beat down on the vehicles so all hatches were thrown wide open to try and alleviate the heat and the smell coming from the men inside. Dave, Charley's Irish replacement, had kept a running commentary for some time on how he was navigating the bumps and holes in the roadway surface. I missed Charley.

'A few big ones coming up, boys,' said Dave in his relentlessly cheery voice.

'Doesn't he ever shut up?' muttered Ian.

I looked down into the tank. 'Put a sock in it, Dave!'

'Just saying,' shouted Dave. 'You want a bit of notice, don't you?'

'No!' snapped Ian. 'It's bloody annoying all the time.'

'But they're getting bigger with all this traffic,' argued Dave. As he spoke, the tank shuddered. 'See, jolted you, didn't it?'

'You're driving a tank,' I said. 'Shut up.' I was exasperated at the man, but his heart was in the right place.

Dave shouted back, 'You'll be sorry, so you will, I'm telling you, other drivers don't care, but I do.'

The vehicles continued to rumble on until we came to a blockade of tanks, lorries and men, scurrying about.

'What's up here then?' Dave asked.

I put my binoculars up for a better look. 'The bridge is being repaired.'

The radio squawked into life, rapid speech tumbling from the little speaker.

'Right, will do,' said Pete into the microphone. He turned from the radio. 'They want us to stay here while they finish repairing the bridge. It will be a couple of hours. No known Germans in the area – blew a few bridges and left in a hurry apparently.'

'Shut down then, Dave,' I ordered. 'Take us off-road a bit so we don't block the traffic.'

After a bit of manoeuvring the tank came to rest and three of us clambered out of the tank and stretched our aching bodies. We gazed around and ahead at the activity at the bridge in the distance, checking the countryside in case we had to move fast.

'I think I need a bath,' said Ian, sniffing his own tunic.

'I wouldn't argue against that,' I agreed. 'Clean out the tank, get some tea going and have a quick dip in that river before eating.'

'Sounds like a plan to me.' Ian slapped Dave on the back, making him stagger slightly; he was not a heavily built man, tall and wiry, but quite strong.

The three of us set to getting stuff out of the tank to air, and setting up the fire and cooking utensils. Pete handed items up to us from the tank so we took very little time setting up. A brew was made and mugs handed around.

'Come on down, Pete,' shouted Ian, standing by the tank with two mugs of tea in his hands.

'I'm fine. Just finishing something on the radio. You carry on.'

'Cup of tea waiting.'

'Put it through the hatch, please, don't want to mess this up.'

'Right, here it comes.' Ian handed the tea through the open hatch and the rest of us sat on blankets and stretched out. It didn't take long for me to fall asleep. It seemed I'd been gone for just a second when the screech of brakes, subsequent loud bang and cursing from nearby brought me to.

'Someone is going on report for that little dust-up,' I said, whistling through my teeth. We stood up by the tank looking down the road towards the source of the shouting. Two lorries had met, head on.

'Wonder which one has the would-be general type in it?' I said.

Dave grinned. 'Not my mess, so I don't really care. Drove a general or two, not my cup of tea. Talking of tea, another brew or a quick dip? We all honk a bit.' He roughed his short hair up as he looked at me and Ian.

I said nothing, but Ian sat down and started pulling his boots off. On past experience I didn't want to get too close when those things came off.

I looked around the tank. 'Where's Pete? Has he come out yet? Pete? Where are you?'

'Here.' The short word emanated from inside the tank.

'Come on out, Pete, a wash and chow coming up,' I shouted.

'No, I'm fine.'

'Come on down, man.' I was tired and didn't fancy an argument, but I was getting a bit fed up with his attitude; I was responsible for him.

'Really, I'm fine.'

Ian looked up at me. 'He is having a bath, don't think he's had one for longer than us, he smells to high heaven, when did he last get out of that tank?'

I nodded. 'You're right, he hasn't been out for a while.' I tried to remember but couldn't recall the last time he'd been out. This wasn't funny. I may have a real problem starting. I rubbed the back of my head.

'Beats me. I've passed him food and drink on occasion.' Ian set his boots neatly beside the tank and began unbuttoning his shirt.

'So have I,' I said, frowning. 'What about you, Dave?'

Dave nodded quickly. 'Same here. A bit reclusive I thought. Being the newbie, I didn't want to say nothing'.

I made up my mind. 'Right, we'll get him out. In you two go and push him up to the hatch and I'll haul him out.'

We all scrambled quickly up on to the tank, Ian and Dave disappeared into the darkness. Shouting and cursing came up to my ears as I stood by the open hatchway. Eventually a head appeared, and then shoulders.

'Go on, grab him,' panted Ian. 'He's heavy and kicking.'

'No!' hissed Pete. 'No, I don't need a bath.'

'Yes you do, mate, believe me,' I said. 'If I need one, so do you.'

I just managed to hold on to him as we hauled and pushed the man out of the hatchway and rolled him down off the tank sides. We three abductors quickly followed him.

'You buggers, leave me alone.' Pete was shouting now. Heads turned towards our vehicle, soldiers curious to know what was going on. Pete was shouting at us, cursing continually as we kept hold of him.

'Come on, lads, let's finish him.' The three of us each grabbed hold of a leg and an arm, leaving one leg trying to kick us away. We made the short walk across the road to the riverbank, to the cheers of more onlookers who, on hearing the commotion, had emerged from their transport. After a count of one, we threw Pete into the river.

'Well done, boys,' I said, dusting my hands together. 'Us next, fully clothed, the sun will dry them off quick. Come on, lads.'

I led the way with a determined wade into the sparkling river. Pete was shouting and cursing at us, but nevertheless, he took his clothes off while in the water and laid them carefully on the bank, then he quickly soaped himself down with a bar that I had thrown at him.

We also took off our clothes and laid them on the bank to dry as we soaped and dived into the water to clean ourselves. Pete didn't join us in our attempts to submerge one another and quietly left, collecting his clothes, putting them out along the sides of the tank to dry in the sun and slight breeze.

As we emerged from the river, a little breathless from our games, I saw we had started a trend of men washing and having fun in the water. I thought it was like one of those open-air lidos we had at home, just the pretty girls were missing.

Clean and refreshed, we returned to the tank. Ian lit the stove to prepare a meal, putting the water on first for a cup of tea. We put our still damp cotton underpants on, and spread our outer garments out on the side of the tank to speed their drying. We had wrung them until squeezing the last drop of water out before hanging them out to dry. I knew they'd end up badly creased but smelling a lot better than they had.

'That was good,' said Ian.

'Yes it was. Where's Pete?' I looked around the tank, I couldn't see him under the tarpaulin.

'In here, you bastards.' Pete's shout came from inside the tank.

'Mind your language, man,' I warned. 'You honked, we all did.' I was exasperated at the man's attitude but I couldn't see how I could change it. I couldn't keep on forcing him out of the tank. I sighed, ruffling my hair to speed up the drying.

'I was alright, leave me alone.' Pete's voice, sounding ever more whiney, filtered out through the turret.

'Fine,' I said. 'Food will be ready soon. You can come and get it, we're not waiting on you hand and foot.'

A grunt came, but no refusal.

Pete eventually emerged, after I'd told him three times his meal was ready. Later, we sat around watching other men sorting their vehicles, and occasionally the men working on the bridge. That was taking longer than anticipated. I didn't mind, but I was fearful the Germans would find us; we were vulnerable, strung out beside the river like this. By nightfall, we were asleep, three of us outside under the tarp, one snoring inside the tank.

Julia Sutherland

Chapter 20

I had made the decision, now I had to put it into effect. 'Ian, you seen the padre?'

'No, need to confess something?' Ian seemed to want to make a joke of everything these days. I wondered if it was a coping mechanism.

When I needed to confess my actions at the chateau to someone, I'd spoken to the last padre, now I needed help on something else and a padre seemed the right person to ask; we had paused in the advance so I had the time.

After a few hard weeks fighting through a succession of small towns, we were enjoying a few days R & R. The Germans had thrown everything they had at us, but we had won through. True, we had lost four tanks and some infantry, though I didn't know how many.

I scanned the infantry soldiers, standing around talking, but couldn't see the padre. 'Just want a word with the padre about something,' I said to my own men.

'Anyone seen him?'

Ian knew where he was. 'He was last seen over by the remains of the church. I heard the locals want to bury our boys in the churchyard.'

I smoothed my hair with both hands. 'I'll wander over. Get the kettle on, will you?'

'I'll do it,' said Dave, picking up the can and swinging it by his side. 'Can never get too much tea.'

Ian made a frown and muttered, 'I tell you, I have never drunk so much tea in my life! Why not coffee?'

'I'll be back soon,' I said as Dave started to fill the pan with water for the tea. The men nodded their acknowledgement.

I wandered towards the church ruins, passing the other tanks and their men setting up tarpaulins and cooking fires. They looked exhausted but seemed to be in good spirits, remembering their losses of friends, but laughing with fellow survivors. Some were quietly writing letters home. I saw the padre in the distance standing under a tree with another man and I made my way towards them. I stopped a few feet away and waited a minute or two. The soldier took a drag on a cigarette while the padre spoke to him. I couldn't hear what he was saying, but I didn't want to intrude. When the padre stopped talking I let out a little cough.

'Padre, can I have a word?'

The padre looked up as if seeing me for the first time, and then patted the soldier's back. 'See you later, son, we are all the same.'

The young soldier smiled somewhat unconvincingly but left the padre to the new member of his flock needing advice.

The padre took a few steps towards me with his arm out, I took it and felt a firm, warm shake.

'Andrew Thomas, isn't it? Seen you at service occasionally, what can I do for you?'

I paused and took out my cigarette packet and offered one to the padre, but he waved a lit cigarette back at me. 'Sorry, didn't realise.'

'Got something on your mind, son?' The padre hitched his trousers up, he looked like he'd lost weight. Most men had lost weight since the 6 June and he was no exception. In a comic way the padre's troubles with his trousers reassured me that we were all human.

'Yes,' I said. 'Something isn't right. I ... we have done what we can, but I think something is really wrong.' I lit my cigarette and put the packet away. I drew heavily on it and spat out the bit of tobacco that caught on my tongue.

The padre smiled. 'I hate it when that happens,' he said, nodding at my discarded tobacco. 'What is it, son?'

'Padre, it's one of my men.' I wasn't quite sure what to say, how to explain what was going on.

The padre looked into my face for a moment, as though trying to see through me. 'A Dear John letter received? We had post last week. A few of the men have had those recently. The war is going on a long time and the women are taking opportunities at home rather than living on hopes.'

I shook my head emphatically. 'No. More serious than that – not that a Dear John letter isn't serious.' I shuffled my feet in the grass, I was still not quite sure what to say next.

'Go on,' said the padre in that encouraging voice they all seem to have.

I took another drag on my cigarette and blew the smoke up in the air over the padre's head. 'It's Pete. He won't come out of the tank unless he absolutely has to.' I took yet another deep draw on the cigarette and coughed slightly. 'We pulled him out a few weeks ago as he stank to high heaven – we all did.'

The padre stubbed his cigarette out on the bark of the tree and put the remains in his cigarette packet for later. He concentrated on my face. 'Pete, you say, will not come out of the tank?'

'No, not unless we force him, or if he wants to, which is hardly ever. He gets one of us to hand food in to him, never the same person all day. We've just realised, he hasn't been out for at least a week.'

'A week.'

'Maybe more.' I rubbed the back of my head.

'Does he give a reason?' Concern now showed on the padre's face.

'Problems with the radio reading, resting. Anything.' I listed a few of the excuses he gave us.

'Hmm, does sound a bit peculiar.' The padre looked around him as if searching for someone. 'I will come over in a bit, have a word with you all, and see the lay of the land.'

I gave a quick salute. 'Thank you, much appreciated.' I returned to the tank, mulling over my actions. Had I done the right thing in informing an officer? The padre would be sympathetic. I had to think of the rest of the crew. Supposing Pete did something stupid.

'Well?' Ian said quietly over his steaming cup of tea.

'He's coming over.' I took a cup of tea and blew over the top to cool it.

'Dave, you got your tea?' I asked.

Dave came around the side of the tank. 'Sure did, I made it, I get first dibs.'

I nodded towards the tank. 'Pete?'

Ian shook his head. 'No, didn't come out, put it on the side, a hand came out, took it, shut the turret up as well.'

'What can we do? I'm all out of ideas.' I sighed and took a drink of hot tea.

Ian smiled at me. 'The padre will have a word, see what's up with him.'

'This bloody war is what's up!' I almost spat out the words.

Ian waved his hands in the air, spilling some of his tea in the process. 'Whoa, mate, I'm on your side here.'

Dave slurped his tea. 'Do you think they would like a cup?'

We turned to follow Dave's gaze and saw the padre striding towards us with another soldier.

'Who's that?' Dave asked.

'The doc, I think,' said Ian. 'The new one. I heard the other had had enough of war, apparently sat outside the medic tent in headquarters and started crying, couldn't keep going, no sleep for days after one of our pushes. He saved a lot of men, but it broke him.' Ian made a small sigh and continued. 'Should be alright after a bit of R & R.'

We stood to attention as the two men approached, shouting out 'Sir!' and throwing up rather sloppy salutes to the two officers.

'Cup of tea?' offered Dave. 'Just brewed.'

'That would be welcome,' said the padre, almost before Dave had finished his sentence. 'Not too strong for me please. This is Captain Reid, the new doctor.' We saluted again.

As Dave approached carrying a couple of teacups, Ian raised his eyebrows. 'Cups?'

Dave flashed a broad grin. 'I borrowed them from our neighbours.' He nodded to a tank pulled up nearby. 'They "borrowed" them from a fallen house a few days ago.' Dave gave a laugh and continued, 'I asked when I heard the padre was coming over. My mum dragged me up to offer the vicar a cup of tea when he visited.'

The captain broke into a beaming smile. 'One of the best brews I've had for a few days, how do you do it? And did your mother send you a boiled fruit cake in the post by any chance?'

Dave grinned. 'No, sir, she can't bake, Dad did the cooking in our house if we wanted decent food.'

By some kind of unspoken agreement the group moved a short way from the tank so we couldn't be overheard.

The padre took a swig of his tea, nodded towards the tank and said, 'Is he ...?'

'Yes,' I said in a low voice to match the padre's. 'Got his tea with him.' I drank the last drop of my tea and held my mug loosely by my side.

The doctor nodded. 'I will just pop over with the padre and listen to what is said between him and Pete. Get an idea.'

I addressed the doctor. 'Do you think it's serious, sir?' I knew it was, but I needed it to be confirmed that I was doing the right thing involving the padre and doctor.

Captain Reid nodded slowly. 'I'm afraid it could be, not been out for a while, you said?'

'No, not really since we gave him a bath. The troop had a day by a river and we all bathed, the whole lot of us, a right sight I can tell you.' I gave a smile, hopefully to lighten the situation and make me feel better, but it didn't.

The doctor grinned and glanced at the padre. 'I can imagine. Did you all good, I bet.'

'That it did.'

The two officers finished draining their tea, then gave the cups to Dave with a grateful nod. He looked so pleased they had enjoyed their drink. He was clearly proud of his tea-making skills.

I watched the two officers walk the short distance to the tank, talking to one another until they came to the tank itself.

'Pete? It's the padre here. Can I have a word?'

A muffled voice came from the tank, but I couldn't quite make out the words. We moved slightly nearer to try and hear what Pete said.

'Sorry, Pete,' said the padre. 'Didn't catch that, open the hatch, will you?'

Another muffled answer.

'Come on, Pete, I need to see a man when I speak to him. I'm not a Roman Catholic priest taking confession, but if you have something you want to get off your chest, I'm quite happy to listen.'

Another muffled answer.

We sat down and watched the officers trying to talk to Pete. We knew we couldn't do anything now but wait and see what happened. I'd tried to talk to him over the weeks, but had got nothing from him. Pete was efficient and able to do his job, but nothing more.

The soothing voice of the padre called out again. 'Pete, I need to see your face. The boys are worried about you, and asked me to come over. I haven't seen you at worship for a long time either, you were a regular I understand.'

'I can't come out, I can't find my bullet.' The voice was a bit louder this time and we could just hear it.

The padre turned his head and looked at us. He beckoned for me over.

I joined the padre and the doctor.

'Bullet? He can't find his bullet, what's that about?' the padre asked.

I nodded. 'Some kind of superstition. My dad told me about it once. He thought it had started in India. I know in the first war they used to write their names on bullets. Charley, he had a bullet with his name on it, said it would protect him. He didn't have it on him when the sniper got him. Didn't realise Pete had one too.'

'Lucky bullet?' the doctor whispered.

'Yes, that's what Charley said, had the bullet with his name scratched on it, and believed he couldn't be shot.'

Padre nodded. 'One of our bullets?'

I looked at Ian who had joined me. 'It was one of ours, wasn't it?'

Ian nodded. 'Yes, sir.'

'OK. I see the problem,' said the doctor confidently.

The doctor inclined his head to the padre and they had a conversation I couldn't hear. They seemed to agree on something. The padre called to Pete again.

'Pete, this bullet, is it one of ours or theirs?'

Dave had joined us. 'What does it matter so long as it has his name on it?'

'Ssh!' I hissed.

'Pete, which is it?' the padre called out again.

'Ours, now leave me alone.'

The doctor nodded.

Other men had become aware that there was something happening at the tank and were now blatantly staring at us. There was nothing I or the officers could do to stop them. I was anxious this was not going to end well, despite my best intentions.

The padre called out to Pete again. 'Well, the doctor says he hasn't found anyone in his surgery with a German bullet with their name on.'

The reply came quickly. 'Really, he said that?'

'Yes, you can ask him yourself.'

'Captain Smythe is here?' Pete sounded excited.

The padre shook his head. 'No, he's on … R & R, been a bit busy lately as a result of you boys pushing forward, given him a holiday.'

Ian muttered, 'Which is just what we all need.'

The voice quavered from within the tank. 'Captain Smythe would know.'

I looked at Ian. Would he stop talking now he knew Captain Smythe wasn't here? We'd seen the doctor around a lot since D-Day, once we'd joined up with the main force.

The padre put a hand on the doctor's arm. 'Captain Reid is here, he can confirm it too, can't you, Doctor?'

Captain Reid took a small step nearer the tank, clearly conscious of the many ears listening. 'Pete, I can call you that, can't I? I haven't found a German bullet with a British name on it in anyone's possessions.'

The padre continued. 'That's where … Charley?' He looked at me for confirmation. '… where Charley went wrong, he should have had a German bullet with his name on it, not a British one. Understand, Pete?'

A wavering voice came in reply. 'Really, sir?'

'That's what I said, soldier. Now can we sort this out?' The doctor was being quite firm in his tone as he spoke to Pete. 'You need a German bullet, yes?'

A muffled answer came, too low for us concerned crew mates to hear.

'No, son, I cannot get one for you,' the captain called back.

Another muffled answer – a little shriller but still inaudible.

The doctor looked at us, beckoning us to come nearer. 'One of you go for the MPs, should be some by the church-yard.'

'Sir?'

'Ssh!' The doctor cut me off, showing me the palm of his hand.

Dave immediately ran off towards the ruined church, watched by mawkish onlookers.

The padre joined in the conversation with Pete again. 'Pete, you'll have to get your own bullet. There are some German supplies over by the churchyard where they were dug in.'

'I don't want to get out, there's a sniper.'

We all heard that answer. The padre, his voice soothing and calm, replied, 'No, son, they've been cleared. We're staying here for thirty-six hours until more supplies come up. A bit of R & R for us all.'

'It's safe to come out, Pete,' said the doctor. 'If you want that bullet you're going to have to come out. We cannot get it for you.' The doctor sounded a little exasperated. I looked at the man's face, he looked tired and worn out.

I stepped forward into the doctor's line of sight. 'Sir, can I?'

'What, Thomas?' the doctor snapped.

'I ... Pete ...' I was stumbling with my words while looking toward the tank. 'We can all go and get one from the churchyard.'

The doctor and padre nodded their agreement, relief on their faces; this may work.

'It's not far to the church – what's left of it. We all saw it when we came in, the Germans are gone now.'

'No, lots of Germans around,' said Pete, his voice

dropping.

Ian stepped up too. 'They're gone now, Pete, even the ones who surrendered have gone. We're just clearing up ammo and stuff.'

As we all continued to cajole Pete from his safe haven, Dave returned with three MPs. The sergeant saluted the officers. The captain motioned them a few steps away from the Sherman tank out of earshot. 'We are trying to get this man out of the tank. Once he's out, you know what to do.'

The three MPs walked a short way and stood in a nonchalant manner, even taking cigarettes out to smoke. I noticed they were watching us the whole time.

'Now Pete,' said the padre, with a little more authority. 'Time to come out before it gets dark and the German shells are taken away. The MPs are here doing that as we speak.'

It was a relief when Pete answered. 'Give me a minute.'

I heard movement from inside the tank and eventually the sound of the hatch being opened. Pete's head appeared, then his body as he clambered through the hatch.

'Sir, sorry to cause a problem, sir,' said Pete, sounding a little sheepish.

The padre softened his voice again, none of his earlier firmness. 'No problem, man, now just get down here with your mates and get that bullet you want so much.'

With his back to us, Pete climbed slowly and deliberately down the side of the tank until his feet reached the grass. Whilst he was doing so, I noticed the MPs had moved quietly behind him.

Captain Reid nodded at the MPs.

'Right, lad. Come with us and let's get that bullet.' The sergeant took his right arm and another MP took the other. I saw Pete stiffen. I made a move towards him but the doctor shook his head at me.

'It's fine, mate,' I said. 'I'm coming, I want a bullet too.'

I looked at Ian and Dave and they said in unison, 'We want one too.'

We followed Pete and his escort to the churchyard. They let Pete search the abandoned bags that had been collected up and piled by the ruins of the churchyard wall. Pete found six bullets and ceremoniously gave one to me, Dave and Ian. Pete looked so happy when we expressed our thanks. After the handout of bullets, Pete was led away to the medical tent for what was explained as a routine medical check-up. I told him that all the men were to have one but Pete was one of the first. I felt I was cheating him by lying, mates in war don't lie to one another.

Later, Pete was put on to a lorry with two MPs as escort. The doctor had told me he would be taken back to HQ and ultimately to England. Ian passed up Pete's bag of personal items he'd collected from the tank and then gave the officer a short, sharp salute as the lorry drove away. The war was now over for Pete. As I watched this unfold, I felt the smoothness of the German bullet in my pocket; later I would write my name on the side and keep it safe.

Julia Sutherland

Chapter 21

Bremen in April was really not the place I wanted to be. The spring flowers would be in full bloom at home. Each year Mother's church organised coach trips to the countryside to see the bluebells; we always took a picnic to eat and I remembered sitting among the flowers and eating cheese sandwiches. Everyone sang hymns on the way home. 'All Things Bright and Beautiful' was one of my favourite hymns. Taking a deep breath, I could almost smell the bluebells. I hadn't noticed any flowers on the journey to Bremen, I didn't realise how I missed flowers in my life until now. They were always there. Mother put a vase of flowers on the big table every Saturday during the winter, and during the summer large flowers were put in the fireplace.

I sighed and hunkered down in the tank, listening to the continual booms from the boats in the harbour as their shells flew over our position. We had no co-ordinates to return fire so we sat and waited for more orders to advance on the dock area. I found myself humming 'All Things Bright and Beautiful' as I sat patiently, shells falling around me. Time passed slowly and I got stiff, and frequently found myself stretching and massaging the cramp in my legs.

'Ian, how much longer, do you think?'

I think I must have woken him, judging by the sleepy reply. 'What? The war? No idea.'

Dave ventured an opinion. 'I think we have them on the run, but some are using everything they have now to stop us advancing.'

A yawn came from Ian then his opinion followed. 'Yeah, they're using sea bombs with no timers now. You think there are no mines, then boom! You drive over one.'

'Yep, been lucky so far,' I agreed. 'Dirty tricks mean desperation. What you think, Ian?'

Ian took a moment before answering. 'Yes, nature of war.'

Silence again prevailed inside the tank, broken only by the sound of shells exploding in the distance.

The radio squeaked into life and our newest member of crew, Big Dave, talked quickly into the mouthpiece. Trust the Army to put two men in one tank with the same name I thought, but it was no problem. It was easy to tell them apart: one was much bigger than the other. They became good mates within hours of meeting each other. Big Dave was a gentle man, thick black curly hair and a sparkle in his eyes, someone you could trust, I thought.

Orders to advance on to the docks were finally received. We made our way slowly through the devastation to the utter destruction of the dockland area. The tank came under fire occasionally from isolated units but we, together with the advancing infantry, soon dealt with the pockets of resistance. We were ordered to stop, regroup and wait for first light before moving on through the city and on to our next objective.

We were settling down for a good night's sleep when Ian tugged at my sleeve and nodded toward a solitary man. It was the padre sitting on a wall, he seemed to be distancing himself from the troop of tanks bivouacking for the night.

'Shall we?' Ian asked.

I shook my head. 'Not sure, he may want to be alone.' I was tired, I didn't really want to sit up talking to the padre all night.

Ian shook my arm again. 'Not a good idea to leave him alone with that bottle in his hand, look.'

I peered at the padre and nodded, noticing the bottle for the first time.

'I see what you mean. He gives that stuff out, told me he didn't drink much, not at all before the war, but gets a lot given to him.' This was unusual, I thought as I stared at the padre taking a long drink from the bottle.

We dusted our uniforms down and began walking over to the padre, we both lit cigarettes as we walked. I didn't really want one, but Ian insisted I took it.

'Padre,' said Ian, throwing up a quick salute.

The padre didn't look up, I wasn't sure he'd heard us.

His head was down, looking at his feet, which he swung slowly, making a slow beat on the wall.

'Padre, cigarette?' I offered.

Still no answer, so we sat down either side of him and just waited, smoking in silence. I stubbed mine out after a minute and carefully replaced it in the packet for later.

The padre began to speak in a low voice. 'I never expected that.'

'Expected what, sir?' Ian asked softly.

'The utter waste.'

I had no idea what the padre was talking about, something must have happened. 'Padre?' I looked sideways at the officer.

'I mean, why do it? War, I know, and soldiers, yes, I can understand. But that?' It didn't seem like the padre was addressing us. He was gazing up into the sky as though searching for something. No planes were flying overhead so I was mystified as to what he was looking at.

Ian and I glanced at each other across the padre. Ian reached out and gently took the half-empty bottle of whisky from an unresisting hand. He raised it to his lips and took a small sip, then offered it across to me. I put it to my lips but didn't take a drink, I then leant forward and placed the bottle on the ground by my feet. I could smell the alcohol on the padre's breath. Ian wrinkled his nose at me and, as I sat back down, I saw patches of wet where the padre had dribbled it down his front.

Ian drew on his cigarette and blew the smoke straight out again. 'What is it, Padre? What's happened?'

'The utter waste of lives, son.'

'I didn't think we lost anyone today, padre, did we, Andrew?'

'Not as far as I am aware,' I answered quickly.

'Not us, son.' The padre's voice was barely audible.

We all sat quietly. I didn't know what to say, nor, I suspected, did Ian. I looked around, not really seeing the ruined buildings surrounding us. In the distance, guns still boomed and thundered.

I didn't feel it was good for the padre to keep what he was thinking about bottled up. He had helped us all through the war, maybe it was our turn to help him.

'Is it the whole thing?' I asked. 'We were talking earlier, surely Jerry won't go on much longer?'

The padre sighed the long heavy sigh of the soul. 'No, son, not the soldiers, the civilians.'

Ian nodded his head. 'I saw civilians today, refugees from the fighting, coming past us, some still in the city, we've heard about the work camps too.'

'No, son, not the camps.' The padre visibly shook from head to toe in a huge sigh. 'I went into the outskirts, where the professionals live. Lovely houses.'

'Yes, we saw them too,' said Ian. 'Not too much damage there, they didn't put any gun posts around them, perhaps because they're away from the main roads.'

'Yes, son, I suppose so, lovely houses.' The padre's voice faded away to almost nothing.

I was really beginning to get worried now, should I get help, or just sit with him? 'Padre?' I put a hand on the man's forearm.

We had to lean towards the padre to catch his words.

251

'I went with some infantry through the streets, just checking, not looting, anyone who needed help after the city fell …'

'Yes?' I encouraged him as the padre faltered in his explanation.

'We heard a shot in one of the houses, lovely houses they are – did I tell you that? – just as we came to it. Beautiful, set back from the road, well cared for.' The padre slipped off the wall and took the bottle from the ground and poured a long drink down his throat. Ian and I looked at each other. This was serious, I thought. For a man who didn't drink he'd drunk almost all the bottle.

I shrugged my shoulders trying to play down my worries by looking relaxed. 'What happened, sir, booby traps?'

'No, the men got in the house where the shots came from, they broke the door down.' He took another mouthful of whisky. 'I followed. While we were in the house, a woman ran up the path, screaming. I think she lived next door. The soldiers stopped her at first, but she must have broken free, she ran in and up the stairs. I went after her.' The padre wiped away a solitary tear which had begun a slow descent down his cheek.

'She was on her knees in a doorway, I couldn't see properly at first … a child's room, two children lay on their beds, a little girl with blond pigtails, typical German clothes, leather shorts, you know, the boy a bit younger.' He took another swig of the whisky, the bottle was almost empty now. 'Looked like they were in their best clothes.' The padre's hand shook as he wiped his mouth. 'The girl lay on a pink rosebud counterpane, except as it got higher up the bed you couldn't see the pink rosebuds anymore only deep red blooms merging into one another.'

I shivered then tensed at the image.

'The woman was screaming, her hands squashed against her face. One of the soldiers took her downstairs. I looked into another bedroom, a woman, the mother I suppose, lay on the bed, shot through the head. A man was slumped by the window, his brains all over the shattered glass.'

He lifted the bottle to his mouth but didn't make it all the way. Some whisky dribbled down his chin. The padre swallowed, wiping his chin on the back of his hand.

'Why do that, why kill the children? We found another house, same thing, members of the Nazi party. Why kill the children?' The padre's voice rose a little more as he repeated the question to us, but we had no answer.

We sat and drank what little remained of the whisky, watching the stars watching us, and I wondered: why kill the children?

Julia Sutherland

Chapter 22

I sat down by Ian. 'I've just been talking to Sergeant Pine,' I said. 'He's been to one of those camps. Saw you earlier talking to him, bad isn't it? Can't believe people can do that.'

Sitting up, I searched through my pockets and found a battered packet of cigarettes. I took one, straightened it slightly and offered it to Ian, who shook his head.

'What's up, mate?' I spoke through the cigarette now dangling from my bottom lip.

Ian again shook his head.

'That Sergeant Pine made it sound horrible, can't be that way, can it, Ian?

The cigarette was alight and the smoke lazily went upwards and sideways into Ian's face. He wafted it away but still said nothing.

'We're heading on to Berlin, finishing up.'

'Fine.' It was all the response I got.

'Sergeant Pine said they had mounds of the dead, all Jews. I don't believe that, do you?'

Ian shifted, shook his head, but remained tight-lipped.

'You're talkative this morning. Something up?' I inspected the end of my cigarette, tapping gently. I stubbed it out, all I needed was a few draws of it and I was finished. I gazed around at the other men relaxing by their tanks and vehicles. I wasn't in the mood to cheer him up. We all needed some time to unwind and maybe it was Ian's day.

'No,' said Ian, suddenly, fidgeting as he sat.

Improvement, an actual answer. I was curious and decided to voice some of my thoughts. 'Well, we may be passing one of the camps. Anneke said there were camps her people were in. You never know, maybe we can leave her name and address for contact with the Red Cross.'

Ian shifted again. 'Hmm.'

I put the stubbed-out cigarette into the packet and back into my trouser pocket. 'Well I think it's a good idea. Sergeant Pine's going back that way. I could give the information to him in case we don't go that way.' I touched Ian's arm. 'What do you think?'

'Fine.'

Ian was being even more unresponsive than usual. I sat upright and glared at him, maybe something was wrong. Ian's eyes seemed vacant and red-rimmed, he didn't seem to be looking at anything in particular.

I wasn't going to give up on my friend yet. 'I'll do that, then. Paper, got some in there somewhere? Want a decent piece if it's to last. Make it look official, maybe get some from an officer, they have nice stuff.'

'Yes.'

'Come off it, Ian, what's bothering you?' I was becoming exasperated. We all had problems to shoulder.

'Nothing.'

I shifted position to get a clearer look at his face. 'Now, I don't believe that, never seen you like this. A moody bugger yes, but this is different. Sergeant Pine's upset you? He can be gory at times telling his stories.'

'No.'

Ian got up, putting his back to me. He stood at the front of the tank for a few seconds, inspecting his hands then he sighed and, as I watched, he moved around the far side out of my view, but I heard the scraping and banging as items were moved and secured. My hand went around the back of my head and rubbed the bald patch that was now a permanent feature. I touched the short hair surrounding the patch and wondered if it would grow back after the war. Following Ian around to the tank front, I stood behind him watching as he finished roping the spade back on. I tried again.

'Ian, come on, mate, what is it? Want the padre for a chat? Caught something from those ladies a few weeks ago?' I flashed a knowing grin. 'Need the medics?'

I put my hand on Ian's shoulder and it was immediately shrugged off. I touched him again but I stood my ground. I didn't want another Pete on my hands.

'Ian, what is it?'

'Those people,' he said through gritted teeth.

'In the camp?' My eyes searched Ian's face for an

answer. This was serious, another incident like the padre finding children dead? That couldn't be it, we'd been together all the time and I hadn't seen or heard any rumours. We'd put Bremen behind us, we had to, or we would go mad just thinking about it.

'Yes.' Ian's voice was barely a whisper.

'I know, it's bad, but—'

'Mounds, Andrew.'

What was he on about? I could see the tension in Ian's neck and shoulders, and bright red rings on his arms where the blood vessels had ruptured from his tightly rolled-up shirt sleeves.

'I don't believe that,' I said.

'I do,' said Ian, beginning to find his voice again. 'They're monsters.'

I didn't believe it, or did I, deep inside? 'Come on, mate. They're hard fighters, but mounds of dead?'

Ian hit the tank side with a clenched fist. 'I believe it! The things they did before the war ...'

I had no idea what he was talking about. I'd heard of a few things, read them in the newspapers. 'Burnt a few buildings, didn't they? Other than that ...' I hesitated as I saw Ian's face change.

'Oh no, much more, much more than that.' Ian fell forward on to the tank. His head sunk on to crossed arms. 'More than that.'

My hand went tentatively on to the man's back. 'Come on, spill it. Get it off your chest, mate, it's killing you.'

'I'm fine.'

'No you're not.' My hand rubbed the back brusquely.

'No!' yelled Ian, slapping my hand away.

Passing soldiers stood and gawked, and a group of officers having a meeting a few yards away looked up too.

'It's …' Ian sucked in a lung full of air. 'The mounds of Jews.'

Not that again, I thought. 'Yes, that's what upset you.' I took a step backwards, giving him space. 'It is over now, Ian.'

Ian shook his head. I noticed, with shock, his whole body was shaking.

'I'm a Jew,' he said quietly, as though worried someone might hear him. 'Well, according to the Germans I am. My mother is a Jew, my father a Catholic.'

'I'm not surprised to hear that, having seen you in the river during the summer, mate. Don't worry about it now.' I slapped his back, relieved it was nothing more serious. But why get so worked up about it?

Ian lifted his head from the tank and looked me in the eye. 'I'm German.'

I jerked my head back as though he'd hit me. 'Oh! I didn't see that one coming.'

'My family was taken after I left.'

'Ah, you're an evacuee.' I nodded in encouragement as I stood beside him, listening. There was clearly a story to tell and I felt it had better come out in one go rather than over a few days. Ian needed to tell it, let it all come out, the secret must have been hell to keep.

'Yes.'

'Your sister and you got out?'

'No, just me. They were to leave later, Papa was

packing up things. I left early.' Ian spoke in a rush. 'One place came up, my mama, papa, two brothers, younger than me, my older sister, all to follow.'

'So who's in that picture?'

Ian's voice trembled. 'My sister. It's all I have.'

'I don't know what to say, mate. I don't know what to say.'

Ian was looking at me with red-rimmed eyes. 'You don't have to say anything.'

I tried a reassuring smile, but it seemed wrong to smile at the distraught man before me. 'I know, but how?'

Ian sighed and began speaking. I listened intently.

'I was a young boy, thirteen perhaps, when we realised and finally accepted what was really going on. In denial, not believing the stories. We thought we would be safe, Father being Catholic. But we were not safe so Father made plans.' Ian wiped his eyes with the back of his hands. 'Enquiries to leave, it took time, Father worked in an engineering company, packed some of his drawings. Told the factory that he was going to take us on a holiday.'

Ian slipped wearily down the side of the tank and sat leaning against it. His face was ashen and his eyes stared out at nothing. He seemed to have shrunk before my eyes. He continued talking in a subdued voice.

'But they were watching us. The Cohens knew, they are Mother's cousins. They'd kept in touch with Mother, they only ones. Going on holiday too, to their house in the mountains, then on out of the country, one man dropped out, so they said I could take his place and be a companion to their son on holiday if anyone asked. One moment I was eating my lunch, the next my overnight bag was in a large car ostensibly to tour the Austrian Alps and lakes, my family were to meet us at their house. I left that afternoon. It was an adventure, hotels and then their house. We did walking trips for a few days in the area. My family never came.' A sob came from Ian, but he kept talking. 'One day we kept walking, over the border.'

I dropped down to sit next to Ian, taking the battered cigarette packet out and again offering him one. I was finding all this a little hard to take in.

'How do you know they're not safe somewhere?'

Ian sighed. 'I sent a postcard when I reached France, and I tried to contact them when we were in Calais. I telephoned the house, and then the factory where my father worked. He had his own telephone. Someone else answered at the house, another family had moved in. The telephonist, she told me they were arrested, gone, and cut the connection immediately. She wouldn't answer me when I rang again. I don't blame her. Beatings, houses burnt to the ground if you were Jewish or if found helping Jews.'

I lit Ian's cigarette and then mine. We sat in silence, just smoking. After a minute, Ian continued.

'I went to London with the Cohens. We were well looked after, we were not the first, nor the last. I kept on looking for my parents, but nothing. No news. I just had to hope they were released. Father isn't a Jew, we all went to Mass. So I'm not a Jew in faith. But I knew. Then the war started, I was too young to join up then, but I perfected my English and cleaned up my accent.

Who wanted to be with a German, right? I'd even been in the Hitler Youth, can you believe it? Everyone was in it. Good fun, camping, athletics. We were fit, I can tell you.' Ian laughed, he looked happy at the memory, then his face fell. 'I was living with a Jewish family in the East End until I joined up, they're still there. A bit bombed around them but they refuse to leave. They enjoyed the sugar and things I brought them, a lot of mouths to feed as they took in more than just me.'

I coughed on my cigarette.

'We heard about the camps. Some who knew, a very few, escaped from Germany. The British Government knows, but I don't think they really know, if you know what I mean. The Red Cross do what they can but very little news got out.'

'You talked to Pine?'

Ian took a long draw on his cigarette. 'Yes.'

Ian confirmed my worst nightmares. I was hoping, praying, that it wasn't true but now I couldn't deny it.

I studied my cigarette, it tasted horrible, worse than usual. 'Will you give your name and address to Pine for the Red Cross at the camp he goes to?'

'Yes. Not that it will do much, but I can hope. I have given names of my parents and siblings too. I wrote to the head office of the Red Cross before we left England.'

I nodded my agreement. 'Good idea, how many camps are there?' I didn't really know what to say, I thought of James and my parents; I couldn't contemplate not knowing where they were or whether they were safe. I caressed my bald patch.

Ian took another long draw on his cigarette and blew the smoke out in a thin stream. 'I don't know, I pray that they're safe, but I fear there's no one to answer my prayers.'

I felt helpless. 'See the padre,' I said. 'Maybe he can help.' What else was there to do? We were in a field in Germany fighting a war.

Ian shook his head. 'He has more on his mind than my small family. They were all I had; Father's family disowned him when he married, as did Mother's.' Ian grimaced, the memory was clearly a painful one. 'The Cohens saw what was coming and helped, but they didn't tell the other family members. My grandmother was still alive when I left, I met her once, on the street by chance. I'm alone.'

I had to stop this downward spiral of despair. 'No, mate, not alone. You have the family in London who took you in.'

Ian stubbed his cigarette out on the ground beside him and got up slowly. 'I suppose,' he said wistfully. 'I think I want to be alone now.'

I wasn't going to let him be by himself for long, but I agreed. 'Right, mate. I'm going to make a brew soon, want one?'

'Yes,' he said, turning away. 'Just going on a short walk, be back soon.'

Ian dejectedly hunched his shoulders and walked away from the tanks parked up and, as he passed the other men, he seemed barely to acknowledge their greetings.

As I watched the forlorn figure walking away I thought

of my family and Anneke. I knew I would be so alone if I didn't have them to think of and fight for. They kept me strong in the darkest moments. What must it be like to have no one?

Chapter 23

'Have you heard, Andrew?' Big Dave's voice sounded shrill. 'They're surrendering!'

'What?' I leapt up, I hardly dared believe the good news recently coming through, but if it was true the war may be nearly over. Had Dave learnt something new?

'Hamburg surrendered yesterday,' he shouted.

I exhaled long and slow, collecting myself, but before I could answer another voice called out.

'Thank God for that, one less place to flatten,' shouted Little Dave from the ground where he was sheltering under the tarpaulin.

The tank was laid up, waiting for infantry to arrive. Orders had been given: we were to support the infantry on the assault on Bremerhaven the next day and the crews were relaxing while they could. We all had our little routines before a battle once the rearmament was completed.

Meals had been cleared away and men were sitting on and by their vehicles, watching the night sky. We could hear the guns in the distance.

'Any news on Bremerhaven?' asked Little Dave. 'No chance they're surrendering too, is there?'

'No news on that,' said Ian. 'The troops are still filing past us for tomorrow's offensive.'

I frowned and looked over to Ian. 'What's the date today?' Sometimes I lost track of the days.

'The fourth, mate, fourth May 1945. Not your birthday is it?'

'Christ!' I scratched my head, gawping at Ian. 'Is it really a year since the invasion?'

We looked at each other. I thought we could see in the other's eyes that we were reliving the landing. Perhaps we had done every day since; we hadn't left each other's company from that day on. I looked away from Ian to see the infantry marching past, and then around to the other tanks. Was there a chance we may actually survive this? I wiped my eyes with the sleeve of my shirt. 'Time flies when you're having fun, doesn't it?

'Not quite what I would call it,' said Little Dave, snorting. 'Lost too many mates, I have. Longest I've survived without losing a mate is with you lot.'

'And long may it continue,' Ian laughed. 'If it's the end, Andrew, what do you think you are going to do in Civvy Street?'

I hadn't given it serious thought before, only that I wanted to return to Anneke. 'Well, I love photography, but I ought to go and help Dad in the shop, I suppose.'

I paused and looked at my grime-laden hands. 'I don't know.'

'A bit more education?' Ian asked.

'Nah, not enough brains. Get ideas for the shop though, expand, specialise maybe. I don't know. What about you?'

Ian shrugged. 'See if I can find my family.'

'And if you don't?'

Ian looked away from me. 'Well, I'm coming to terms … I may go to the Middle East. When I was in London there was talk, in the synagogue, of returning to the Promised Land.

'But I thought you were raised Roman Catholic or something.'

Ian nodded. 'Yes, Father was. But now, I'm not anything. I cannot come to terms with any religion that rejects another so violently. Mother's parents rejected her, Jew against Christian there, then Adolf, he was what, Roman Catholic? Lutheran? He was against anyone or anything, not that religious unless it suited him.'

Little Dave sat up, leaning on his elbow. 'He's a right politician, says what the crowds want to hear, uses people and ideas to his own ends. Nasty piece of work, he is. Nasty.'

'That's the reason we're all here, isn't it?' said Ian. 'Fascism, Hitler, the enslavement of whole sections of society – the infliction of another person's will and thoughts on another.'

I shook my head. 'What does it matter what God you worship and how? Just don't say you have to believe the same as me, or you die.' I rubbed the back of my neck. This was a heavy conversation, the first one we'd had. Up till now we were just intent on surviving.

Ian nodded. 'I saw it in Germany. Didn't know about the camps, but looking back, where were all those people going? Denial, I suppose. The women didn't have a good time either, stay at home, cook and have babies – whether or not you wanted to – if they had a good job, bye-bye, go home.' Ian nearly spat the words out.

'What do you think, Ian?' asked Dave. 'Wasn't the Nazi party a form of religion – hero worship?'

'Yes, I suppose it was, ideals, superiority over others. Same thing, I suppose.'

After a few moments of silence, I called up to the top of the tank. 'Big Dave, what do you want to do?'

A curly-haired head emerged from the tank, then a hand holding an oily rag, wiping the other hand so it too was covered in an oil. I smiled; Dave seemed to get dirty the more care he took of himself.

'Me? Well I would like to go into engineering. I like making things. See if I can get a job in a car factory.' The dirty rag was dropped inside the tank. Dave smiled. 'Would like to be in on designing new ones, not just making them, but doubt I'd get the opportunity. So long as I can potter on I'll be OK.'

I looked at the large man, who was still beaming, then he disappeared from view. I thought for one moment of Pete and his wish to be in the tank all the time, but Dave wasn't like him. When this was over, I would look Pete up, see how he was.

Little Dave sat up. 'I have absolutely no idea. Just put food on the table and enjoy myself. But I'll have to get a job of some sort. Dad was killed in an air raid and Mother has only myself left.' He paused for a moment. 'My brother, he was in the RAF, Bomber Command ...' His voice trailed off.

'Sorry, mate,' said Big Dave. A silence descended on us as we became lost in personal thoughts for a minute or two.

I rubbed the back of my neck. 'Letters home, tonight, I'm going to write to Pamela. I'm going to tell her I don't love her. I don't think of her much. It isn't right.' I gave Ian a defiant look.

Ian sighed. 'If that's your decision, go with it, but don't rely on hooking up with Anneke again.'

'I don't accept that!' I gritted my teeth. 'I will find her and I will ask her to marry me.'

Little Dave looked. 'Anneke, who's that then? I've heard about Pamela, seen her photo.'

Ian replied before I had a chance to say anything. 'Oh, a woman he met, soon after landing. Had a nice little holiday, didn't we, mate?'

I gave Ian a long hard look. 'Yes we did.' I walked off, hands in pockets, shoulders hunched against the world and the rain. My mind was in turmoil.

The camp continued its preparations for the next day's offensive, more supplies were brought up and distributed. Letters from home, some weeks or even months old, were handed out to grateful recipients.

I sat and looked at the three letters in my hand. Two

from Mother, one from Pamela. I agonised over which I should open first – date order, of course, it was obvious. But I was too tired to think straight. I looked at the dates and opened Mother's first letter.

Dear Andrew,

> *We have had one or two letters from you. You sound well, but I do worry about you and getting wet and cold, silly really, but that's your mother for you. Father is well; James is still growing and is following the news reports on where he thinks you are. I do pray the war is over soon so he doesn't have to join up too. It will be over soon, won't it?*
>
> *Pamela is well, I saw her yesterday. Looks a little tired but Mr V is busy despite the rationing, I expect that's the reason. Her mother is not good, but is still out and about. Father has planted all the vegetables now; we hope to have a better crop than last year. I do get tired of carrots every meal but they grow so easily. Amazing the number of recipes you can make with carrots.*
>
> *The church started a knitting bee, did I tell you? We knit things for men on the front line and camps for the Red Cross, did you get anything from them? It would be nice if you got one. I knit the scarves. Your grandmother would have been good at this but I couldn't get her to go to the meetings, she would have been quicker than me even with*

her hands, I do miss her but at least it was quick.

I crumpled the letter a little and then smoothed it out on my leg. The last letter I'd received had told me of Grandmother's death. A stray bomb, one jettisoned after a bombing raid on the factories. It had happened just before the invasion but they had decided not to tell me until months later, to spare me the sorrow when so much was going on. A small tear meandered down my cheek as I remembered Grandmother's silver hair escaping from its bun, the feel of the silky hair as I brushed it for her, once her arthritis got too painful for her to do it herself. I would never do that again. I returned to the letter.

I have no other news, very quiet here. Most of the American soldiers have gone now. Some were very polite but others, well, I would not tolerate that behaviour from James or you. I hope you are behaving and remembering that the people you meet are wives, mothers and children. But if they are trying to kill you then I suppose that is different.

The rationing is not good, the few things you brought have all gone now, they did last well. I used them for special occasions, birthdays, Christmas, you know. Pamela has been around for a meal a few times. Not so much lately. Have you thought about what you will do after the war? Father would love for you to work with him again, but it's your decision.

I look forward to receiving another letter soon.
Keep safe, my darling boy.

Love Mum

I smiled. Mother was not the best letter writer in the world, but it was comforting to receive them. I tore open the next letter in date. It was from Pamela.

Dear Andrew,

    I have had a few letters from you, I am sorry
I have not written so often. Mr V is keeping me
rather busy and Mother is not well.
    I saw your mother a few days ago. She said
she had a letter from you. The Americans have
nearly all gone now; Cynthia is upset her boyfriend
has gone too. She seems to get a letter every other
day. They had hoped to marry before he went over-
seas, but his CO would not give permission. Appar-
ently a lot of boys have been getting married.
    I have been out a few times with Cynthia
as I told you last year. Her mother asked me to.
Daniel Wilson, his friend, came as company for me,
a blind date. I was not that taken with him but I
was there as a chaperone so could not really leave.
We had such a gay time dancing with all the GIs. If
you had not been in my mind I would have had a
wonderful time. I danced and danced even though
I told them I was engaged. It made them somehow

*even more insistent. I think they thought of me as
their sister that they had left behind.*

*I have put the wedding suit idea on hold, I
still have my coupons saved, but there are dresses
you can borrow.*

*I follow where you go on the continent, very
exciting seeing all those foreign towns. I looked
some of them up in the Library. They look beautiful. Don't forget if you see any shoes do buy me
some.*

Your Pamela

I stared at the letter. It seemed short, even for Pamela.
Not so giddy about things either. I slipped the paper back
into its envelope and put it on top of Mother's first letter.
I picked up the third letter and eased open the envelope

My darling Andrew,

*So much has happened since I last wrote.
The news from Europe is so much more positive,
the army is making such good progress. I do believe
it will soon be over, at least in Europe, they won't
send you to the East will they? Not if you stay in
tanks. Do you still have Maisie?*

I told her we'd named our fourth tank 'Maisie', though
we hadn't named any of the others. I wasn't sure where
the name had come from.

*Have you taken a photograph of her and
your crew? We are all well, and we are glad the
warmer weather has come at last, we finished our
coal ration a long time ago. One of our windows
broke, we had a hard time getting replacement
glass, not like before the war, but I suppose they
only have a limited supply, after all that bombing
we had.*

*I am sorry to say that Pamela's mother died,
all of a sudden, outside Mr V's shop of all places.
She had just been in talking with Pamela, some
said arguing, and as she walked out the door, she
fell and was dead before she hit the pavement they
say. A lovely way to go, I suppose, but a big shock
to everyone there. Pamela has taken it well, but she
says she will not come and live with us. The funeral
was well attended.*

*I must tell you. Pamela has taken up with
a GI called Daniel. I am sorry to tell you but she
doesn't seem to want to write to you, I think in
case he doesn't marry her. He has asked her and
she has said yes. I do not think it is right, you
should know, you would not do the same would
you?*

I looked up and gawped into the distance. After a moment
I looked around and saw fellow tank members reading
their letters, oblivious to my stunned reaction. It hadn't
crossed my mind that Pamela might find someone else,

not a serious friend, marriage and all that.

> *Well, I have told her she should, but with her mother gone she seems to have gone a little wild, out every night, whether or not Daniel is around. He is a clerk on the base, it seems unlikely he will go overseas. He does seem a nice man but I am trying not to like him, but who would go out with an affianced woman and then ask her to marry him? I am so sorry to tell you this news but I felt you should know so it will not come as a shock when you come home.*

> *Do write and tell me you are fine. Come home safe.*

> *Your loving mother*

I carefully folded the letter and put it back in its envelope. I then opened up Pamela's letter and reread it. Now I understood the briefness. I sat and gazed at the tanks and men around me going about their business, their doings; I hadn't thought of that phrase for a while. Like Their doings were nearly over; like us, they just had to survive and get back home. I rubbed the back of my head. I felt a little lighter somehow. I was free.

Julia Sutherland

Chapter 24

The infantry had marched past our position and found places to sleep the night before the advance on the town. Organised chaos all around us, men talked, made final adjustments to their arms and munitions, a gentle hum and activity that every army made before action, filled the air. I looked at it with new eyes: would the end of the war in Europe come soon, would this all be over in the coming days, weeks or even months? Would I able to come home safe to mother? I had promised, but half of me hadn't really believed that I would. The German people surely could not take much more of the relentless advance from the Allies.

Late afternoon drifted into early evening, and the men sat and talked. A quietness came over the encampments. I even heard the evening song of birds, it felt so still as if we were waiting on something – a huge storm maybe. I anxiously scanned the sky; it was a little overcast, with a light drizzle that certainly hadn't come from the huge black clouds usually around when it thunders. Meals and the inevitable cups of tea were drunk, men began to lay down to try to sleep.

I heard it first, I couldn't sleep, my mind running over and over the letters I'd received, and the ones I hadn't. No reply to the letters I had sent to Anneke, but it was a lottery whether or not letters got through anyway, so I tried not to worry. But I did worry; at least one should have come. A bang broke through my thoughts. I looked up into the sky.

'Look at that!' I shouted.

The distant sky was lighting up. Hundreds of Verey lights and rockets were blasting away. Searchlights pierced the sky for planes that we couldn't hear, but the lights had no pattern of search, they were moving so fast and haphazardly. Men got up, stood on tanks, vehicles, anything to get a better look. I thought of Caen, and the offensive we'd waged on the town. This was different. There was no artillery noise, no ground shaking. The display continued and, after what felt like hours but was only minutes, the radios crackled into life. Seconds later, all the radio operators were running around the encampment, shouting the news.

'It's over. Germany has surrendered this evening. Six-thirty they signed the surrender to Monty, it's over. No advance, it takes effect tomorrow.'

The radio news spread like wildfire between the men.

We all stood, at first in disbelief, then in enormous relief. We had talked about it, hoped for it, prayed every day and night for it, and the end was real. Soldiers slapped each other on the back, gave hugs, regardless of rank. A feeling of euphoria, some cried. My eyes filled with moisture, but nothing ran down my cheeks. It was over. Over. I could go home.

The firework show lasted nearly all night. Bottles were produced from hideaways and drunk into the late night. It was over, our doings. After a few hours I walked away from the throng of men and had a few minutes of reflection. Charley, gone, the sergeant on the bridge, gone, and many more I hadn't known. The horror of D-Day, young men cut down before they'd begun to live. It could have been me. I raised a mug of wine to the sky and drank deeply. I returned to my crew and celebrated again until the sun came up and the new day began with the dawn chorus of birds announcing a new day, and peace, at last, in Europe.

Julia Sutherland

Chapter 25

I stared up at the chateau as the lorry made its bumpy progress up the gravel driveway. I'd managed to bribe my way into the cab with the driver rather than sit in the back with the other men and Ian. I'd decided my battered body needed a rest and I also needed peace to reflect on the future without Ian advising me all the time.

The house didn't appear much different to me after a year away. The river still ran alongside it, but no Nazi flag dipping and diving in it this time. Upstairs the shutters remained mostly closed against the heat, but the front door was wide open. A smattering of golden-coloured gravel shot up from the tyres as the driver spun the lorry in an arc in front of the chateau and brought it to a sudden halt.

'You could have avoided that,' I muttered as I was enveloped in choking dust drifting through the half-open window.

'Yes I know,' Harry the driver said. 'But it's my one pleasure from driving this heap around to make you lot suffer as much as I do. The seats are awful and the machines are beasts to drive.'

I brushed my face free of dust. 'Fine, you try it in the back sometime. It's a dust bath in weather like this.'

Harry pulled the hand brake on with a hard yank upwards. 'Oh I have, believe me, and sometimes I wish I was back there.'

I shook my head in disbelief that anyone would wish to travel in the back of the transport lorries.

Harry shouted at the top of his voice, 'Everyone out. Terminus reached.'

I dropped to the ground and reached in for the kit bag that had rested at my feet for a long hundred miles. I pulled it out and it fell to the gravel with a resounding thud.

'So what are you doing now if everyone's off?' I asked Harry.

He didn't answer me straight away. Harry had been watching in his mirror as the men appeared behind his lorry, and when all were safely off he gave a small grin.

'I, mate, am having a wash, some grub and a forty-eight hour sleep to catch up on the thirty-six hours of nonstop driving I've done ferrying you pansies around the countryside.' With that, Harry released the handbrake and drove, with another scattering of gravel, away from the chateau forecourt, leaving a set of bewildered men scurrying to pick up their kit in the dusty wake.

The sergeant sidled up to me and Ian. 'You two have

been here before, ain't that right? Nice gaff, no wonder you wanted to come back. Food good?'

I looked at the small Scottish man; I hadn't warmed to him on the journey. He was another reason I'd blagged my way into the front with Harry.

I looked for Ian, but he had chased after his bag that had rolled away.

'Food was OK,' I said. 'Just after D-Day, so not a lot, but better than rations.' I looked around. We'd heard that the chateau had since become the staging post for tanks being shipped home. A wonderful piece of news for me. I'd immediately volunteered for collecting tanks for shipping. A little more time in the Army but an opportunity to find Anneke.

Ian made his way back, bag in hand, and clapped me on the back. 'Don't fret, son. She'll be here. I can feel it in my bones.'

'Wish I was feeling it.' I pulled my lips into a nervous smile.

The small group of men finished collecting their belongings and followed me as I walked into the familiar hallway of the chateau.

A sergeant appeared from the drawing room where I'd been taken after being hit all those months ago. The sergeant immediately gave us our orders.

'Right, men, tents out the back for the use of. Inside in the staff quarters for food. Not so many of us here now so the mess tent has gone. Food quality has gone up. Get to it, stow your gear and report back in thirty minutes. Go.' The sergeant shouted the last word and it reverberated around the chateau like a shell firing.

We left the hallway as quickly as we could, our heavy boots leaving soil and long black skid marks on the polished floor. I knew Armande wouldn't be amused by the dirt on the floor, but I wasn't about to get on my knees and start scrubbing. Instead I filed out with the other men to find the tents.

The tents stood forlornly in short ranks, having been well used in the weather since the invasion, but they still kept the rain and sun out. We found empty ones with campaign beds and tied the entrance flaps back to air the tents. Some men flung themselves down and closed their eyes.

Ian and I found beds next to each other and we set our kit bags down.

'No time for those beds, boys,' said Ian. 'That sergeant means business.'

'I haven't slept for days, that bloody driver was a sadist,' groaned a voice from one of the beds.

I felt I had to protect Harry. 'He has his issues too,' I said. 'In fairness, he hasn't slept either, but had to get us here.'

I felt uncomfortable giving orders now the war was over. 'Come on, lads, let's be having you.'

A lot of grumbling and sighing filled the air but the men got themselves ready to return to the house for orders. One man had to be shaken awake amid much cursing when he finally came to.

Ian sat on the bed opposite me while the men sorted themselves out. 'How are you going to play it then, Andrew?

She must still be here, surely.'

I shook my head. Despite my time alone in the lorry and all the thinking I'd done, I hadn't thought of any plan, what to say, do. My only plan was to find Anneke. 'I don't know.'

Ian frowned. 'Why don't you find Armande and then see the lay of the land. Madame won't help you, but I think Armande had a soft spot for you.'

'Yes, I will, he should be in the kitchen. Once we find out what's going on army-wise, I will sort things.' I knew Ian was trying to be helpful, but it was beginning to make me uneasy. Did he know something I didn't? But how could he?

Ian reached across and laid his hand on my leg. 'She'll be here, mate. Are you sure that is what you want? You still have Pamela to go home to, you know.'

I looked at Ian; his eyes did show concern for me. I hadn't told him Pamela was no longer my fiancée, I wanted to keep that information to myself. Something made me feel that if I told anyone, fate would turn against me finding Anneke.

'Find out first before starting to beat yourself up for what you have done to Pamela. You never know, Anneke may have run off with some romantic Frenchman who's made lots of money in the war, seem to be lots of them around.'

I glared at Ian. There was no time to comment as we began to move into the chateau to receive orders. We joined the other men and reported to the sergeant standing in the hallway.

'Right, all here? Good. Now, the transporters are already here for the motor vehicles, and two of the tanks are now roadworthy to go back. Andrew, yours is a non-runner, never found out why. Still here, believe or not, up the hill. Load and be off in the morning. A convoy will pick you up ten miles west. You get yourself and the other low-loaders there by fourteen hundred. Breakfast in the kitchen staff quarters, a bell will sound.' The sergeant cast his gaze around the assembled men. 'Jump to it!'

We all gave a rather limp salute in reply and retreated from the hallway.

'Now what?' I muttered to myself.

'Go find her. I'll see the lay of the land for the tanks.' Ian hit me quite hard on the back. 'Go find her!'

Relieved I was actually going to do something to find her, I walked around the side of the chateau to the kitchen entrance where I could hear the traditional swearing and shouting of the army cook. This time there was a familiar French voice answering as robustly. Armande still had control of his kitchen, no army was going to take that over. Having survived the German invasion, he was not surrendering now. The door swung open at my touch and I tentatively put my head around the door.

'Armande, are you there?'

'André is that you.' A happy voice greeted me. '*Entré*. Come in.'

I walked into the familiar kitchen; the large enamelled stove had pots steaming upon it and the smell of fresh-baked bread met my nose. I hadn't had breakfast, and now realised how hungry I was.

'Armande,' I shouted, smiling broadly. 'How are you, well?'

The old Frenchman came rushing to me, he hugged me hard and kissed me in the continental manner on both cheeks. I still felt a little uncomfortable with this unfamiliar greeting, but not as much as my first encounter just after D-Day. Was that a whole year ago? The army cook pushed past the two of us and picked up a metal rod, which he rotated around a metal circle hanging by the doorway. A piercing, ringing sound broke the silence of the morning and I only just heard Armande's reply.

'I am well. Come eat something.'

Before I could answer, I heard the thunder of army boots behind me on the flagstones outside the doorway. The rest of the tank drivers had arrived for their long-awaited breakfast.

'Easy, lads.' The cook beamed at us all. The cook was clearly happy now he had a proper kitchen and fresh food to supplement the rations he was sent.

The men obediently moved through into the kitchen and into the room used by the long-gone servants. The well scrubbed table still stood on the flagstones, a bench along one side and individual chairs on the other. A chair with arms stood proudly at one end; I'd seen Armande sitting there on occasion, eating his meal in solitary splendour. It had a faded green cushion, well worn and indented with use. Not one of the men sat in that chair. The cook stood protectively behind it, barking orders at his assistant as he loaded food on to the table. Coffee, with tinned milk, was poured; a sugar bowl, already on

287

the table, was soon emptied as the men spooned it into their drink. Two baskets of freshly baked bread rolls were put on the table with a plate with individual pats of butter. Then larger plates followed, each with bacon and a solitary sausage and egg. And then two tins of jam landed on the table with a bang.

Silence reigned as each man ate his way through the food before him. As they eagerly ate, an easy atmosphere prevailed and conversation started between the men who had just arrived and those who had already been at the chateau a few days. I sat, ate and listened.

'Fine gaff,' said Taff, a small Welshman from the valleys. I didn't know his real name.

'Sure is,' another soldier agreed. I think his name was Tom. 'Survived quite well.'

'How come?' asked someone else.

'Germans used it for officers visiting the defences,' answered the cook's assistant as he began clearing away a few empty plates.

Taff spoke. 'Who owns it?'

A soldier who had been here when we arrived paused as he took a mouthful of coffee then said, 'Some lady. Don't upset her.'

Tom's head nodded slowly. 'Oh, one of those, I have a grandmother like that.'

The soldier continued, 'Well, the Jerries didn't want to upset her.'

The speaker lifted the last piece of bread from the basket and smeared butter all over it.

Taff wanted to know more. 'How come? They didn't

mind upsetting those they put in camps.'

 More bread was produced and immediately taken by the hungry men.

The soldier who seemed to know most about the house answered. 'Related to some high-up German. By marriage.'

I stopped eating and swallowed. This surprised me and I listened a bit more carefully. I didn't know all the men talking but they seemed to know more about the chateau than I did.

'How come the military police didn't arrest her?' Taff was insisting on more information.

The soldier laughed. 'She wasn't a supporter of Hitler, and she did help the locals. No one has a bad word against her in the area so not a shred of evidence as a collaborator. The opposite, I suspect, but I ain't asking her.'

'Battle axe, just like my gran, do anything for you, she would. I wonder how she is, been lots of bombs where she lives ...' The soldier's strong voice faded away as perhaps he thought of his grandmother. I know I thought of mine at that moment.

'And some,' another voice agreed.

A few minutes of silence ensued as we finished eating.

'We had some senior officers here before Christmas, no it was autumn, late October. Big chinwag between them and an elderly man, he kept to his bedroom, not well, but think that was a ruse myself. Arguing, they were.' The soldier shook his head. 'He's gone now, a big plush car came and they bundled him in, and he was protesting all the time, but he went. His daughter stayed.'

I listened a bit harder. Anneke, she was here until at least October. I looked at Ian; was she still here?

'How come?' Ian asked, trying not to show too much interest in the conversation.

'Something about leaving and going to England. He didn't want to go.' The soldier reached for another piece of bread.

A younger soldier snorted. 'Maybe he and Madame were sweet on one another.'

A ribald laugh and a smattering of coffee hit the table.

'Hey, cut it out,' shouted the cook, throwing a cloth for the mess to be cleaned up.

The subject changed to tracks and exhaust fumes. I felt a mounting tension as I hadn't been able to talk to Armande – well, talk was an exaggeration! Pidgin English and a smattering of French was hardly a conversation, though we had both learnt a little more in the ensuing year. It would have to do.

Breakfast was finished at last and the men, more or less as a company, stood and left to go about their jobs. Only I remained at the table having had a nod from Ian to remain seated.

'Don't you have work to do, lad?' the cook snarled at me.

Armande shouted at him in French and motioned for me to follow him out of the room into his back office. The Army hadn't taken that over either. I stood in the doorway of his office looking at Armande. Here was my answer.

'Armande … Anneke, is she still here?' I asked.

'She leave. Go city.' The older man sat on his chair by the desk he used to collate the chateau's household accounts.

'When?'

'Two, non, three weeks ago.' Armande shuffled a few pieces of paper into a neat pile.

'Come back, return?' I moved my hands in the air.

'Uh, *non* ...' Armande stuttered and shrugged his shoulders. He didn't seem to know what to say. '*Madame comprend.*'

'*Oui.*' I agreed. I sighed and rubbed the back of my head, the hair had stopped growing there after the year of continual rubbing. Ian had his doubts it would ever return, and called it a monk's haircut gone wrong. The bald circle had slipped, like my morals, apparently, with two women waiting for me. That's what Ian had told me, at least.

'Madame is here?' I asked.

Armande nodded his head quickly. 'Oui, secretariat.'

I understood and muttered, 'Office.' I nodded my thanks to the man, who watched me intently.

Walking through the chateau I was struck by how much lighter it felt, a better atmosphere, no traces of the Germans remained. The downstairs windows were wide open, glinting in the sunlight, fresh air was being drawn through the building, cleansing it.

I knocked on Madame's office door. The large double doors had always been firmly shut when I last stayed here. I understood the German commanding officer had used it during the war and as soon as they'd left Madame had retaken it, and locked it every time she left. I noticed the paint was peeling at the edge of the door where boots had scuffed it, shutting it without use of hands. The black marks had never come out despite Armande's efforts, but the brass door handles shone brightly, they were cleaned every day. I smiled at a memory: I remembered seeing Armande and Anneke going about armed with a polishing cloth and, in quiet moments, rubbing the brass till it gleamed.

I knocked again, a little louder this time. Standing close to the door I heard the rustle of papers and a brisk '*Entré*.'

'*Madame, bonjour.*' My accent was improving, although the different dialects I'd encountered made it a little hard to be understood two or three villages from where I'd learnt a new word, but I was fine with that one. Sometimes I mixed it up with German and Dutch, but I usually got it right – and I had to with Madame.

To my left Madame was sitting at her desk by the large windows, her back not fully to the doorway. She didn't immediately move, she was intent on moving papers into files and I noticed several framed photographs standing on top of the desk. It was too far away to see the figures clearly but, in most, the chateau appeared in the background. Madame looked up, her eyes narrowing slightly as she saw me for the first time. She pursed her lips briefly.

'Bonjour, Ian. How are you?' As she stood, she knocked the desk slightly and wobbled a small picture frame. She put a hand out to steady the photograph and placed it picture face downwards.

'Fine, Madame, and you?' I walked across the room and stood by the desk where she sat.

'Well, a little tired. The Army still here but not long now they go. Then we can rebuild our lives. My family, that has survived this horrible war will arrive soon, I feel it.'

'Family, Madame?' I didn't know she had family until the conversation in the mess. Anneke hadn't mentioned it. Then again, if she were connected to the German High Command, she wouldn't have shouted it from the rooftops when the invasion had begun.

'Yes I … I have a daughter who lost her husband, *mort*. He was in Berlin at the end. She has two daughters, and one son. They live in Bavaria, once they have the travel documents they will come. My son, I know not where he is, Angleterre, I thought. I did not want to know. The Germans watch me like a hawk. I was lucky Monique married well, for *amore*, but he was a Nazi. Saved my home. But at what price to my honour?'

'Madame, I did not know that you had family.' I smiled sympathetically. I knew I had to be charming and considerate or she wouldn't help me.

'I do not tell. The Germans. My son. He will come soon. They not learn my secret but now it is free.'

'Madame …' I paused and looked down at booted feet, dusty and worn, on her fine carpet. I didn't have a good record at keeping her floors clean: vomit and now dirt from the battlefields of Europe. But I no longer cared about her floors, once it would have worried me, but not now.

'Now, what is it you want?' Madame looked at me; she knew what I wanted but she wasn't going to help the man before her.

'Anneke.'

'She is not here.' Madame turned away from me and picked up some letters that she then put over the photograph she had laid down. It seemed a natural movement but I thought there was something deliberate in her actions.

Madame spoke quite firmly. 'She is no longer here. Anneke leave, to join with her father and his assistant.'

'The assistant came back?' I was a little surprised. The man in the woods, he was the assistant, I was sure. Kurt.

'Yes he was not far. He hide,' Madame quickly answered as she dismissively waved a hand in the air.

I looked at the wall behind Madame. The wallpaper had faded in places and not in others, where pictures had hung. My eyes drifted down to the photographs on top of the desk. I could see them more clearly now. There was a picture of Anneke and her father with a man beside Anneke. He looked familiar. The build was right.

'The assistant, was he the man in the wood who hit me, Madame?'

'Yes.' There was no hesitation in her reply.

'When did they leave?'

'Oh, a month ago, I think. I been busy.' Madame moved the papers on her desk again, putting them into a pile.

'Do you have a forwarding address I may have?' A bead of sweat ran down my back. I had to be polite and not scream and shout at the woman. She would not give me what I needed if I lost my patience, although I began to doubt she would even if I kept my composure.

Madame looked me straight in the face. I got the impression that she wasn't going to lie to me.

'They said they would write when they were settled.'

'Did she get my letters?' I shuffled from foot to foot, clenching my fists.

'Non.'

My shoulders slumped. 'Do you know which town or city they were going to?' Keep trying to get information, I told myself, anything to help find her.

'I do not.' Again an emphatic answer, which I felt was true.

'Madame, I want to find her.' I rubbed the back of my head, running out of ideas.

Madame hesitated as if searching for the right words. 'Does she want to find you?'

I was certain she did, but I answered, 'I think she does, Anneke told me to come if I wanted, if I could.'

'Anneke is not here.'

'Where is she? Where has she gone, Madame?' I felt there was a hint of desperation in my voice, which I could do nothing about.

Madame glared at me. 'I do not know where she has gone. They talk of America when they leave.'

I felt myself sink a little further within myself. 'America, not England?' I had a chance of finding her in England.

America was a long way away, how could I go there? I was beginning to lose hope.

'Non, the Americans and the English they talk, they discuss many days. America is the place, they decide.'

'America. How can I find her in America? A letter, did she leave one for me?'

Madame looked at me then away out of the window. 'I do not know how to find. Does she want to be found?' Madame then looked down as she spoke the words, 'Anneke left no letter for you.'

I could hardly believe my ears. No letters? I felt my throat contract. I somehow did not believe there was no letter. I was becoming distraught. What could I do? I paced to the half-open French window and looked out over the terrace and up the hill, desperately trying to clear my mind.

I said in a clear voice, changing the subject, 'You could see our tank when we were here.'

'Yes, I could see you,' Madame quietly agreed.

I pivoted on my heel and looked at the immaculately dressed French woman. Our eyes met.

Madame stood. 'She is not here. She has gone. With her father and Kurt, they were married.'

'Married?'

'Yes married.'

I sank on to one of the chairs set a little away from the desk. Married. My brain tried to process this news.

'I am sorry, Andrew, but they marry before they leave.' There was a hint of softness in the voice, but not much.

As I spoke I didn't really believe it. 'I was nothing to her then?'

Madame inclined her head at me. 'I know not. Maybe, but she has a new life.' Madame then turned away from me and moved papers around her desk; she looked up at me again. 'Nothing.'

Madame tried to smile reassuringly at me, but it didn't work. 'She went with her father. All the family she had.'

I couldn't stop myself crying out at her, 'I have a family she would have joined.'

A sharp reply came back at me. 'A Jewish family?'

'No, but ...'

'Andrew. *Comprends*.' She shook her head at me.

'Madame. I loved her and I thought she me.' I didn't believe it, I refused to believe it.

Madame sighed; I didn't know if it was in sympathy or exasperation.

'Maybe she did in June, but now she must think of the future. Would you come back, *enh*?'

'She knew I would,' I insisted.

'Anneke has gone, Andrew. Now please leave, I have work ...' Madame's voice trailed off.

I stared at her. 'Yes, Madame, I am sorry. But gone, no letter?'

'No. Leave now please, Andrew. Start a life with your girl at home.' Madame pulled more papers towards her and started reading.

Slowly I drew myself up. I gave a little head bow to the lady before me. As I did so I saw Madame clear the papers from the photograph and set it up again. I left the room quietly, deep in thought. A girl at home, how did she know I had a girl? The letter to Pamela I had lost, had she found it?

Ian was waiting for me in the hallway. 'Well, mate, how did that go? Did she tell you where she is?'

I shook my head. 'She's gone, Ian.'

Ian touched my arm. 'So, where?'

I shook the arm off. 'She doesn't know. America.'

Ian gave a little whistle. 'That's a bit hard, left a letter?'

'She says no, but I don't believe her. Can't say definitely but I think she has one.' I shrugged my shoulders in defeat. 'No way I can get it, can I?'

'No, mate. Come on outside, have a smoke and a think. Maybe one of the officers that are still lurking know where they went, even a city would be good. Jews are a tight bunch so you can write to the local synagogue and find her that way.'

I just looked at Ian. 'She has married too.'

Ian whistled through his teeth. 'Not expecting that one, mate.'

We walked through the hallway out of the fateful front door where I first saw Anneke and on to the gravel terrace. I indicated to the left with a nod of the head and we each found a cigarette and stood looking up the hill to the barn. As we were outside Madame's office, and her windows were open, we spoke in hushed voices.

'Now this is all over, when I get home, I'm going to give up this filthy habit.' I held my cigarette up and looked

298

at Ian, who took an extended drag on his.

'Good luck with that, mate, not sure I can give it up now.' Ian nodded up the hill. 'She's got a good view, didn't appreciate that when we were here.'

'Nor did I,' I said. I moved away from him. I wanted to think.

But it seemed Ian wasn't going to let the subject go. 'How much do you think she saw?'

'Enough.' I threw my cigarette down, disgusted with it. I ground the remains into the gravel.

'Hmm.' Ian drew on his cigarette again, looking thoughtful.

We stood looking at the countryside around us, both silent. Wild ideas chased through my mind, then I heard a door shutting behind us. We turned to look through the French windows and saw it was the office door closing. We heard the click of a key and we looked at each other, I think we both had the same idea at the same time. Ian moved to the half-open windows.

'Go on, mate,' said Ian, opening the French windows. 'You know you want to.'

'I can't do that.'

'Sure you can, I'll keep watch.'

I looked around; soldiers were nowhere to be seen, so I quickly stepped over the threshold into the room, closing the French windows behind me. I stood in front of the desk, looking down at the tidy piles of papers and folders, making a quick survey. I then went quickly and methodically through the envelopes placed in the small cubbyholes in the desk. I couldn't find the letter, I was convinced there was one, then I realised I was looking for something unopened, not the ragged edge of a letter that had been opened and read. I scanned the desk contents again and found a blue envelope unopened but, by its look, had something inside. I tentatively turned it over and saw with relief my name inscribed in neat handwriting. I sat down at the desk and weighed it in my hand. Do I open it now or later? I got up suddenly, the thought flitting through my mind how I didn't want to be caught by Madame in her private room. I must leave. As I turned, my elbow caught one of the photographs on the desktop, and it clattered to the floor. Reaching down, I picked up the photograph and went to place it back on the desk. I saw it was a photograph of a young woman holding a baby. It was Anneke.

Tap-tap, the noise hardly penetrated my frozen mind, I couldn't think of anything but the sight of the baby. Tap. Louder this time. I looked up at the French windows, Ian was gesticulating madly. I had to go. I gathered myself, put the photograph straight and, clutching the letter, hurried to the French windows and let myself out.

'Did you find it?' Ian hissed.

I didn't answer.

'Did you find it?' he asked, more insistent.

'Yes.'

Ian exhaled. 'Come on, mate, let's walk up to the barn.'

He took a few steps then looked back at me. 'What's up?'

I stared blankly at Ian but started to walk with him

away from the chateau.

We crossed the bridge in silence. Ian went to say something but one look at my face seem to stop any more questions. He let me walk in silence.

Perhaps struggling to keep quiet, Ian started to speak. 'Armande looks well, a little tired, don't you think?'

Having no reply from me he continued. 'Madame is looking good too, got things running well, waiting for family to come back, who knew? Son in England, a good country, taking every one in.'

The words fell on my deaf ears. I glanced at him but said nothing, I thought only of the letter I held tightly in my hand. He didn't give up talking to me though.

'I've been thinking more about what I shall do after demob. The Cohens are going to go to the Holy Land. I'm going too. I've written to all the agencies about the family,' he continued. 'Other than travelling around the camps, I can do no more. I just have to wait and pray.'

I just walked and listened to him.

'Big Dave said when he demobs he's going to Rolls Royce, he sent letters and has an interview all set up, he should get a job there, don't you think? But Little Dave still has no idea. Lots of men I've talked to over the past few weeks are excited, but you can tell are a bit concerned, frightened even about their return home – a few new babies that shouldn't be there.' Ian gave a little laugh.

I shot Ian a cold look but he didn't appear to see it.

'Well, here we are,' said Ian as he put his arms in the air and twirled around. 'It does feel good to be back.'

'Yes.'

'I'm going to have a look around.'

I nodded, and I sat down in the barn doorway, looking down at the chateau. Ian paused a second then walked off around the barn.

As soon as he left, I tore the envelope open, a photograph fell to the floor, but I didn't look at it. I read the neat handwriting, spaced evenly over the page.

My dear Andrew,

I am so happy you are reading this as it means you are alive.

You know now that I am no longer at the chateau and that I have married Kurt. He is Father's assistant. He was hiding in the woods. Kurt was the one who attacked you that day. He loved me before you came but I did not return his regard.

I will always have a place in my heart for you but I must be realistic. I have a daughter to think of. Kurt accepted what happened, he tells me to forget you, but I cannot forget you are the father of my daughter.

Father has been asked to go to America to join the other engineers on developing planes and rocket engines. He was coerced to do this for the Germans. We are going with him. Kurt is a talented engineer too and as Father is all I have left I shall be with him, Kurt proposed and I accepted. It is for the best.

Please do not try to find us, I could not cope

*with the turmoil this would cause. A hard decision
but for our daughter it is for the best. She will have
all the things we can buy for her. She will be raised
a Jew, I have named her Elizabeth.*

*One thing I feel in my heart which is like a
dagger, why did you not write when I wrote of our
child?*

A daughter, Elizabeth. I dropped the letter to the floor
and I couldn't stop the tears falling from my eyes on to
the paper. I heard a rustle: Ian had crept back and now
stood beside me. He lent down and took up the letter
and photograph, pausing only to look at me, and when
he saw no dissent, he read the words quickly.

Looking down at me he said in a soft voice full of
compassion, 'I cannot say anything that will help ,Andrew.
You must accept this, she's gone.'

I stood up and looked Ian in his eyes. 'You go to the
Holy Land and find your family. I will go to America to
find my daughter.'

I took the letter and photograph from Ian's hand,
replaced them in the envelope, and put it in my breast
pocket. I would read the rest of the letter later. I had a
daughter named Elizabeth.

I nodded at Ian and then began to walk away from the
barn to the chateau. I realised these were my first real steps on
my journey to home and family. I would keep my promise to
come home safe, but I knew I wouldn't stay; I had two people
to find in America. The tug of war had been satisfied, but now
I had a tug of love that was stronger and couldn't be denied.

Acknowledgements

I want to thank the Forest of Dean Writers for their support, and in particular Claire Hamilton. Tania, for reading my opus when I could no longer. Ian Young, for putting up with me. But most importantly, the men and women who fought in the Second World War. During my research, I read many books on D-Day and the battles that followed, and I've been enthralled by the biographies and blow by blow accounts of those that took part. I am amazed at what they did and what they lived through. Although the characters depicted are completely from my imagination, some friends will recognise their names. Big Dave, you are greatly missed by the Earle of Stamfords. The book is inspired from a conversation with a World War II veteran who told of how his tank broke down following the D-Day landings and how he and his crew were looked after by a French family, having been told by HQ to wait where they were. Thank you Mr Jones for sparking my imagination.

Julia Sutherland's life-long interest in history led to her involvement with a re-eactment society, and an extensive collection of history books. A chance conversation with a D-Day veteran revealed a very personal account of a man caught up in a war, and inspired the human story that became *The Tug of War*.

Julia lives with her family on the English-Welsh border.